The Cause and Cure Is You 1 ended with chaos and bloodshed, and the finale starts the same. Steve Valentine stops at nothing to protect the Valentine's clan against Theodore Jones, who is determined to be the only metahuman left on the earth.

Will Steve be able to save Keys in time?

In the meantime, Ivy struggles to start a new life without the leading men in her life. She moves to Dallas, away from the heartache and pain, only to find out that it has come along with her to Dallas.

This is a work of fiction. Names, characters, places and incidents are either the product of the author's imagination or are used fictitiously, and any resemblance to actual persons, living or dead, business establishments, events, or locales, is entirely coincidental.

Previously on The Cause and Cure is You
STEVE VALENTINE

"Pops, you gon' have to chill on all this drinking," Esco preached.

"Right," Reese chimed in. "Last thing he needed was a son that owned a bar."

"Just because you motherfuckers are decades old doesn't mean that you can tell me what the fuck to do," I barked. "I'm still your father."

They were still talking shit as we pulled up to *Dreams*. Reese began to park, and my eyebrows narrowed in confusion as I noticed that the club was pitch black.

"I thought they opened at seven," Esco said.

"Me too," I responded slowly.

"Well, looks like they're closed. Where you wanna go?" Reese asked.

I sat staring strangely at the bar. "Let's check this out first. Your brother always makes sure that his club opens on time. Something ain't right about this."

I jumped out of the car before Reese turned off the engine. I could hear Esco closely behind me as I marched quickly toward the door. Once upon it, I peered inside.

"Fuck!"

I immediately kicked the glass door in. The glass shattered around us as Esco and I hurried through it. I ran over to his body and watched the blood around him with confusion. Brain matter littered the pool of blood like confetti. "No, no, no," I panicked.

I heard Esco gruff, "What the fuck is going on? He's dead!"

"This can't be," I said as I dropped down to my knees and looked at Keys' lifeless body. I felt for a pulse, but I couldn't find one, but his body was still very warm. "She's here," I said standing to my feet.

"Who?" Esco asked.

"Ivy. She's here. She has to be here somewhere."

I left Esco standing over Keys' body as I ran through the club looking under bars, tables, and in closets. "Where the fuck is she?!" I shouted. I knew that she was there somewhere. She had to be. That was the only way that I had lost my son.

"What happened?" Reese asked once he finally entered the club.

But I couldn't answer him. I had to find her. I ran toward the back of the club and barged through the men's bathroom looking for her. Then I rushed inside the women's bathroom, but I found no one.

Then I heard faint crying close by. I turned and kicked down the first door that I saw. It fell to the floor with a thud. Just as I thought, Ivy was on the other side, tied to a chair in the office and gagged with obvious bruises all over her. She was crying, and her terrified screams were muffled by the gag in her mouth. Her eyes were pleading for help as she attempted to get out of the chair, despite her restraints. As I ran toward her, I stumbled. After falling to the floor, I jumped right back up. My adrenaline was pumping wildly. I looked back to see what I had stumbled on, and it was yet another body. The boy lying on the floor looked young, feminine, and almost pretty, despite the gaping hole in his head that had been gushing out blood for so long that it was now running dry.

Ivy's eyes were red with agony as she stared at him and screamed through the gag.

My heart ached for the dead boy's soul. He was a casualty of a war that he knew nothing about. My worst fears had come true. This was Theodore's doing. The Jones boys were back.

JESSICA WATKINS PRESENTS

The Cause and Cure Is You 2

by JESSICA N. WATKINS

CHAPTER ONE
STEVE VALENTINE

"Shit!" I cursed as I stared oddly at Ivy in front of me, quivering and terrified. "Reese! Esco! Get in here!" I hollered.

Being in Chicago, I had seen my fair share of bodies, but this was so brutal, so horrific, that I wouldn't wish it on my worst enemy.

Ivy looked terrified, as she sat there, bound and gagged. She had obviously been beaten bad, and this young man was laying on the ground by her with a hole in the back of his head. I could tell that he meant a lot to her by the way she cried while staring in disbelief at his body.

I finally snapped out of the shock and rushed towards Ivy to set her free.

"What happened?!" I heard Esco snap as he and Reese came running in.

Esco hurried over to help me untie Ivy while Reese took in the scene in front of him.

"I don't know," I told Esco. "Right now, we just need to get her the hell out of here and as far away from Keys as possible." Then I told Ivy, "Sweetheart, listen to me..." As I went on, she stared at me with wide, red, and tear-soaked eyes. "We're here to help, so you don't have to be scared, okay?" She didn't look sure in whether she should trust us or not, so, as we continued to free her, I added, "I'm Keys' father, and these are his brothers. We're not going to hurt you."

First, her eyes squinted curiously. Then she finally nodded, and I took the gag from her mouth.

"They shot hiiiim!" she started screaming. "Oh my God! I wanted to help him, but they killed my cousin to shut me up! Oh my *Gooood*," she sobbed. "Kyaaaaan! Please, God, no. Please..." She started babbling uncontrollably to the point that I couldn't understand what she was saying anymore.

Reese and Esco looked at me with horrified looks amongst their bearded faces.

"Pops, we gotta do something. We gotta move quick," Reese said.

"Is he okay?" Ivy asked. "Please tell me Keys is okay. Oh my God, please don't let him be dead." Her tears were flowing so heavy. She was shaking nonstop. Her teeth were chattering with fear. "He just can't be gone," she said as she continued to sob.

"And he won't. Not if I can help it," I told her, trying to reassure her. "He's going to be okay. But you can't be here. You need to go and get checked out at the hospital."

"No!" she argued. "I need to be with him. He just lost his mother, and...and...and he doesn't need to be alone."

I gently grabbed her by her shoulders, attempting to calm her down the best I could. "He won't be alone. I'm gonna be with him. I can help him," I told her. "Now, I know that Keys cares about you a lot, and I know that you care about him. But if he has any chance of surviving, I need you to leave ...*now*. Go to the hospital. You've been beaten badly. You need to go and make sure that you're okay. Keys is gonna be fine, but you've GOT TO GO."

She looked at me with a look of confusion and fear. "How do you know that he's going to be okay? I heard them. They said that he was dead."

"Just trust me on that." I then turned to my sons. "Take her to the hospital now. I'm going with Keys."

"Pops, you sure?" Esco asked.

"Yes, gawd damnit!" I barked. "Y'all are wasting time. Go! Once she's been checked out and everything is good, take her to the house."

He nodded quickly as he walked out the room back to Keys. Ivy kept crying, and I watched as she looked down at the dead young man.

"Ky," she whimpered.

I motioned to Reese, who took her by the arm and guided her towards the back door. She turned back to me and gave me a pleading look that actually tore at my heart for a second.

"Please?" she sniffed. "Please don't let Keys die."

Looking at her, I could see why Keys was so head over heels. She was obviously a beautiful, curvaceous woman. But, in addition, any fool could see that she truly cared about him. Even bruised and beaten, she seemed to only care about him.

My son was lucky. It was no wonder why he had put his life in danger for such a beautiful girl.

"I won't," I promised her.

Reese took her out of the office and then out of the back door. Then I sprang into action.

My adrenaline was still pumping as I ran back into the bar area, with Esco right behind me. I knew we didn't have a lot of time.

Once we were standing over Keys' lifeless body, Esco knelt next to him and checked his pulse. His eyes were big with anxiety, but I saw a little hope in them as he said, "He's getting warm."

"Good. That means we've still got time," I said. "Esco, listen to me; go with Reese and help get Ivy as far away from this motherfucka as soon as possible. I can't risk shit else happening to Keys. Take her to the hospital, make sure she's good, and then take her to the house. I don't care how you do it, just get it done."

"Aight," he huffed, walking to the door.

"Esco," I called after him. He turned and looked at me as I added, "Be careful. 'Cause this has Theodore's name written all over it."

Esco paused, questioning my accusation. "You think he was behind this?"

"Hell yeah."

"You sure?" Esco asked with a questioning squint. "We haven't had any smoke from him in years."

The Cause and Cure Is You 2
by *Jessica N. Watkins*

"I believe he's behind this," I told him. "But until I know for sure, we gotta keep her away. I don't think Theodore knows me and the rest of your brothers are here. If he does, all hell 'bout to break loose. I'm gonna take Keys somewhere safe long enough for him to heal."

I reached down to check Keys' pulse. He didn't have one yet and he hadn't gotten any warmer, which meant that Ivy and Reese were still in the vicinity.

"Go," I urged Esco. "Get out of here, stay low, and stay out of sight."

He ran out, and I looked at Keys. As strong as I was trying to be for them, I was petrified. I had just found my son. I damn sure didn't want to lose him now.

I reached down and touched Keys again. I knew that Esco had pulled off with Ivy because Keys was getting warmer now.

I hastily picked him up and raced towards the back door.

"Just hold on, son." He was still unconscious, and I knew that he couldn't hear me, but I needed him to know that I was there.

Fuck! This was the first time that I had ever come close to losing one of my kids. This was the exact reason why I had left Chicago twenty-eight years ago. Back then, I had left because Theodore had ignited a war against me, and I knew that he had now started one with Keys. His beef with Fredrick decades ago had left him so angry that he wanted to be the only metahuman left on this planet. As soon as he found one of us, he wasted no energy getting rid of us, even if it meant killing all of the mortal loved ones around us.

I had to make sure that Keys was safe. I knew that he would probably be pissed that I sent Ivy away, but it was for his own good, especially now that Theodore had surfaced.

How the hell could Theodore have known about Keys when I had just found him myself?

I weaved through the crazy, Chicago traffic towards the University of Chicago. Since I didn't know how long it would take for his body to change from human to supernatural, I thought it was best to get him medical care. I looked over at Keys and could see a little bit of color returning to his face.

"Come on, hang in there, son," I coached him. "Everything's gon' be all right."

God, I hoped so.

****

After what seemed like forever, I finally got to the hospital and pulled him out of the car.

"I need some help!" I barked, carrying his bloodied body inside.

A nurse saw that he was bleeding from his head and rushed over.

"What happened?" she asked.

"He was shot," I told her.

The Cause and Cure Is You 2
by *Jessica N. Watkins*

Several nurses and doctors rushed over with a stretcher, and I laid him on it. Then I followed behind them as they hurried to an available trauma room.

The nurse started asking me questions, and I answered them the best that I could as I followed close behind. I watched as they checked his vitals and was relieved when I heard one of them say that there was a faint pulse.

It's working. He's going to make it.

"Sir, we need you to stay here in the waiting room," one of the nurses told me. "We'll have someone out shortly to speak with you."

I nodded my head. "Okay. Thank you."

Then I went into the waiting room and sat in an available seat, tapping my foot nervously.

Keys *had* to make it. Ivy was gone, so he had a chance. The fact that there was a pulse let me know that he was coming back to life, considering that he had no pulse at all when I first found him.

My thoughts then went to Theodore. He had to be stopped. I needed to find his ass; fast.

I couldn't figure out how he'd found Keys. Theodore being blood, he knew just as much as I did that being around your soul mate is the one thing that makes us mortal. Ivy had been bound and gagged to that chair, not Dream. For that to happen, he had to have been watching Keys closely for some time.

It was fucking with me that this motherfucker had been around, but I didn't see it.

I wasn't about to lose my son. Theodore had messed with the wrong one. My blood was boiling. I was seething in that uncomfortable chair as I waited to hear if my son would live.

If Theodore wanted a war, he was going to get one. I was going to take him down; for good.

CHAPTER TWO
IVY SUMMERS

Keys has gotta be okay. He's just gotta be. He can't die.

I kept saying that in my head repeatedly while I was sitting in the backseat of a car with two dudes that I didn't even know. I could see them looking as scared as I was and talking lowly.

All I could think about was Keys. I needed to know that he was okay.

I didn't want to go to the hospital, even though I was sure that I probably looked as bad as I felt emotionally. I wanted to go home. But I knew that probably wasn't going to happen. Then, with that thought, I realized that if I'd gone home, I would have to be there without Kyan. I would have to tell his mother that he was gone. I regretted that more than the hospital, so I just took the ride.

After a thirty-minute drive, we had passed so many hospitals that I was starting to think that these motherfuckers were kidnapping me. Just as I was about to hop out while the car was still rolling, we were pulling into a hospital that was oddly on the other side of town.

Once inside, they rushed me to a triage room. Nurses began to check me out while these two guys stood watching over me. I felt like I was in some witness protection program or something. I tried to relax, but it was hard. I couldn't stop thinking about Kyan. I wondered if Keys was in the same hospital.

I needed to tell my aunt that her only son had died because of me. I had asked him to go with me to Dallas. If I hadn't have asked him that, he would be at home scheming his next lick, not laying in a pool of blood. And, even though Travis and I weren't back together, and he had done some pretty fucked up things, I didn't want to see him dead. Now, Keys was fighting for his life, if he was even alive. All of this was my fault.

I felt helpless.

Now, I was lying up in a hospital bed waiting on the doctors to come back in to give me my prognosis. These two guys were sitting and texting in their phones heavy. I was surprised the cops hadn't shown up yet. I needed to get out of there. I physically felt fine. I was a little banged up, but I didn't need to be there.

"Look," I spoke for probably the first time since I'd gotten in the car with them. "I really appreciate the help and the ...uh...the ride and everything, but I'm good. I need to get home. I have a lot of calls that I have to make, and I gotta make sure that my family knows that I'm okay. I gotta tell my aunt about Ky–" I choked saying his name. I took a deep breath and forced out, "Kyan."

It was hard to even say it without new tears stinging at my eyes. One of them, who I think I remembered his name being Esco, cleared his throat and scratched at his head.

"I think it's best for you to stay here and get checked out and everything," he said.

"I'm fine," I pressed.

"Well, I drove," he said so short that it stung a little. "So, when the doctor says you're good, I'll take you home."

I grimaced at the way he shrugged like I didn't have a fucking say so. Smug motherfucker shrugged his shoulders and leaned against the wall like I didn't have a damn choice.

I didn't like his attitude. The other guy, whose name I didn't catch, nudged him and gave him a look that let me know he didn't like how Esco had come at me either.

"My bad," Esco mumbled to me. "I'm just fucked up over this. I'm worried 'bout Keys. Man, what the hell happened?"

I knew that question was coming eventually. I replayed everything that happened in my mind and shivered from the sheer terror, as if it was happening all over again.

"Honestly, everything happened so fast," I said. "I was leaving to go to Dallas. Me and Kyan were on the way to the airport when Travis showed up."

"Who's Travis?" the other guy asked.

"He's my ex fiancé," I told him. "Anyways, he showed up, and, at first, I thought he was there to start some more drama. Him and Keys had gotten into it before, and Travis had shot him."

I stopped because thinking about that made me see Travis' body, dead and cold, on the ground. Esco's jaw clenched, but he didn't say anything.

"Um..." I pressed on. "Travis apologized about everything, and I forgave him. He said he would go with me to Dallas and I... I really didn't have anything keeping me here since Keys decided to-to..." I hesitated.

"Decided to what?" the other guy urged.

"He decided we weren't going to work."

I couldn't bring myself to tell them the whole story, that Keys told me that he could never be with me and that I basically told him to kiss my ass. I couldn't believe that that was the last thing I'd said to him, that *we'd* said to each other. And now... now we possibly wouldn't ever have a chance to fix it.

I wiped my eyes, not even realizing that I was crying again.

"Anyway, we were heading to the airport and Travis had to stop for gas. One minute, he was at the gas pump, and me and Kyan were looking in our phones at stuff to do in Dallas for the weekend before I started work on Monday. The next minute, these two guys came out of nowhere. They started beating the shit out of Travis. Kyan and I started to get out and help him, but another guy came out of nowhere and jumped in the driver's seat, pointing a gun at my head. So, Kyan and I just sat there frozen. Once Travis stopped putting up at fight, they shoved him in the trunk. Then they got in the back seat." The fresh, horrific memory was making me hyperventilate. I took a deep breath, forcing myself to calm down so that I could get the words out. "The guy behind the wheel sped off, and the others kept their guns pointed at us. They took us to *Dreams* and tried to force us inside. Once they grabbed Travis out of the trunk, he put up a fight, and they shot him dead. They just—they just shot hiiim!" I couldn't stop crying at this point. I had literally watched my ex-fiancé take his last breath, trying to protect me. For so long, I thought he didn't love me because of the way that he treated me. But him trying to save me told me maybe he really had started to change for the better. It was like it was his way of trying to prove to me that he was serious this time and finally figured out how to love me the right way... but it was too late.

As Esco led me out of the club a little while ago, we had to walk by Travis' lifeless body like he was just roadkill. It was unbearable and felt like a terrible night terror.

"I tried to fight them off, but one of them punched me in my face. Kyan tried to defend and protect me, but they just beat him up too. Finally, we just stopped fighting and let them take us inside. They forced us into the office and told us not to make a sound. Then Keys' partner, Trouble, came in, and I thought I was saved. But when I asked him to help me, he wouldn't. I thought he was cool with Keys. I didn't know that they had beef," I cried.

As much as I didn't want to go on with it, I had to.

"Then this older guy showed up, and he started talking about how he had been looking for Keys. He said that he was going to use me to get to him. I begged for him to let us go. I didn't know where Keys was. I didn't know what was going on. I hadn't seen him or talked to him since he left my house. But the older guy didn't believe me. He had one of his boys hit me so hard that I could taste blood. He swore he was gonna kill Keys..." I swallowed hard, swallowed the vision of Kyan's brains splattering all over the room. "I heard somebody come through the front door, so I just started screaming for help. And then-then-then," I struggled to speak. "One of them shot Kyan right there in front of me. They shot my cousin."

I broke all the way down. All I kept seeing in my mind was Kyan's body hitting the floor. He was the only family that I had, the only person that looked out for me. We had been through so much, and he lost his life because of me. So did Travis. Everybody that I knew was getting killed. And the worst thing is, I still didn't know if Keys was okay.

"This is all my fault," I sobbed.

I couldn't take anymore. My life had been turned upside down in a matter of a day. Everything I knew had changed.

One of the doctors came in and concern crossed his face as he saw my tears.

"Is everything okay?" he asked, eyeing Esco and the other guy.

"Yes," I answered quickly. "I was just telling them what happened to me."

THE CAUSE AND CURE IS YOU 2
by *Jessica N. Watkins*

Esco stood up and walked over to the doctor. "I'm Esco, and that's my younger brother, Reese. We just wanted to make sure that she's okay."

The doctor nodded, but my eyes were bugged. At the mention of the word 'brother', suddenly, I recalled the older guy back at the club who helped me saying that he was Keys' father and that these guys were his brothers. But Keys didn't have any brothers. Not to my knowledge. Where the hell had they been? Was he telling the truth?

"Well, Ms. Summers, you are going to be okay," the doctor said. "Aside from the obvious bumps and bruises, luckily, there were no broken bones. I am concerned because it looks like there might be a slight concussion, so I think it's best we keep you overnight. But as long as that checks out, you will be able to go home tomorrow. Now, due to the nature of events, the police should be here soon to ask some questions."

I nodded my head. I figured they would want to keep me overnight, but the minute they released me, I was out. I was so ready to go home... wherever that would be now.

"I'll be back in a few," the doctor announced. "Try to get you some rest."

As he walked out, Reese stood up and walked over to my belongings. He grabbed my clothes and tossed them on the bed.

"We need to move. Now," he said.

"Huh?" I asked, confused.

"Cops is comin'. So, we gotta move. I gotta get you out of here," Esco explained.

"Wait. I need to tell the cops what happened," I stressed. "I can't leave."

"No, you don't. And trust me, yes you can."

Reese had opened the door looking for an exit as I asked, "Why not?"

"I'll tell you later," Esco told me.

"No, you'll tell me *now*," I said.

I was sick of this guessing game. What were they not telling me? He looked at me like he didn't care about my rebellion at all, and I was getting pissed off.

"I swear to God, if y'all don't tell me what the fuck is going on, I will start screaming and tell the damn cops y'all kidnapped me," I threatened. "Now what the fuck is going on?!"

Esco's jaw clenched as I got loud. Reese looked at Esco, who sighed and shrugged his shoulders. Reese then closed the door and stepped back in.

Esco stared into my eyes and said, "We know who attacked you and killed your people. But we have to take care of it. The cops can't. So, they can't know what happened."

I don't know why I believed him, but it was something in his eyes telling me that I should.

I was still so confused, however. What in the hell was going on? Why couldn't I tell the police what happened?

I opened my mouth to speak, but Reese cut me off. "The less you know the better. We just gotta keep you away from Keys."

"What?" I frowned.

What kind of shit was that to say? I had enough of niggas pushing me around. I had enough to deal with. I had just watched my ex fiancé and cousin get killed, and now they were trying to tell me that I couldn't see Keys?!

"Just leave it alone for now," Esco spoke up.

"I ain't gotta leave shit alone!" I snapped. "You know what? Fuck this. I'm going home. ALONE. I'm going to tell my aunt that her son is dead, and then I'm going to check on Keys. I don't need your permission. He needs me. Somebody needs to be there with him."

"Somebody is," Esco said. "His fiancée, Dream. Not you."

My heart stopped and dropped down to my stomach. *Fiancée? He proposed to that damn girl?!* I had completely forgotten about her. I felt so stupid for even acting the way that I had, considering that he was with her. I felt sick to my stomach. I didn't know what was bothering me more. The fact that I couldn't see him, or the fact that he was now getting married to the girl that was never there for him.

I guess my face must have read how upset I was because Esco's expression softened.

THE CAUSE AND CURE IS YOU 2
by *Jessica N. Watkins*

"I'm sorry," he apologized. "I ain't mean to say it like that. But talking to the cops is not a good idea, and you can't see Keys." Then he asked Reese, "Bruh, we clear out there?"

"Yeah," Reese answered. "Not for long, though."

"Aight. Don't scream," he warned me.

Esco grabbed me before I could say anything else and rushed me out the door to the elevator. I tried to break free from his grip, but it was pointless. He was strong, and it was as if my feet weren't even touching the floor, as if he was running so fast that we were floating.

Once on the elevator, it started to go up, and I was confused.

I thought he said we were leaving. I knew I shouldn't have trusted him!

Once at the top floor, I started to panic. As the elevator door opened, my heart started to pound so hard and fast that it hurt. There was nothing in sight, except a door that led to the roof. This nigga was about to push me off the roof of the hospital! I knew it! I started to put up a fight, but Esco was easily able to drag me out of the elevator and towards a door.

"Noooooooooo! Somebody heeeeeelp!!!" I started screaming like crazy, but he covered my mouth with one hand and cuffed me tight. He reached in his pockets and tossed Reese the car keys.

"Go back to pops," he told him. "Let him know we left. Tell him I'll call him soon."

He walked back to the elevator, and I struggled to get free as Esco continued to drag me towards the door. I kicked and screamed into his hand as he pushed the door open. I clawed at his hand around my mouth, but it was as if my nails couldn't even penetrate his thick skin.

As he walked me to the edge, I knew my life was over. I regretted those dudes not killing me back at the club because a bullet to the brain seemed a lot less gruesome than being thrown off of a building.

I kept trying to get away. I kept fighting as we inched towards the edge of the building.

"Noooooooooooo!" My screams were curdling, and my legs fell limp with fear.

Then, before I knew what was happening... we were airborne.

"Ahhhhhhhhhhhhhhhhhhhhhh!!!" I screamed as my eyes widened with immense fear.

What was happening?! I was fucking flying in the air! I clung to Esco so tight as we soared between buildings. I looked down with bulging eyes to see houses and trees underneath me that were all the size of ants. It was like flying in an airplane, only I had a close-up view of everything. This strange ass man was holding me and flying like he was Superman, and I was blown. I couldn't breathe. I was trying to scream, but it was like the breath left my body completely.

I'm not sure how long we were in the air, but eventually, we were getting closer and closer to the ground, and I was somewhere completely different. I didn't recognize anything around me. I was shook. I couldn't catch my shaking breath. My heart was still dangerously racing, and I was trying to make sense of what the hell had just happened. I thought I was going to pass out. Esco held onto me tight, and the minute my feet were on the ground, I opened my mouth to scream but his hand covered it again quickly.

"Shhh," he whispered in my ear. "Don't scream. I'm gonna move my hand, but you cannot scream, you understand?"

I just nodded my head yes. I don't think any sound could come out anyway.

He let me go and stepped away a few feet looking at me cautiously as I freaked the fuck out.

"Why the fuck can you fly?!" I suddenly spazzed.

He rushed towards me. "Would you be quiet?"

I backed away from him with bucked eyes. "No, fuck that! Why can you fly, my nigga?! People don't fly! Did those doctors give me some bad drugs or something? Oh my God…" I started to hyperventilate. I bent down, resting my hands on my knees as I took slow, long, deep breaths.

This is a dream. Yep, this is a dream, and I am going to wake up soon.

"Look, be cool," I heard Esco say. "I told you that we had to get you as far away from Keys as possible. Being in Chicago would have been deadly for him."

I spun around, taking in my surroundings as if it would give me an idea of where we were. "Where the hell am I?"

I looked around for anything that could be helpful in telling me where we were, but there was nothing. All that was in front of me was a brick house with a few lights on.

Esco cringed and frustratingly ran his hand over his head.

"Nigga, you got me in front of some random house, I don't know where I am, and my black ass was just flying! You better start talking!" I screamed.

I walked up on Esco like I was a damn giant. Fuck the fact that he was at least eight inches taller than me. I wanted to know what the hell was going on.

He studied me and shrugged. "Aight, fuck it... I'm a metahuman."

I stared at him, wondering had I heard him correctly.
Yeeep, I'm high. I gotta be.

I blinked slowly like it was going to wake me up from this bullshit nightmare, but it didn't. "A meta what?" I asked.

"A metahuman. It just means that I'm not one-hundred percent human. I can do things that other people can't, as you can see," he said motioning towards the obvious flight that I'd just taken.

"No shit," I whispered.

"I have certain... abilities, and so does my pops and my brothers."

"Whaaaat?" I asked slowly. I gave him a judgmental glare. Clearly, this dude was a psychopath. But I was the one that could have just sworn that I was flying in the air.

He groaned and shook his head. "There's no use in me repeating myself because you aren't going to believe me anyway."

I couldn't say a word. I just stood there with the slow blink again like a damn idiot.

Somebody pinch my fat ass so that I can wake up.

I didn't believe it. I wasn't crazy. This wasn't a damn Marvel movie. People did not have special powers for real. This wasn't real. Maybe those dudes *had* killed me, and I was actually dead.

"We don't have a lot of time. Right now, you just gotta trust that we the good guys," Esco told me. "It's some shit going on with Keys right now that he done got in the middle of unknowingly, and they out for his ass."

"Why?" I asked. Nothing that he was saying was making any sense to me. "I don't get it."

"I know you don't," he said. "As soon as we know Keys is good, you can do whatever the hell you wanna do. But, for now, you gotta stay here. Away from him. Real shit. If you care about Keys like you say you do, you'll do that for me."

I was getting real tired of hearing that from everybody. I didn't know what the hell was going on. They just expected me to stay at some random house in the middle of God knows where. I still didn't understand what he meant by me being around Keys being the key to his destruction. The last thing I knew, he had been shot. Was he okay? Did this mean he'd lived? Why the fuck wouldn't they tell me?

I didn't think I could handle anything else.

"Fuck it. Whatever," I conceded. This was too much, and I was tired of fighting every minute. It was too many unanswered questions, and I needed to gather my thoughts.

I followed Esco into the house, and he led me to one of the bedrooms.

"You can crash here. I know you probably tired," he said.

He was right. This had been an emotionally draining day. I had nothing left in me.

As I flopped down on the bed, Esco's cell phone rang.

"Hey, Pops," he answered. "How's he doing?"

I stared at his face intently, listening, praying for some type of confirmation. I saw the tension ease in his face, and I knew it had to be good news. He listened for a couple of minutes before he said anything. "Okay. We're here at the house now. I'll let her know." He talked for a few more seconds before hanging up. "Keys is going to be okay," he assured me, and finally his intense demeanor that he'd had all day lightened up.

"Oh, thank God," I whispered in a rush of relief.

I felt fresh tears stinging my eyes. These were happy tears though. I was so happy knowing that Keys was going to make it. I couldn't lose him too.

"I'm gonna be in the living room, if you need anything," Esco said, closing the door.

I sat back, looking around the barely decorated room and turned the television on for some type of noise. The silence was killing me. I couldn't get the visions of dead bodies out my head, no matter how hard I tried. The images of Travis and Kyan just wouldn't stop burning through my brain. I couldn't take it. I broke down and cried like a baby.

Today had been the worst day of my life. I felt like I was cursed. Everybody that I loved and everybody that I held close was either hurt or dead because of me. The only thing I had left was Keys, but he belonged to somebody else.

CHAPTER THREE
DREAM FRANKLIN

Keys had spent a grip on this ring!

I had been snooping around the house and found the receipt from the jeweler he'd bought it from. This nigga dropped damn near ten grand on it. I hoped he knew that he was going to get me an even *bigger* wedding ring. I was expecting him to break the bank on that one!

I had finally gotten Keys to propose and give me my ring. I knew it was only a matter of time, and now I was on my way to being Mrs. Valentine. But that didn't mean that I still wasn't going to get mine. While this nigga was at the club handling business, I was about to go and finish what I had started with Keys before he left.

I had given him some head so good, I damn near sucked the skin off his dick. I was trying to show him with my mouth how grateful I was for this ring. I was about to get fucked from the back over the kitchen table when Trouble called him, telling him to get to the club. Of course, he dipped, promising to dig my walls out when he got back, but it had been hours and a bitch was tired of waiting.

So, I hit up Zeek, and that nigga sent me to voicemail after two rings. I called him again, and it went straight to voicemail this time.

"Fuck this shit."

I was going to pop up on his ass. On my way out of the door, I hoped he didn't think that because I was engaged that he wasn't still going to give me the dick. I know that sleeping with Zeek was shady as hell, and I was playing a dangerous game, fucking with Keys' best friend, but I played the game well.

I got to Zeek's house in no time and started banging on the door. I could hear him inside moving, but he wasn't coming to the door.

I started banging harder. "Nigga, you better open the damn door!"

The door swung open and he stood there shirtless in some jeans looking pissed.

"Yo', what the fuck?" he growled.

I laughed at his ass. "Move out the way," I dismissed him as I pushed past him, walking into the house. He slammed the door behind me.

"What the hell are you doing here?" he asked. "Shouldn't you be celebrating your engagement?"

"I should, but the nigga had to handle some shit at the club," I told him. "So, I got some time."

I walked over to him and started tugging at his pants and licking his neck, trying to get to business.

"Stop," he refused.

"For what?" I smiled. "Oh, wait you got a bitch in here again? I think we both know I can chase any hoe that you got up in here away...unless..." A slick smile spread across my face. "She wanna join..."

"Nah, it ain't no bitch here," he frowned, swatting my hand away. "But if I did, I can do that. I'm single, Dream. *Your* ass is engaged."

"I know, right?" I giggled, looking at the ring. "I swear this ring is bad as hell."

He shook his head and shoved past me. "Yo', real shit, you got some serious fucking mental issues," he told me. "Do you hear yourself? You ain't even been engaged twenty-four hours, and you already over here trying to smash your man's homie."

"And that same homie been fucking his best friend's fiancée, so what the fuck you sayin'?" I shrugged. "You act like I'm the only one in this shit."

He was getting on my nerves with this 'holier than thou' act, wanting to be reformed.

"Man, I'm saying that this is foul as fuck," he said. "I can't keep fucking with you. It was one thing when y'all were just a couple, but this nigga is talking 'bout you being his wife."

I sucked my teeth and laughed. "You are gullible as fuck if you actually believe that shit." I huffed. "You don't think I know that he fucked that fat bitch?"

I didn't actually know that for sure. But with Zeek being his best friend, I'm sure he knew. He looked away and that gave me the answer that I needed. I wasn't expecting him to actually confirm it, but it just made it easier for me to fuck him and not have an ounce of guilt. Keys could act like he was this good boy all he wanted to, but I knew better.

Once a hoe, always a hoe. He'd cheated on me before, and this shit was no different. Only this time, he cheated on me with a bitch that wasn't even on my level, and he'd tried to cover that shit up with a ring.

"So, how am I foul as fuck when this nigga out here fuckin' around with this Snuffaluffagus looking bitch?" I questioned.

"Man, I didn't say he fucked that girl," he said, fidgeting.

"You didn't have to. I'm not stupid, baby." I shrugged and gave him a seductive smile. "Now, are you gon' sit here and keep talking about this shit, or you gon' come get in this pussy?"

I raised my dress up, so he could see my semi-wet cove. Walking up the stairs in his hallway, I sat at the top and spread my legs.

"I want you to come fuck me right here," I suggested with a smirk on my face.

He can act like he didn't want to, but the bulging dick in his pants said otherwise.

"Yo', Dream we can't keep doing this shit," he groaned.

His ass was walking up those stairs, though.

"Mmhmm. Yeah okay," I told him.

"This the last time I'm fucking with your ass," he told me.

I knew that was a lie. He would keep getting this pussy as long as I let him.

THE CAUSE AND CURE IS YOU 2
by *Jessica N. Watkins*

I pulled his dick out, put it in my mouth, and went to work. I loved sucking his dick. It was so pretty that I couldn't help but put it in my mouth. He could swear up and down all day long that he couldn't stand me, but he dicked me down like he did.

I was never going to let this shit go.

"Fuck!" he mumbled, fucking my mouth and thrusting his pelvis back and forth.

I knew he was enjoying this head. He was watching his dick disappear into my mouth over and over as I slobbed all over it, spit dripping from the side of my mouth while I jacked his dick. I know the sight of that alone was making him wanna bust.

"Shit," he groaned, trying to hold his nut back.

I was on a mission. He was going to give me what I wanted. I sucked harder, and it was only but so long before he pulled his dick out of my mouth and turned my ass over right there on the steps. He shoved his dick in my pussy and started taking his frustration with me out on my walls. It was feeling so damn good.

"Oh shit!" I screamed. "Fuck this pussy!"

I started throwing it back on him and squeezed my walls as tight as I could, trying to smother his dick.

"Ooo, fuck! Take that shit!" He started pounding me harder, and a bitch was in heaven!

Wanting him to give me all of it, I started talking shit. "Fuck this pussy."

He smacked my ass so hard that it brought tears to my eyes. "Shut the fuck up," he growled.

Grabbing me by my waist, he plowed me so damn hard that I thought I was going to go through the wall. With all of the screaming, I barely heard his phone ringing. He pulled his phone out of his back pocket, and I looked over my shoulder at him like he was stupid.

"Are you fucking serious right now?" I snapped. "I was about to cum!"

"Shut up," he said, wiping sweat from his brow. "It could be your *fiancé*. I'm supposed to be meeting up with him." Then he answered his phone, "Hello?"

Fuck that. I kept grinding and throwing it back on him. He wasn't going to stop me from getting mine. The idea though of fucking him with Keys on the phone was exciting. It reminded me of the night that I was at the office hiding under his desk.

"Wait, whoa. Hold on what?" he said into the phone, suddenly pulling out of me.

I turned around and opened my mouth to put his dick in, but he stopped me quick and pulled his pants back up. Then I saw he had panic all over his face.

"What the fuck you mean he got shot?" he asked the person on the other end.

My eyes got big, and I knew he was talking about Keys. I gave him a questioning look, and he held up a finger, letting me know to be quiet.

"Nah, I ain't talked to Dream," he said. "I'll try to call her, though, and let her know what's up. Do you know what hospital he at?"

I sat there listening, trying to figure out what was up.

"Aight, well just let me know soon as you find out."

He hung up the phone, and I waited on him to say something, but his face was frozen.

"What happened?" I asked.

"That was Keys' brother, Esco. Keys got shot," he finally said. "Something happened at the club, and they said he was shot."

"Oh my God, is he okay?" I asked him.

My heart was pounding, and I'm not going to lie, I was scared. I may not have been committed to Keys, but I didn't want him to die. Keys had already been shot once before, and now he had been shot again? What the hell was going on?

"Was it random? A drive-by? Was somebody after him or something?" I asked him.

"I don't know," he answered with a shrug. "I'm waiting on Esco to let me know what hospital he's at. But he said it's bad. Yo', I gotta get to the club and find out what the fuck happened," he said.

For some reason, as fucked up as it seemed, I was still slightly disappointed that I didn't get what I had come for. I guess it must have read on my face because he looked at me like he was actually disgusted.

"Keys is my boy," he reminded me. "And your fiancé. Both of us did some foul ass shit. But the shit stops today. I can't fuck with you no more. Despite what you think, that nigga love you enough to put a damn ring on your finger. If he even knew how you got down, yo'..." He just shook his head and continued to get dressed. Then he went down the stairs, shaking his head.

I don't know why I got so mad because he was right. Keys was shot, and we didn't know if he was gonna live or die, so my mind should have been on that. But this nigga was sitting here trying to make it seem like I was just some dirty ass thot.

"Hold up, Zeek," I said, following him. "I'm not the only one that's doing the foul ass shit. Now that he's been shot, you got a fucking conscience? Just as fucked up as it is with me fucking around with his homie, the same goes for his homie fucking his fiancée," I told him. "You know if Keys found out, he would murk your ass."

"Why the fuck are we talking about this shit?" Zeek snapped. "I didn't say that I was blaming everything on you. I said both of us was foul as shit for doing it. You so worried about getting dick, but you ain't even give a fuck that your nigga might not make it."

I decided to let that go. I needed to find out what was going on with Keys, so for now, I was going to just leave it alone.

"I'm going to go find out what's going on with my fiancé," I said pulling my dress back down and straightening my clothes.

"Yeah, why don't you do that?"

He opened the door, and I smirked at his cocky ass as I left.

His ass would be back. Hell, if I wanted, I could probably get a ring out of his ass too. I would let him throw his little temper tantrum because some serious shit was going on. Eventually, he would come to his senses. But for now, I needed to find out what was going on with Keys. He was up to something. Even when he was hustling, he was never in this much trouble. He never had folks coming after him. This was the second time now that he'd been shot, and it hadn't even been a month. I hoped to God that he was okay. I didn't know if I could make it out here without him. I didn't even want to try.

ANTONIO 'KEYS' VALENTINE

Beep. Beep. Beep.

I could hear a monitor making this loud noise, and I knew instantly where I was. I'd heard the same damn noise not too long ago the first time I got shot at *Dreams*.

I felt something on my head and opened my eyes to see a bright light above my head.

This wasn't a hospital. It looked like I was in a house.

"Yo', what the fuck?" I grunted, sitting up.

"Son."

I looked around to see my pops sitting in a chair and Reese in another. It took me a minute to see that I was in a house in a bedroom. There were machines hooked up to me, but I didn't see a doctor nowhere.

Pops stood up and walked over to the bed that I was laying in with worry all over his face.

"Good to see that your ass is finally up," he said as he gripped my shoulder. "You had us scared for a minute."

I was still trying to figure out what was going on. My head was throbbing a little, but otherwise, I felt fine.

"Yo'. What the hell happened? The last thing I remember I was going to the club and Trouble was there with the security team," I told him.

"Yeah," Pops agreed. "And so was Theodore."

Things started coming back to me. I remembered Theodore coming out of nowhere and introducing himself like shit was sweet. He was over two-hundred years old, but of course, like the rest of my family, he didn't look anything over forty-five. What I couldn't figure out for the life of me, though, was why I actually felt pain when he put a gun to my head and pulled the trigger.

"How did I end up feeling that pain?" I asked him. "I thought as long as I was away from Ivy, I was good. The last time I saw her, she was with her ex, and they looked like they were on their way out of town. So, I shouldn't feel any pain."

He raised his eyebrows in surprise.

"So, you talked to her?" he asked.

"Not today but I ended things with her a few days ago," I told him. "I told her that I couldn't be with her. I told her that I was gonna be with Dream. She didn't take it too well, of course, and she popped off and told me to kick rocks. I went back over there to apologize, but I just couldn't make myself get out the car. And then I saw that nigga, Travis, pull up, and she had luggage in her hand. I figured they were both going to Dallas. So, I left. I was at the crib when I got a call to come to *Dreams,* and the next thing I know, a damn gun was at my head. Last thing I remember was Theodore's smiling ass. And then I woke up here. How the hell did that happen?"

"Ivy was at *Dreams,*" Reese told me.

My eyes bucked. "Wh-what? When? How?" I rattled off. "I didn't see her."

"She told us what happened when we took her," he answered.

I sat up, slightly, "What the fuck you mean you took her?!"

"Calm down, son," Pops said.

"Nah. Fuck that! I wanna know what the fuck you mean by you took her! Where is she?!" I spat.

I started ripping off the monitors that were attached to my body. Pops raced towards me and, before I knew it, had slammed me down on the bed with such a force that I felt like I was going to go through it.

"Watch who the fuck you talking to," he growled. "I know you mad and everything, but your ass needs to be thanking us. We took her away to save you. If we hadn't, your black ass would be dead right now. And I ain't one of your fuckin' employees, so you better watch who the hell you speaking to. She's safe and ain't shit happening to her. So, calm the fuck down."

I didn't have a choice but to relax. I had never had a reason for him to put his hands on me, so I didn't know his strength until now. I'd gotten my strength honest. His eyes, which usually appeared drunken, were now dancing with fire.

He let me go and cleared his throat. "Ivy is safe, and now so are you."

"Yeah, you welcome," Reese added sarcastically.

I shot him a stare that let him know I would fuck him up if I could get past Pops.

"Where is she?" I asked them.

"She's with Esco," he said. "He said she's been bugging the hell out of him about you. But right now, it's better for her to stay there than be here. Because now that Theodore knows who you are, he's going to come looking for you again. He has no idea that you're alive right now. I took you out of the hospital and brought you here to my other house. I couldn't chance him finding out that you made it."

"You took me out of a hospital?" I asked.

"Yeah. You were healing too fast for someone that had been shot in the head. It would draw too much attention. It's only been...roughly twenty-four hours and the wound had almost healed. So, we brought you here. I have a friend that practices medicine that helps me out from time to time, so you're good. But you're staying here."

"Why was she at the club?" I asked.

"Think about it, son," Pops said simply. "Theodore must know who you are. He knows what it takes to bring us down. He brought her there to ensure your death."

"Yeah," Reese agreed. "She said that her, her cousin, and some dude, Travis, was supposed to be going to the airport because she got a job offer in Dallas."

I frowned hearing him say that. She never told me anything about a job offer. But then again, I couldn't blame her. Hell, I basically told her that I would never be with her. I just couldn't tell her why.

"They stopped at some gas station, and her ex got blindsided by a couple of Theodore's boys. Your security," Reese explained. "They ended up dragging them to *Dreams*. Honestly, bro, they beat her up pretty bad… and they killed her peoples."

I was pissed. Looking at the two of them, I could tell they were pissed too. I could see the anger behind my father's eyes, and I knew this was fucking with him.

Damn. I knew Ivy was probably going through hell. I could only imagine the type of pain she was dealing with. I really hated myself for hurting her so bad. I knew how much her cousin meant to her, and I knew she was losing her mind.

"She's going to be okay," Pops assured me as if he was reading my mind. "She doesn't hate you. She understands that you care. She's got her own grief that she's dealing with right now."

"Okay, then, where is she? I need to go talk to her. I need to try to make some sense of this for her and apologize."

"Boy, you were shot in the damn head!" Pops bellowed. "Me and your brother had to sneak you out of a damn hospital because our own fuckin' blood is trying to kill you. What part of that is unclear?"

He was beyond stressed. It was reading all over his face. He took a few deep breaths and calmed down.

"Look, son, I get it. Believe me, I understand. When you love somebody so much and you see them hurting, you want to do everything in your power to stop it. In my case, the best way for me to stop the one that I love from hurting, was to leave and never return," he admitted. "Sometimes the best thing to do is just walk away. I know you love her. But I'm telling you, if Theodore finds out that you're alive, he's not going to stop until he kills you. Now, trust me, I will find a way to shut him down for good, but I'm not about to lose my son. Not after all of this time. I spent years looking for you. My own selfishness made me abandon what was the most important thing to me, which was my boys. So, no, I'm not just going to let you get yourself killed because you want to protect her."

"Plus, bruh, what you think Dream is gonna say when she finds out that you left to go see some chick that she's been suspicious of this whole time after you just proposed to her?" Reese added.

Shit. I had completely forgotten about Dream. I felt like shit because I knew she was probably going crazy trying to get to me.

"Yeah, that's true," I admitted. "I know Dream's worried."

"It's been taken care of," Pops told me. "I called your friend, Zeek, and told him what happened. I didn't tell him exactly how serious it was, but I told him that you were at the hospital as a precaution. He said he would tell her. I've been buying you some time by not answering their calls. I just texted Zeek and told him that you would hit him up soon. Dream may be pissed at you, but it'll give us time to figure out what the fuck to do and for me to find Theodore's ass."

This was beyond infuriating. I had been shot three times in the matter of a few weeks, and I'd damn near died. I was thinking about Ivy so much that I had forgot that I had a fiancée now. Although I knew she probably wasn't as worried as Ivy. That girl loved me. There was no questioning that... But I had proposed to someone else.

"You aight?" Reese asked.

"Yeah." I sighed. "Just tired."

"Well, yeah you probably do need some rest," Pops suggested.

"Man, Rip Van Winkle was just asleep for like a day and a half," Reese joked.

I cracked a small smile, but my mind was somewhere else. This was a lot to deal with. I had everything mapped out. But it had been turned upside down. Pops' words resonated with me. This Theodore motherfucka wasn't going to stop until he killed me. How the hell could I live a normal life with a damn target on my back? Theodore knew that Ivy was my soulmate. It wouldn't be long before he found out I wasn't dead. Would he come after Dream next? Zeek? The club?

I couldn't deal with all the damn questions in my head. Instead, I chose to think about Ivy until I dozed back off.

*****

THE CAUSE AND CURE IS YOU 2
by *Jessica N. Watkins*

When I woke up, the room was dark. I could hear Pops and Reese talking in another room. The light illuminated the hallway. I got up to go to the bathroom and walked down the hallway. I could hear my father talking to Reese about Ivy being at a house in Michigan. Why the hell did they take her all the way to Michigan? She didn't know anybody there.

I coughed, and they stopped talking.

"You good, son?" Pops called out.

"Yeah, just going to the bathroom," I told him.

He must have known that I had heard too much because he jumped up and walked into the hallway. I ducked into the bathroom and closed the door before he could get to me. I didn't care what Pops said. The first chance I got, I was going to Ivy. Whether they liked it or not.

I went back to bed and lay there wide-awake, thinking about Ivy. Eventually around midnight, the house died down and I took my opportunity. I got up and started getting dressed. If I was going to leave Ivy for good, I was going to do it my way. I had to let her know why. I had to tell her the whole truth, no matter how crazy I knew it would sound to her. I owed her that much.

I crept into the kitchen, looking for the car keys without making noise.

"You just not gon' make this easy, are you?"

I jumped, seeing my father standing at the entrance. He turned on the light, and I froze like a kid getting caught in the cookie jar.

"I got to go see her pops," I shrugged.

"Son, you almost lost your life again," he reasoned. "You may be immortal to a point, but you not invincible. If you're not careful, you're going to start bringing attention to yourself. And the more attention that you bring to yourself, the worse it's going to be because then people are going to start wondering why in the hell this man keeps getting shot and surviving. Look at you, you're up walking around and you were shot IN THE HEAD."

He was right. I knew that he was trying to stay under the radar, but I needed to make sure that she was okay. I couldn't just leave it alone.

"You really love her that much?" he asked.

I just stood quiet. He already knew the answer to that. A small part of me felt guilty because I knew that I was still doing Dream dirty. Here I was expecting her to be here for me, when I was already on my way to another girl. But Ivy wasn't just any girl. She was mine.

I knew that I would never care for Dream the way that I did for Ivy. Dream was going to be that girl that I had on my arm, but Ivy would forever be the woman that I had in my heart.

Pops frowned a little and shook his head.

"Clearly, I can't stop you. If you are going to go see this girl, you need to be safe. Because the minute that

Theodore finds out your ass is alive, he's going to do everything in his power to kill you. And he may very well kill her too. So, I hope she's worth it."

My eyes told him my answer. She was worth all of that and more.

He tossed me his car keys and gave me a knowing look.

"You better lay low, boy, and get your ass back quick. We're about to be at war."

I nodded my head and walked toward the door.

"Text me the address," I called over my shoulder.

I left out and rushed towards the car, eager to get to Ivy. I hopped in the car, and as I peeled off, I got the text message from Pops with the address to where Ivy was. It was in Detroit, which was four and a half hours away, but it was nothing to me. I would have rather flown, but my abilities weren't that strong yet. But I would have drove four days to be with her.

I put the address in the GPS and drove, thinking about everything that my father had said and everything that happened. It seemed like no matter how much I tried, me and Ivy were always drawn back to each other. I couldn't get rid of her, no matter how much I was trying to. I had proposed to Dream, knowing that my heart was elsewhere. Truthfully, me nor Dream were going to be good to each other ever. I was always going to be thinking about Ivy, and Dream was always going to be selfish. I couldn't blame her, but at the same time I hated her for not being Ivy. I was going to be miserable for the rest of my life. I might as well risk it one more time for the one that I truly loved.

CHAPTER FOUR

ANTONIO 'KEYS' VALENTINE

I finally got to the address my pops gave me, and the door opened before I could make it up the stairs. I could see my brother, Esco, standing there, looking at me with a disapproving look on his face.

"I already heard it from Pops," I said. "I don't need to hear the shit from you too."

"Bruh, I ain't trying to stop you," he replied. "You the one rolling up in here at damn near five in the morning."

"She okay?" I asked, walking into the house, ignoring his sarcasm.

"Yeah. She's back there sleep," he told me. "I'ma be outside smoking a cigar. Figure I'd give y'all some space."

"'Preciate that, bruh."

I walked to the back room where Esco had pointed and opened the door to see Ivy curled up asleep. Just looking at her, I felt weak. She was so beautiful. Why did this shit have to end this way? Why couldn't we be together?

I walked over to her as quietly as I could. I admired the way her locs fell into her gorgeous face as she slept. Her cliffs of curves were barely covered by what looked like one of Esco's shirts. Her juicy thighs sipped from underneath the white tee.

She must have been sleepy lightly because she opened her eyes and jumped up out of bed when she saw me.

"Keys?!" she screamed in a whisper. "Oh my God!"

She wrapped her arms around me tightly, hugging me, crying uncontrollably, and stuttering over her words. I could barely make sense of what she was saying because her head was buried in my chest. It wasn't until she pulled back that she started making sense.

"I was so scared. I thought you were dead," she sniffed.

I hugged her again and for a few minutes, everything was straight. Things were right again for as long as I held her. It felt good. I'd needed this; to feel her. I just wanted to take all of her pain away.

She started looking me over, touching me everywhere, with so much confusion in her eyes. "Your…. your brothers said you were shot in the head."

"I was," I told her.

"But… how? How are you here? Walking around?" She was rambling, shooting off question after question. "You were shot in the head, Keys. What the hell is going on?"

"Ivy, sit down," I told her. "We need to talk."

She sat down on the bed and stared at me, worry all over her beautiful face.

I took a deep breath. Now that I was getting ready to finally tell her my truth, I realized that it was going to be harder than I thought.

"Look, I'm about to tell you something that's probably going to seem crazy as hell. But I promise you, it'll make sense later. Well... somewhat."

"What?" she pressed.

I took another deep breath before saying, "Aight, look, baby girl. There's a reason why I can't be with you."

Her eyes bucked dramatically. Then she sucked her teeth and snatched her hand away from mine. "Seriously, nigga? You came all the way to wherever the fuck I am to tell me why you *can't* be with me? I know you can't be with me, Keys!" she hissed. "I already know that you're getting married to your little girlfriend, okay? You didn't have to come tell me that. You didn't have to come rub it in my face on the day that I lost everybody that I loved."

"Ivy, no. That's not it," I said, reaching for her, only for her to push me away. "I wouldn't just be here to throw it in your face. You know me better than that. Just listen..." I stressed. Her nostrils flared as she folded her arms. I took advantage of her being pissed to silence. "What I was saying was there's a reason why I can't be with you that has nothing to do with Dream."

"Okay, what possible reason could that be?" she sighed.

"Ivy, you're my soulmate," I answered.

"What?" she asked with her pretty face balled up with irritation. "You think this shit is funny? Seriously, Keys, I been worried about you all this time, but now you're starting to piss me off."

"I'm not trying to do that, ma," I promised her.

She sucked her teeth. "How *aren't* you? So, if I'm your soulmate, then why are you pushing me away?" she urged. "If I'm your soulmate, then why the fuck are you getting married to another woman? Yeah, that makes sense," she said, rolling her eyes.

"Ivy, baby, from the day that I met you, it was some type of feeling that came over me. I didn't even know you, but something in me said to stop and help you. And I knew I was taking a risk knowing Dream wasn't feeling it, but I didn't care," I admitted. "I knew that I should have walked away from you and focused on my relationship with her, but I couldn't. Every time I tried to, you would enter my mind and I would find myself wanting to see you, touch you, feel you."

"Okay, and that's a bad thing?" she asked.

"Yeah," I told her.

She frowned again, and I tried to explain further. "It's only because when I'm with you, my life is in danger."

She cocked her head to the side, obviously confused. She opened her mouth to say something, but I cut her off. "Ivy, I'm a metahuman," I blurted out quickly.

Her eyes rolled as she slapped her thighs in frustration. "Ah hell, not you too!"

"What?" I asked, caught off guard.

"Now you trying to feed me that same bullshit that your brother told me earlier," she ranted. "Talking about how he was some kind of weird human or some shit."

"It's true," I told her. "I'm a metahuman. What it means is, that for the most part, I'm immortal. I can live forever, as long as I stay away from my true love. That's the only thing that can make me mortal. It's the only thing that could kill me. It's my kryptonite."

She sat quiet for a few seconds... and then scared the hell out of me when she started laughing, loudly. "Haaaaaaaaa!" She stood up from the bed and laughed hard as hell, clapping her hands. "Bravo, Keys! Bravo! Nigga, this is one hell of a performance," she laughed. "You seriously expect me to believe that your ass can come up in here after you told me that you never could be with me, and tell me that I'm your soulmate? Then turn around and say that in order for you to live some long ass life and be some metahuman or whatever the fuck you call it, that you have to stay away from your soulmate? You gon' get an Oscar for this one! Ha!"

"Ivy, I'm serious." I sighed. "Before meeting you, I had never gotten shot, never saw my own blood. I thought it was luck. Then the first time at your cousin's house, the bullet grazed me, and I was bleeding for the first time. Then standing next to you at the club and getting shot in the chest, I thought I was gonna die. And then I healed the same day, once I was away from you. I just got shot in the head yesterday and damn near died because you were there, but now I'm standing here in front of you in no pain. No wounds. Think about it! What does that tell you?"

She looked at me like I was insane. "Okay, so you're immortal."

"Yes."

I was relieved, feelings as if I was finally getting through to her... until she said, "Prove it."

I groaned. "What?"

"You heard me. Prove it," she repeated.

What the hell did she think this was? Ripley's Believe It or Not?

"How am I supposed to prove to you that I am immortal?" I questioned. "When I'm with you, I am mortal. I bleed."

"Well, you the one talking about you healed when you away from me. So, prove it."

I looked around the room and saw a box cutter sitting on a small table.

"Aight," I said walking over to it and picking it up. "Stab me as hard as you can with the box cutter in the hand. I'm gonna bleed. Take a picture with your cell phone. But I'm gonna leave and go as far away as I can and come back in a half hour, and I bet you my hand will look like it never got cut."

"You want me to stab you? Are you serious, Keys?!" she shrieked.

I handed her the box cutter. "You said you wanted proof. Just do it. I can take it. I took getting shot in the head, so this won't be shit."

"I can't," she said, shaking her head and cringing.

I grabbed her and pulled her to me trying to comfort her. "It'll be okay. I promise."

I put my hand on the table and she looked at me with an uneasy expression. I nodded, urging her to go on, and she raised the box cutter. Then she paused for several seconds before bringing it down hard.

"Argh!" Instantly, blood started pouring from my hand. She dropped the box cutter, backing away, and I grunted from the pain. "Shit."

"Oh God," she whispered.

"Take a picture with your phone," I instructed as I winced.

She grabbed her phone, hand shaky, and took the picture.

"Aight. I'm gonna be back in thirty minutes."

I left out the room and towards the door. Esco was still on the porch, smoking his cigar.

He gave this odd look, with his eyebrows furrowed, and he asked, "What the fuck were y'all in there doing? And why are you bleeding?"

"I'll tell you about it later," I promised. "I'll be back."

I hopped in the car and drove as far as I could for fifty minutes. By the time I parked my car, my hand had already healed. I took a picture and sent it to Ivy's phone and headed back.

When I walked back in the room, the first thing she did was look at my hand and her mouth dropped open when she saw again that it was completely healed. All the color left her face, as if she had seen a ghost. She snatched my hand up, bringing it closer to her eyes, and examined it closely. Finally, she gave me this look of fear and curiosity.

"So... you're some kind of like-- I don't even know what to call you," she whispered. "What the hell is going on?"

"I know it's crazy as fuck," I told her. "But I had to be real with you so that you know that I am not doing any of this to hurt you. This is why I can't be with you, baby. It's not that I don't wanna be with you. I just... I just can't."

I walked over to her and pulled her to me. She was hesitant, which was understandable.

"So, I really *was* flying..." She was staring off into space, speaking to herself.

"What do you mean?" I asked.

"Your brother fucking lifted me in the damn air and flew me through the city like superman. Then we landed here," she told me.

I rolled my eyes at that. I was strong and could sling my brother across the street, but this nigga was flying to different cities? Shit wasn't fair.

"I guess so," I told her. "It's just a lot of crazy shit going on right now. Theodore isn't gonna stop until I'm dead. So, we gotta take him out."

"Who the hell is Theodore?" she asked. "What did you do to him?"

I told her the story that my father told me, and she listened with wide eyes. I could tell she believed me because of the way that she so intently listened.

When I finished, we both sat quiet for several minutes. It wasn't much left to say.

"So, he knows who I am to you?" she asked after a while.

"Yeah," I answered. "He knew that you were my soulmate. When Trouble told him about how fast I had healed after getting shot, he knew. That's why he kidnapped you. If you're anywhere near me, I become mortal. I'm more likely to be killed. But when I'm away from you, I'm stronger. I am immortal. As long as we're together, neither one of us is safe."

Her eyes flooded with tears, and she pulled away from me again. The reality hit both of us in that moment.

"And you're just gonna settle with Dream? With a woman that you know you will never truly love?" she asked.

"Ivy... I'm sorry. I know none of this probably makes sense. I know you're probably confused right now. It hurts me too. I want to be with you. You're all I think about. I *know* Dream isn't the woman for me. But I can't bring you any more pain, baby. You've lost so much because of me. I can't stand to see you hurting anymore," I confessed.

"So! It's still not fair that she gets to have you and I can't!" she snapped.

"Ivy, don't you get it? There are people after me. They're going to do anything they can to kill me. They know what you mean to me! Everybody knows what you mean to me! If we are together, we are dead. I'm not going to let anything happen to you," I stressed.

She started wiping her tears away and pacing the floor. "You know the funny thing, Keys? I was leaving! I was leaving you alone like you wanted. I was taking my ass to Dallas and trying to forget about you because I felt so bad about expecting a man to leave his relationship for me after he stood in my face and told me that, despite his feelings for me, he didn't want to be with me. That he would be with his woman, but not the woman he *wanted* to be with. Now, you're standing in my face trying to make it seem like you're not trying to cause me no pain, but you keep reminding me that even after everything that's happened, we *still* won't be together?! That hurts just as bad as watching Kyan die. So, fuck you!" She was panting and going off so bad that her pancake colored skin was turning red. "Yeah, I said it. Fuck you, Keys!"

I reached for her, and she snatched away.

I don't know what came over me... Maybe it was the way that she was crying and still managed to look so beautiful. Or maybe it was just the fact that she just brought it out of me, but I needed to feel her. I pulled her closer to me and placed my lips down on hers. I feared that she would resist, but she didn't. She fell into the kiss and accepted it eagerly.

For a few seconds, all of the bullshit and drama disappeared as our tongues tangled into a web of unknown. Everything was forgotten momentarily.

I could taste the salt from her tears. I needed her bad. I fumbled with her clothes to remove them and she let me. I laid her down on the bed and she welcomed it.

Once our clothes were off, I spread her legs slowly, taking in all of her. Even with a tear stained face, she was still strikingly gorgeous. Bringing myself down to her, I kissed her again and entered her slowly. I could feel her warmth clenching around me as I stroked her.

I propped myself on my elbows and locked my eyes on hers, exploring her warm cave as deep as I could. Something was different about this time. It felt like I was reaching her soul. Not a word was said between the two of us. I don't think anything could have been said. I noticed silent tears falling from her eyes and softly kissed them.

How could I live without her?

How could I just walk away from her?

I needed her as much as I knew she needed me. I couldn't be with Dream. Ivy was the one. I didn't want to be miserable for the rest of my life. If it meant being mortal, then so be it. It was what I was going to have to do.

I started to speed up. I knew she was near the point of cumming because she started to clinch me tighter, her nails digging into my back. She still refused to cave and make a sound, and I could feel myself getting that tingling sensation.

Her eyes stared into mine, and I didn't like what I saw.

"Stop," she said suddenly.

I didn't listen. I kept stroking, trying to persuade her with this dick to change her mind.

"I don't want her. I want you; only you," I whispered.

"Stop," she repeated with a begging plea.

I finally stopped and looked at her, concerned. "What's wrong?"

"You need to go," she choked out.

"What?" I asked, coming down from my high, hard and fast.

I pulled out and sat up as she covered herself.

"You need to go," she repeated. "Keys, I love you. But I can't let anything happen to you. I can't be the reason why you die. Not you too. So, if it means keeping you alive by staying away from you, then, I'll never see you again. You need to move on and live your life. Go marry, Dream. Do you."

"Ivy –"

"No," she cut me off. "I'm going to go to Dallas. There's nothing here for me anymore. You won't hear from me again."

She stood up, and I watched her walk to the door.

"I'm going to take a shower. If you really love me, then you won't be here when I get back."

With that, she walked out of the door, closing it behind her, and I sat there, for the first time feeling like I had lost it all. I knew that she was right, and I knew that I had to go on and live my life.

But, for once, I didn't even know if having my life was going to be worth it if she wasn't going to be in it.

CHAPTER FIVE

IVY SUMMERS

After all the crazy things that had happened the last couple of days, I never thought I would miss Chicago so much. It actually felt good to be back.

However, I was still in my head about all of the things that had happened between me and Keys. He wanted me. He didn't want Dream, he wanted *me*... Yet, choosing to be with me would have been the death of him. Now, I knew why he had been playing games. It made my heavy heart smile through the sadness it was drowning in, to know that that man loved me and wanted me. But I couldn't live with his choice on my conscience. No matter how much laying eyes on him made my life better, made me breathe easier, I could not be the reason why he was hurt... or even worse, dead.

Now that Esco had finally given me permission to leave Michigan, I was on my way to tell Aunt Christine that Kyan was dead. After learning what Keys truly was, my mind was so blown that I hadn't even thought about telling her. He'd let her know that he was coming to Dallas with me. Since I had his phone, I knew that she hadn't called. She probably thought he had landed in Dallas and was enjoying her house being all to herself. She probably was partying it up.

Kyan was everything to me. And even though he and Aunt Christine had probably the most fucked up relationship ever, that was still her son. Yeah, she cussed him out and called him every dirty ass name in the book, but Kyan was her only child. I was scared to go to the house and tell her this, but I knew I had to.

When Esco dropped me off, it felt weird walking up those stairs. The last time I had been there, I was excitedly on my way to a happier, better life. It was such an eerie feeling knowing that that ended up being so far from the truth.

I could hear my aunt inside yelling at the TV. I tried to go over in my mind what I was going to say. I didn't know how she would react. She could hate me, blame me. She could break down. She could not give two fucks. I didn't know what to expect, considering her tumultuous relationship with Kyan. They say that the tough ones are the ones that love the most. If that was the case, she loved the *hell* out of Kyan.

I nervously used my key to unlock the door. I took a deep breath and walked inside. Our eyes met, and she grunted at me, then put her attention back on the TV.

"What the hell yo' ass doing here?" She asked. "I thought you and that faggot was in Dallas."

Yeah, so she isn't going to make this shit easy.

"Um, Auntie, I gotta talk to you," I said, walking over to her.

"Well, can you fucking talk away from the damn TV?" she snapped as she moved to look around me at the TV. "I'm trying to watch Family Feud and you in the way," she fussed grilling me. "And what the hell happened to you?"

My bruises hadn't completely disappeared. I still looked like I had gotten my ass whooped.

"What the fuck y'all done got into now?" she snapped. "And where the hell is that damn fruitcake? Nigga think he gonna leave this motherfuckin' house and leave me with these God damn bills so he can go trollop his hot ass off to Dallas. What? He sent your ass over here to try to apologize?" she rambled. "Well, tell that little punk ass motherfucka I said he can kiss my black ass and let him know not to be calling me when his ass getting arrested for doing dumb shit again."

"Aunt Christine, please!" I shouted. Her eyes bucked, and she continued to grill me as I went on, "I really gotta talk to you."

It was to the point that tears were forming in my eyes. How the hell could she just sit here and talk about her son like this?

Okay, I got to get myself together.

She sat on the couch glaring at me with her arms folded across her chest.

I took a deep breath and forced myself to say it, "We never made it to Dallas."

"What? His ass in jail again?" she asked.

"No." I shook my head. I could feel my heart dropping into the pit of my stomach, trying to get the words out. I sighed, long and deep, and started, "The other day, on our way to the airport, we stopped for gas and these two guys came out of nowhere and held us up at gunpoint and took us to *Dreams.* Long story short, they were looking for this guy that I was dating, and for lack of better words, he got into some shit, and ... these guys tried to use us as leverage to get to him." My voice was shaking, and I was trying to hold it together, but it was getting hard to do. "First, they killed Travis. Then they started hitting me. I kept screaming for help and..."

I had to stop. I couldn't get the words out. And it didn't help that she was sitting there looking like none of this was phasing her.

"They shot Kyan." I barely got the words out. My words were almost at a whisper.

"Stop all that damn mumbling girl and speak the hell up!" she snapped.

"He's dead!" I yelled. "They killed him. I tried to stop them, but they had me tied up. He's dead."

I was trying to watch to see if she was going to give me any kind of emotion, but she just sat there. Here I was literally in tears, and she was just silent. Did she hear what I'd said? Did she not understand that her only son was gone? I hoped so, because I did not want to have to go through telling her again. I couldn't bring myself to.

The only sound was coming from the TV. I stood there watching her stare at the TV with zero emotion in her face with completely dry eyes.

I couldn't take her silence anymore. "Are you okay?" I asked.

"I can't afford no damn funeral for this boy," she finally said.

"Huh?" I said.

I was caught completely off-guard. I knew I couldn't have heard what I thought I did.

But I had. "I ain't got no money to be buying caskets and all of that," she went on. "That boy barely gave me money as it was 'cause he was always up some other niggas ass and too busy to help his own mama. And the money I do get, I gotta try to keep the bills paid around here. I ain't got money for all of that."

My eyes bucked as I stared at her in complete and utter awe. I could not believe her. I just told her that her son died, and she was sitting here talking about how she couldn't afford a funeral!

"Wow." I huffed. "Is that all you can say? I just told you that your son was killed. He was shot! And all you care about is paying for the funeral?"

"That's what I said, ain't it?" she replied, pulling a cigarette out of the pack.

I shook my head and threw my hands up. "This is un-fucking-believable."

I just looked in amazement while she lit her cigarette and smoked like everything was cool. I had to get the hell out of there. It was too crazy for me. This woman clearly didn't give a shit. I needed to clear my head.

I started climbing the stairs to head to Kyan's room, but I stopped mid-stride.

She needed to know how I felt. She was too chill for me.

"You know what?" I started. "It's no wonder that Kyan hated being here. You treated him horribly. You made him feel like he was nothing. He had to act like shit didn't bother him because his own Mama couldn't accept him for who he was. But it did bother him, yet he still stayed. Quite honestly, I don't know why he didn't get the hell out of here sooner. All you did was talk shit about him and treat him like shit until he got some coins. Oh, the minute that he had money or the minute that he could do something for you, that's when you wanted to be all up in his face."

"That nigga owed me!" she yelled. "Don't come up in my damn house and try to tell me what I felt about my son. I don't give a fuck what you think! Hell yeah I made his ass contribute, 'cause he was a grown ass *so-called* man living in my damn house. And I find it funny that you wanna sit here and try to judge me and your ass is the reason why he's dead in the first God damn place."

She stood up and looked up at me, dropping ashes everywhere. "You wanna sit here and judge me when you the reason that boy is dead? You can take all that attitude and get the hell out of my house!!"

"Gladly." I told her.

All I needed to do was get what little I had left in his room out, and then I could get the hell out of her house. The only problem was, I didn't have a place to go. But anything would be better than this.

She stomped back to her chair and sat down, turning the TV back on, mumbling under her breath about how trifling I was and how I was such a bitch. I didn't have time for this shit. This was all the more reason why I needed to be away from here. I literally had nothing left in Chicago for me. As soon as I could make sure that Kyan got a decent burial and attend Travis' funeral, I was going to Dallas and starting over. Soon, Chicago would be a distant memory.

ANTONIO 'KEYS' VALENTINE

"Keys! Oh my God! I'm cummin!"

"Cum for me baby girl. Squirt all over this dick."

I was lost in her walls. God, she felt good. Every stroke that I made in her, it seemed like her pussy pulled me in a little bit more. I could tell she was about to cum the way her lips clenched my dick. I was spellbound inside of her. Her whimpering only made me want to go harder. I couldn't get enough of it.

She started to shake, and her walls were caving in on me.

"Oooo! I love you, Keys," she cried out.

"I love you too, Ivy," I whispered, tasting her sweet lips.

It was something that was different about the way that we made love. I knew her body inside and out and the more that I stroked, the tighter she got. I could feel myself ready to explode.

I looked in her eyes and released, giving her every last seed. Her pussy tightened around me once again, and she gave me that sweet ass nectar that I craved.

Then suddenly, the door burst open, and Theodore ran in firing his gun. Bullets riddled the room, and I could feel them striking my body. I tried to cover Ivy, but I was too late. I heard her scream as a bullet pierced her right in the heart. She looked at me with fear in her eyes, and I watched her soul leave.

"Keys," she whispered.

"No!" I screamed.

She was slipping away, and Theodore was laughing as bullets flew everywhere.

"Keys!"

I woke up sweating with Pops standing over me. I had to look around a couple times to remind myself where I was.

That dream was so crazy. It seemed so lifelike.

"You all right, son?" he asked.

I could see Esco and Lucky standing at the door. Lucky smirked and walked in the room.

"I know your big ass ain't in here having no damn nightmare like some little ass kid," he taunted. "Was you cryin' too?"

This lil' nigga was really starting to get on my nerves. He had a way of getting under my skin. If he didn't shut the fuck up, he was going to find himself getting tossed to fucking Africa somewhere. I chose to ignore him for the time being.

"What's going on?" Pops asked me.

"I just had this crazy ass dream." I told him. "I dreamt that I was with Ivy, and we were...making love, and right after she said I love you, the door burst open and Theo was there all of a sudden. It was crazy. I actually felt like I had gotten shot for real."

I looked down at my body just to check to make sure that I wasn't bleeding.

"Well, you ain't dead," Pops said. "But this shit with Theodore isn't."

"I know. I just don't want him to hurt Ivy," I said sitting up.

"What happened with that anyway?" Sincere asked, wanting to know about my conversation with Ivy.

I filled them all in on what happened last night. I told them about how she and I talked, how I told her everything, stabbing myself in the hand, and the look on her face when she saw me healed a half hour later.

I couldn't forget how she responded to everything. I thought about her pained expression. I thought about how good she felt when I was inside of her when we made love for the last time, and how I really wanted to be there to protect her.

"Basically, she told me that I needed to stay away from her and that she was letting me go," I summed up.

"Well, son, it sounds like she wants the best for you."

"Yeah," I said dryly.

"Look, I know it's hard right now, but eventually you'll understand, and it won't hurt as bad."

"She said she's going to go ahead and take the job in Dallas," I told them.

"Well, that's good for her. It'll give her a chance to start over," Sincere spoke. "I know shit is probably hard for her right now, between things with you and the death of Travis and Kyan."

I mumbled, "I guess."

"So, what are you going to do about Dream?" Pops questioned. "Are you going to let her go?"

"Yeah, bruh, what you gon' do, 'cause your ass can't stay hidden forever. It's already been a day and a half since you've been shot," Sincere pointed out. "Now you're sitting here in wrinkled clothes, smelling like Jack. Dream ain't gonna sit tight too long. You know that girl quick to go off."

Lucky snorted, walking over to the wall at the other end of the room and leaning against it. "Man, if I had a chick like that, I'd be blowing her back out every night," he boasted.

This nigga really wanted me to whoop his ass! I jumped up out the bed and went straight to him.

"What the fuck is your problem?" I asked.

This wasn't cool. She may not be my soulmate or no shit like that, but at the end of the day, this motherfucker needed to respect me and mine.

"You better watch your motherfuckin' mouth," I growled.

I was right up on him and could see low key his ass was scared. Pussy ass nigga.

"It ain't like you love her ass anyway," he said breaking his stare.

I was two seconds away from choking the living shit out of him.

"All right that's enough," Pops said. "Lucky, you gone keep pushing it and get fucked up and ain't nobody gone feel sorry for your ass either. I don't know what the hell it is with you and Keys, but you need to stop this. If anything, you should understand."

"Why I gotta understand?" he snapped. "You didn't."

This is the kind of shit that I didn't need to worry about. This lil' nigga was too bitter on some shit that pops did and couldn't get over this. He was walking around with this big ass chip on his shoulder. But I wasn't his problem. He needed to take that shit somewhere else.

I walked back to the bed and started putting my shoes on.

"So, what you gon' do?" Sincere pressed, changing the subject.

I'm guessing this shit with Lucky and Pops was a regular and he was used to it.

"I mean, shit, I'ma go back home," I told him. "Handle shit with Dream and deal with her crazy ass. Ain't nothing else I can do. By now, Ivy's probably already halfway to Dallas."

"Nah, she hasn't left yet," my father said. "She's getting everything together for her cousin's funeral."

I looked at him surprised. "How the hell you know that? Did you talk to her or something?"

"No," he said. "I've got eyes on her. And before you ask, she's fine. She's not in danger or anything. I just got people watching her just in case. I think Theodore still thinks you're dead, but I'd much rather not chance it, so I've got people watching her. Don't go after her," he warned.

"Don't call her. Just leave her alone. Let her grieve and let her move on."

"Look, Pops, I know this. But this is still fucked up." I admitted. "I don't know I'm just... sitting back and thinking about how my life is gonna be with Dream, and knowing I'm literally going to live forever with a chick who I know ain't the one. All I'm thinking about is how I'm going to end up marrying this girl and probably having kids with her, and she's gonna age and the kids are gonna get grown, and eventually they're going to start to wonder why their dad isn't looking older. And knowing that I still can't be with Ivy just doesn't make sense to me."

"You right." Pop nodded. "None of it does. But that's just how it is. As long as Theodore is around, as long as there's evil around, then it's what must be. But you have a choice, son," he said looking at me concerned. "Now, I'm not saying that I want you to be looking over your shoulder for the rest of your life, but I don't want you miserable either. They are many of us Valentines that have chosen the regular mortal life, and we're fine with it. But I can't let you live obliviously either, son. If you do choose that life, it's going to be a short-lived life, as long as Ivy's around. You know this."

I sighed, "Yeah, I know."

I didn't think it would be, but it was really hard for me to deal with this internal battle. I knew that I needed to stay away from Ivy, but I just couldn't stand the thought of what life would be like without her. How could I spend countless years knowing that the reason why I'm around so long is because I'm not with her? It was a hard pill to swallow.

Everything in me was saying to go see her, to hold her and make her let me choose her, but I knew what I would be giving up. I knew that choosing her was giving myself a death sentence.

I was forced to make choices that I didn't agree with. Still in all, I wanted Ivy.

"Why can't we just get rid of Theodore?" I asked, frustrated.

"Good question," Sincere agreed.

"Trust me, I want that motherfucker gone as much as you do," Pops told us. "But since we can't just kill him, it's not as easy as it sounds. We have to think of a plan to make sure that he stays away. He's made his whole life about torturing this family. But the one thing y'all gotta know about evil, is that it's not always easy to defeat. He knows that I'm gunning for him. So, to attack now would be stupid. Right now, I need to find out *how* he knew how to get to you. I found you on accident. So that's got me a little worried that he could have had eyes on you before I even came around."

What Pops had said made sense. After all, Trouble was the one that had set that shit up at the club. And Trouble had been around for a minute.

"I don't know how he found me, but I know who brought him to my club," I said.

They all turned and looked at me, and I stood up to get my shit.

"We need to get to Trouble. He had Theodore in my shit. We get to him, we get some answers."

CHAPTER SIX

STEVE VALENTINE

"So, how we gon' go about doing this?" Esco asked.

I was sitting at the table at my home with all of my son's around me; except Reese. He volunteered to go to Miami to keep an eye on Bridget and the other kids until we were sure that they weren't on Theodore's radar.

We had left the hideaway and decided to get together at my house to try to figure out how we were going to get rid of Theodore. Keys had to go back home soon because it had been two days, and I could only keep Zeek and Dream at bay but so much longer, so we had to have this meeting now. Theodore had to go down. The only way that I could see any of us being remotely safe was to run him and his entire operation out of Chicago.

"However we do this, it has to be meticulous," I told them. "Theodore's not stupid. We got to get inside his head, we got to get inside his organization. Get rid of them one by one. Once we do that, then we get to Theo. But we can't be out here doing anything reckless. So, Lucky, that means your ass can't be out here wildin' the fuck out," I warned him.

Everybody looked at him, and, of course, he got in one of his little childish moods.

"What the fuck y'all looking at me for?" he barked.

"Because you the damn firecracker out of everybody," Esco spoke. "You always got something to prove. And nine times outta ten, somebody gotta save your ass."

"So, that means don't be out there doing nothing stupid," I added. "Just cause your asses are immortal don't mean he just gon' back down. And don't be bringing no attention to yourselves either. If you start doing dumb shit, then you gonna have folks hunting us. All we gotta do is get rid of Theodore. If we don't, this nigga will keep fucking with us for the rest of our days, and he knows how to get to some of us. So, watch yourself, cause I ain't got time for the stupid shit."

"We got it, Pops," Sincere said.

He was the calmest one of all my kids. I could never know what was going on in his mind. Lucky; he was easy to read. He hated my ass, but he knew that no one would have his back like me and his brothers did. Esco was reserved, but he had his moments. Reese was in his prime, and the only thing I really had to worry about with him was knowing that women were at his disposal. But Sincere was hard to read sometimes because he was so calm.

"Did you find out anything about Trouble?" I asked Keys.

"Yeah," he nodded. "Got word that he's puffing his lil' chest out. They said that nigga already acting real stupid like he the boss."

"Well, it sounds like the boss needs to be checked then," Esco spoke.

"Hell yeah," Keys agreed.

"All right. So, what's the first step?" Sincere asked.

"We need to get Trouble alone, 'cause he seems to be the direct link to Theodore. Now, Keys, you gon' have to rein that temper of yours in. I know that you wanna take him down, and you will in good time. But we need to get all the information out of him and may need to use him for a bit. If you kill him, then it'll ring alarms for Theodore."

"Okay," Keys agreed.

I could tell by looking at him that he was just telling me what I wanted to hear. Much like Lucky, I could see he had that hard-headed nature where he thought he knew it all. The only difference was, Keys could rein his in better.

"I'm serious, son," I told him.

"I said okay," he gritted.

"Good. Now once we can get inside his operation, we tear down from the inside out. Theodore will have no choice but to get the hell out of Chicago."

"And if he doesn't?" Lucky asked.

"Then I'll take him out myself." I meant that with every fiber of my being.

"Pops, how the hell you gonna do that?" Esco asked.

"Yeah. That nigga just like us. And he been around a lot longer too," Sincere added.

"This is true," I said. "But age means nothing. It's all about strategy. That's why we got to get inside his organization. We got to study him. We need to know everything about this nigga's moves. Find out his weaknesses. We do that, we get him. Nobody is perfect. He's bound to fuck up. And the minute that he does, I'll be right there to catch him."

"I don't understand why we can't just go and kill this motherfucka right now," Lucky said, jumping up out his seat.

I couldn't do nothing but shake my head. I knew he was going to do something stupid. Why the hell did I put him in on this shit? He was so fucking hard headed! The funny thing is, he reminded me so much of myself.

"Because he won't just die, you stupid motherfucka," Esco explained. "Did you miss the whole 'this nigga is a meta human too' part?"

"Fuck you, man," Lucky mumbled, sitting back down. "I'm saying. It's more of us than it is him."

"You're right, son, but that don't mean shit when he is *immortal*," I told him.

"So, the planning is good and all, but we need to get to Trouble while his guard is down. While he thinks I'm dead. Right now, he thinks he's won," Keys said.

"Yeah, you right," I admitted. "We do."

"Aight, so, why don't we go pop up at the club?" Esco suggested.

I saw the stone-cold expression on my son's face.

"Sounds like a plan," Keys agreed. "But the minute that he gives us what we need…"

I nodded my head. What was understood didn't have to be discussed. Trouble's time was about to be up. And so was Theodore's.

DREAM FRANKLIN

It had been two days since Zeek had told me about Keys. The only thing that he knew was that Keys had been shot again, and that he was in a coma. I tried calling hospitals to find out where he was, but nobody had him in their system. I was actually starting to get scared because it wasn't like Keys to just disappear like that. He used to do that kind of shit when he was hustling, but he said he wasn't doing that anymore.

He had been sending me these vague text messages telling me not to worry, which only made me worry more.

I had been seeing stories on the news about bodies being found at *Dreams*. When I rode by the club, it was police tape everywhere and camera men snapping photos. I didn't know what I was going to do. I wasn't able to take care of myself! Keys had been taking care of me for three years. I didn't know how to work. I wasn't going to either!

I was sitting there trying to figure out what I was going to do when I heard the front door open. I jumped up and ran to the living room to see Keys come strolling his ass in the door! This nigga was about to hear me today!

"Uh, nigga, where the fuck you been?" I snapped on his ass instantly.

He came through the door like he just went to go run errands. Fuck the fact that he was gone for two days!

"I know, baby," he defended instantly, tossing his keys on the table.

But I ignored how truly sorry he looked. "What the fuck, Keys? I thought that you were hurt. I've been going crazy trying to figure out what happened!" I shrieked. *How the fuck could he be sitting here acting like ain't shit wrong?* "Nigga, you left outta here to go to the club TWO DAYS AGO, and then Zeek is telling me that your daddy is telling him you got shot and was in a coma!"

"Yeah, and I bet your ass has just been so worried about me," he replied mockingly as he looked around. "Look like you chilling to me. You're having a drink and watching Love and Hip Hop?"

My mouth dropped as he flopped down on the couch.

I know his ass was not coming up in here trying to make me feel guilty? Oh hell nah!

"First of all," I hissed through narrowed eyes. "You don't get to come up in here and try to tell me how I'm supposed to be feeling," I snapped. "Did it ever occur to you that maybe I was doing all of that because I was trying not to worry about what the fuck was going on with your ass?" I asked. "You the one walking around here with a God damn target on your back lately. Every time I turn around, you're getting shot," I said. "I'm watching bullshit TV 'cause I was tired of hearing about this on the news while not knowing where you were. Why the fuck couldn't I know where you were, Keys? Why the fuck did I call every fuckin' hospital and nobody had you registered, huh?"

Something was up that he wasn't telling me. He was sitting in front of me and I didn't see a mark on him. If he was shot, there would be some type of damn scar or something. But he was sitting in here flawless.

He sat back and started rubbing his head.

"Look, my bad for coming at you like that," he apologized. "I'm just stressed the hell out. It wasn't as bad as my pops or Zeek made it sound. The bullet barely grazed my head. It was just a lot of blood, and it looked like I was really hurt."

"So, then what the fuck is everybody talking about on the news, huh?" I pressed. This nigga was lying about something, I know it. "I been seeing stories about bodies being found at *Dreams* and somebody being carried out of the club. And now you're sitting here talking about how you good. If you so good, then why in the fuck your ass been gone all this time, huh?"

I wasn't stupid. This nigga was fucking around with another bitch or something. He had to be. Looking at him, he looked totally fine. And the only reason that I could think of for this nigga to be gone that long was because he was fucking with somebody else or hustling again.

"Who you fuckin', huh?" I asked. "You fuckin' that fat bitch?"

"Yo', you buggin'. You seriously need to let that shit go," he said rolling his eyes and getting up, walking past me to the kitchen.

But I was right on his heels. "And you seriously need to tell me what the fuck you were doing! I ain't got time for this shit, Keys. I can do bad by my motherfuckin' self."

Truthfully, no, I couldn't. But I was proving a point right now and was on a roll.

"How the fuck you gon' sit up here and propose to me, and then turn around and just disappear for two gawd damn days? Then you stroll your ass back up in here like everything is all cool and expect me to be straight with it?"

I was pissed the hell off. He was acting all nonchalant like he didn't give a fuck, and I was not about to have that. This nigga was not about to make a fool out of me after all this that I'd dealt with.

"Ain't nobody expecting you to be straight with shit," he said. "I don't need no extra shit right now."

My eyes bulged. "Oh, so I'm extra shit now?" I asked. "I'm getting real sick of this."

I walked over to the refrigerator and opened it, looking for something to drink. I couldn't even look at him right now. This is exactly why I kept Zeek on standby. Keys was becoming too unpredictable. That nigga worshipped the ground I walked on at one point, and now he was acting like I was some mere afterthought.

I got another can of Lime-A-Rita out the refrigerator, popped the top, and took a long sip. I heard him walking towards me, but I kept my back to him. I was not trying to hear anything else that he had to say.

Before I knew it, he had his arms around my waist, his dick pressed up against my ass.

"I'm sorry, baby," he whispered in my ear, kissing my neck. "A nigga fucked up. But I ain't out there fuckin' around."

I knew he was lying. I'd already heard from people that be in *Dreams* that some chick had been up at the club that sounded a lot like that fat bitch that he picked up on the street in that wedding dress. She was really starting to be a problem for me. But if he was going to lie about it, then I damn sure was going to have some fun.

He turned me to him and pushed me against the refrigerator. "You hear me?"

I loved when he got rough with my ass.

"You scared me," I said, giving him my small and helpless voice. "I thought you were gone."

I'd even managed to work some tears. They didn't fall, but still, it worked! He kissed me hard, and I knew I had him right where I wanted him.

"Let me make it better," he murmured in between kisses.

"I'm just saying, baby," I whined. "It seems like you're getting into more shit now than you did when you were hustling. You've been shot twice in like a couple of months. Like what the fuck are you not telling me? It's got to be something going on."

THE CAUSE AND CURE IS YOU 2
by *Jessica N. Watkins*

"It's nothing," he said. "I know it's been a lot going on. I'm just stressed out. And I ain't mean to take it out on you." He actually looked sorry.

"You sure you trying to get married?" I asked him.

"Why? You don't want to marry me now?" he asked.

"Can you blame me?" I replied.

He nodded his head. "Aight."

"I ain't saying that I don't want to marry you, Keys," I told him. "I'm saying that I'm done dealing with this bullshit. It's not cool for you to just string me along. If you gon' be with me, then be with me. You asked me to marry you. And then the next thing I know, you disappeared. How the hell am I supposed to take that?"

"You right," he admitted. "And I'm sorry. It ain't right the way shit is going down. But I'm gonna do better."

"Okay," I said.

I needed to get him back in my grasp. He was going to give me the lifestyle that I deserved, and hell, the one I worked hard for. So, I needed to play nice for a little bit.

"Well, how about we finish celebrating our engagement?" I purred, grabbing at his dick.

I started massaging his dick in my hands, and within seconds he was hard. "You got some making up to do."

For some reason, he was reluctant, which only made me even more confident that he had spent the last two days with another woman. But that was okay. Finally, he wasn't the only hoe in this relationship.

The Cause and Cure Is You 2
by Jessica N. Watkins

Despite his reluctance, he swung me around and bent me over the table, smacking my ass so hard that tears came to my eyes. I liked this kind of behavior from Keys. He was acting like my nigga again. He had been acting like a bitch lately, but this Keys was the one that I fell in love with. This Keys right here was the nigga that had me twisted.

Once he put that dick inside me, it was a wrap.

"Shit!" I moaned.

His dick fit perfect in my pussy. He started fucking me so good that I temporarily forgot that I was mad at him. I could hear him grunting, and he grabbed my neck grinding deeper into me.

I started to throw it back on him and clenched tight, sucking his dick with my pussy lips.

"Ooo, I missed this dick!" I cried out. "Fuck, Keys. Fuck me hard, baby. Take your pussy."

He growled, and I could feel his sweat against my skin. He was putting in work on my pussy. He grabbed me by my waist and thrust so hard with his big frame, that my body was pushing the kitchen table across the floor.

"Shit!" I screamed. "Keys, baby, you trying to make me cum!"

"Then cum then!" he growled.

He smacked my ass hard again, and I started to play with my pussy while he dicked me down. I was throwing it back so hard, he was bucking like he was riding a mechanical bull. All that you could hear in between my moans and his grunts was the sound of his balls hitting my ass and the screech of the table legs dragging the floor while he took all his frustrations out on my walls.

It was a beautiful fucking sound.

I exploded all over his dick, my cream dripping down my thighs and lubricating our session. That only made him go harder. My legs were about to give out from under me and then I felt that familiar hot lava entering my womb before the excess came sliding out mixing with the sticky cream on my thighs.

CHAPTER SEVEN

IVY SUMMERS

"Now, Ms. Summers, we've got a lot of different options and packages that you can choose from. The caskets start as low as five-hundred and go up from there. If you know that you have a lot of family and friends that will be in attendance, then we can accommodate that here or, if you prefer to, have a church. Do you have a pastor in mind?"

I heard the man speaking, but I couldn't bring myself to answer him. He was rattling off all these questions at me, but, for some reason, there were no words. I was still trying to deal with the fact that I was sitting here at a funeral home trying to make arrangements for Kyan. This was getting harder to deal with. It's been hard to deal with. But being here was breaking me down.

Since Aunt Christine put me out the house, I'd been holed up in a hotel for the last couple of days avoiding this. I knew eventually that I would have to make arrangements, since she had made it clear that she wasn't paying for anything, but I didn't think it would be this hard.

Sitting in the funeral home, all I could think about was Kyan laying on that cold slab, alone, and no one to mourn him but me. Now, this man, Mr. Ross, was sitting across from me telling me all of this stuff at one time, and it was just too much.

"Ms. Summers?" he said, getting my attention.

"I'm sorry," I apologized trying to focus. "Um...it's just a little bit too much right now."

"I understand," he nodded his head. "It's a difficult process for anybody to deal with. Do you need a minute to yourself? Or do you want to try to do this another time?"

"No," I said shaking my head. I let out a big sigh and straightened myself up. "I need to go ahead and take care of this now." I cleared my throat and looked him in the eye. "I don't think it'll be a large funeral or anything like that. So, I don't want to do anything too extra. But I want to go ahead and get him taken care of. He needs a proper burial."

"Yes, ma'am," the director said. "I know this is probably a little unorthodox, but I actually heard about your cousin's murder on the news. And let me just say that you have my deepest condolences," he offered.

"Thank you," I replied.

"It's so unfortunate," he continued. "These two young men cut before their prime."

Travis and Kyan's faces had been all over the news. Every media outlet had been talking about the shooting at *Dreams.* Of course, people had all kinds of versions as to what happened. I had heard everything from a drug deal gone bad, to a secret relationship between Travis and Kyan. It was ridiculous. Not to mention that the news had also reported that there was a third person involved that had been seen running from the scene of the crime. I had a feeling they were talking about me. Good thing is, nobody got a good description.

The director kept rambling about how the world was going to hell if it continued in the direction that it was going, and I cleared my throat to steer him back. I guess he must have realized that he was not really helping the situation because he finally stopped talking about it.

"My apologies," he said. "Well, I have a couple of catalogs that I'd like you to look at, and then maybe that'll kind of help you get an idea of what you want," he offered, setting the books in front of me.

"Okay," I said.

"I'm going to give you a few minutes to look everything over. If you need me, I'll be right outside."

He got up and walked off, and I started thumbing through the pages of the catalog. Could I even bring myself to look at Kyan's body lying in a casket? What about Travis? Did he have anybody helping with his arrangements aside from Renee? I knew his mother was probably a basket case. When I told her what happened, she broke all the way down. I remembered having to catch her, and for once, I actually felt sympathy for her, which was very hard for me with his mother because she always looked down on me.

My phone rang, and it snapped me out of my thoughts. I looked to see that Sara Robinson was calling me. Shit. It hit me that I forgot to call the hospital in Dallas.

"Hello?" I answered.

"Hey, Ivy, how's it going?"

"Hey." I huffed. "I am so sorry. I forgot to call and let you all know what happened."

"Yes, the hospital called and said that they were expecting you yesterday," she said.

"Yeah," I said. "I'm going to have to give them a call."

"Is everything okay?" she asked. "This is a good opportunity, Ivy. You said you could do this. I would hope the only reason for you not to show is because of something life-threatening."

"Well, it kind of was," I told her. "My cousin and my boyfriend were both killed this past weekend."

I could hear her breathing drastically. "Oh my God, Ivy! I am so sorry," she rushed. "I know I probably just said the dumbest thing."

"It's okay," I assured her. "You couldn't have known. It was just a lot going on, and I didn't even think to call. But I'll call them and see if they can give me a couple of extra days."

"No, no, no, it's okay," she told me. "I'll give them a call and let them know what's going on. I hope I don't sound too insensitive, but do you think you can start next week?"

"Yes." I told her. "I just needed to have enough time to make the funeral arrangements for my cousin and attend their funerals. But if they can let me start next week, that would be great. I'll definitely be there I promise."

"Okay good." There was a pause before she spoke again. "Ivy, I'm really sorry."

"Thank you."

She was probably one of the few people that had said that, and it sounded sincere. Everybody else that knew of what happened was giving fake condolences because they wanted to know what happened, or like the funeral director, they had said it so many times that it became meaningless.

"You just make sure that you take care of yourself," she added. "And call me if you need anything, okay?"

"Okay," I said. "I really appreciate it."

"Of course. I'll talk to you soon."

I hung up with her and dropped my head in my hands, trying to gather my thoughts. Everything was just happening so fast, and I felt like I was drowning. Here I was by myself trying to make these funeral arrangements, and I knew that not a lot of people were going to be there for Kyan. I didn't even know if his own mother would be there.

I kept thinking how life would be if we had never stopped at that gas station and gotten kidnapped. Kyan would have loved Dallas, especially the nightlife. I could just see him ready to tear up the streets and party.

Damn, Kyan was supposed to be here. He was supposed to be right there with me starting over. It was supposed to be an opportunity for *both* of us. But because of some bullshit that Keys was mixed up in, my cousin was gone.

As much as I loved Keys, there was a small part of me that resented him for that. I knew that he wasn't directly responsible for pulling the trigger, but because of all of this shit that he had going on with his family and this Theodore guy, my cousin and Travis died a miserable, painful, and terrifying death. Travis hadn't been the best man to me, but he didn't deserve to go out like that.

I looked down at my phone at the screensaver of me and Kyan posing outside of the club. He had the biggest smile and was serving face, and I was looking at him laughing. He always knew how to bring the fun, no matter where we were. It wasn't fair. He didn't deserve it. He deserved a new life more than I did.

Mr. Ross walked back into the room and gave me a small smile.

"Have you seen anything you like?" he asked.

I didn't know where the thought came from, but him walking in was perfect timing.

"Actually," I started. "I don't think that I want to do a casket. I want to have him cremated."

"Well, Ms. Summers, if it's a matter of cost, then, I'm sure we can find something that's affordable in the form of burial. I don't want you to think that cremating him is going to be the best option because of financial situations."

My finances were strapped, but, not to that degree. I had saved most of my money since I started working. It was easy because I was staying with Kyan and didn't have to worry about a lot of bills. Plus, the day that we left for Dallas, Travis pulled out all the stops to show me he had changed and was being supportive and gave me and Kyan money for a shopping spree when we hit the streets of Dallas. I had been hesitant about taking it, while Kyan looked like he had hit the lotto. "Bitch, you better take that money," he'd fussed.

I smiled thinking about it. Lucky for me, it was still in my pocket, and the morgue had returned Kyan's to me, so money would be tight, but I had enough to make it.

"No," I told him. "I think this is the best way to keep my cousin close to me."

"Okay," he said. "If that's the direction that you want to go."

"Yes," I nodded. "We can still have a nice little going away ceremony and let everyone say their goodbyes if they wish."

Cremating Kyan would be perfect. When I left for Dallas, I was going to take him with me. He would still be able to start over. If I was going to start my new life in Dallas, then I was still going to have my cousin right by my side... just like we planned.

ANTONIO 'KEYS' VALENTINE

"Keys, baby, I'ma be back in a little bit. I gotta go pick my homegirl up from work, and then we're going to go look at some wedding dresses."

"Aight," I nodded.

Dream was standing behind me, smiling hard as hell and looking at me in the mirror in our bedroom. I was glad that she was leaving because I'd been in the house since I got back home the day before yesterday and was itching to get out. She had been doing everything to keep me there. I was actually trying to take Pops' advice and put forth the effort to be more involved with her. Dream was even starting to act like she had some sense. She hadn't been whining and complaining like her usual self or just outright getting on my damn nerves, so things were actually pretty good.

But, like always, my mind always managed to find a way to think about Ivy. I knew she was still dealing with the death of her cousin and Travis. We were still friends on Facebook, and I'd been finding out what was going on with her through looking at her page. Every post she made was about Kyan and Travis, and about losing the one you loved. I wondered selfishly if any of those posts were about me.

"What are you about to get into?" Dream asked, noticing me getting dressed.

"Not much," I told her. "Probably get up with Zeek."

I noticed that she frowned up a little bit when I said that, but I let it go. I wasn't about to get into it with her about me leaving to go hang out with my boy.

"Oh okay," she said. "Well, did you want to go get something to eat or anything later on? Or I can cook."

I actually turned around on that one and looked at her amused. "You? Cook?" I laughed.

"Fuck you, Keys," she smirked, flipping me the finger. "I can do a little something. I know I don't cook that much, but I can do the basic stuff."

"Yeah, all right," I laughed.

She smiled again this time, holding up both fingers.

"Whatever," she dismissed. "You just wait and see."

It felt good to joke with her. Maybe this wouldn't be so bad. Maybe I could live a life that was somewhat happy, as long as things stayed like this and wasn't full of her dramatics all the time.

"What?" she asked, noticing me staring at her.

"Nothing. Just looking at how fine you are, is all," I told her.

"Boy, you better quit before I get your ass back in that bed," she teased.

"Don't worry; I'ma get that ass later," I replied. "I gotta re-energize, though. You been trying to wear me out. Gotta save something for the honeymoon."

She pouted slightly, but I ignored it, turning back around.

"Have fun dress shopping," I told her.

"All right," she shrugged. "I'll hit you up in a little bit. Love you!"

"Cool. Love you too," I rushed.

Then she yelled out over her shoulder as she walked out, "And don't be going out there getting shot!"

And just that fast, things had gone right back to normal; her saying shit to irritate the fuck out of me. That shit wasn't funny. I wasn't about to let it ruin my day, though. I just shrugged it off and went back to getting dressed. I was going to meet up with Pops and just chill for a little bit.

I'd been laying low like he said, but I was starting to go crazy, even though it had only been a couple of days. I wished it could go back to the way it was. Even before Ivy. If I had never met her and never stopped to help her that day, I would just be numb to all of this. I probably wouldn't even know what I truly was.

But I could never forget about Ivy, even if I wanted to. She was embedded in my mind.

I felt like shit because I knew she was going through it, but I couldn't be there to help her. I went back on Facebook and went to her page. I saw that she had this long post about her and Kyan with a picture of them attached to it. I started reading it, guilt once again consuming me.

It's so hard to wake up every day and know that the one person that loves me no matter what, and the one person

THE CAUSE AND CURE IS YOU 2
by *Jessica N. Watkins*

that has always had my back is gone. I wish I could understand why he had to be taken from me. I wish to God that I can understand, but I can't. He died protecting me. He died trying to keep me safe. That's always going to stay with me. Kyan, I miss you so much. Why did you have to leave me? We're supposed to be in Dallas taking over the city and making waves. It was going to be our time. Those that knew Kyan knew that he was the closest relative I had. We had a time where we barely spoke, but when we got back into each other's lives, it was like we didn't miss a beat. Kyan was more than a cousin to me. He was my brother. He was my best friend. I hope to God that the person that did this will feel this kind of pain for the rest of their life. I hope that every person that they ever loved is taken from them. I know that may sound selfish, and I know I'm supposed to forgive and let go, but sometimes it's okay to be selfish. We can't be a hundred percent perfect all the time. That was something that Kyan taught me. I'm just so angry. I want to get over this. I want to stop hurting, but all I can think about is my cousin being taken from me. I love you so much, Kyan. I miss you. Not a day goes by that I don't think about you. Sleep in paradise and hold it down for me. Until we see each other again, fam. I'm always going to make you proud.

Damn, man. This was all my fault. I wanted to comfort her. I wanted to call her and tell her that I was sorry. She probably hated me right now. I had to do something. I needed to keep my distance from her, but the least I could do was make this right with her cousin.

I had seen where she had checked in to one of the funeral homes in a previous status where she said she was making funeral arrangements. I grabbed my keys and headed over there. If I couldn't be with her physically, then I was going to be there for her emotionally. I figured if I could take the stress of paying for everything off of her, then it would be a start.

I drove the half-hour to the funeral home and walked in to find a short, black man with a name tag reading Maurice Ross. He reminded me of the funeral director from Tales from the Hood, Clarence Williams III. It was kind of ironic that he was in a funeral home his damn self since he looked dead. He looked at me and offered me a warm smile.

"Can I help you?" he asked.

"Yeah," I said looking around. "I... uh...I think I'm in the right place. A friend of mine is burying her cousin here. Her name is Ivy Summers. Um, I know money is kind of tight for her, so I was going to pay for the funeral and any other arrangements that needed to be taken care of."

"Okay what's the name?"

"Kyan ...Summers," I assumed.

"Okay," he nodded, typing the information into the computer. "Yes, the young lady was here not too long ago. Are you a friend of the family?"

"Yeah, something like that," I answered.

THE CAUSE AND CURE IS YOU 2
by *Jessica N. Watkins*

He gave me this weird look, and it was just something about him that seemed a little familiar. I couldn't figure out what it was, but the way that he was looking was somewhat unsettling.

"She desires to cremate him," he told me. "She said she is still going to have a service, but ultimately, he will be cremated."

Somehow, I could see her doing that.

"That's fine," I told him. "Whatever she wants. I just want to make sure that he has a good home going. Money isn't an issue."

"Uh huh," he smiled.

As soon as he heard that, he perked right the hell up. That's one thing I never could get about folks that worked in the funeral business. It was like they got off on people's pain and misery.

"Well, we do have several packages that you can choose from. I would probably recommend the golden package. A beautiful casket made of 100% Oak, lined with gold. And we also offer—"

"Whatever," I dismissed cutting him off. "Like I said, I just want to make sure that he's taking care of and she doesn't have to stress it."

"Absolutely Mr.?"

"Valentine," I answered.

I pulled my wallet out and handed him one of my credit cards and ten one hundred-dollar bills for him as a courtesy.

He slipped the cash in the pocket of his suit jacket with a smile. Then he began to stare at me, and, again, that weird feeling returned.

"What?" I asked annoyed.

"She means something to you," he answered. "I can tell by looking at you."

I didn't know what to say. I was not about to spill my feelings to some strange man. He stood up and walked towards me.

"I'm glad you're here. Actually, I could use your help," he said. "I'm not as young as I used to be, and I was actually headed to bring his body downstairs to begin preparations. I could use some assistance."

Looking at the feeble man, I could understand. It was a little odd to be helping him with her cousin, but I felt like I wanted to help him.

"Aight," I agreed.

I followed him down the hall to a room full of bodies inside of drawers. It was spooky as hell. I had been around a few dead bodies during my stint in the streets, but those bodies had at least still been warm.

"You know," he spoke as he led me to Kyan. "In life, we all meet that one person that makes us change our way of thinking. They make us change our actions and our behaviors for the better. Now, you may think I'm getting in your business, but I can see that this young lady has had that effect on you. I can tell that you really love her."

He opened the drawer, and Kyan was right in front of me. He looked a lot different than I remembered him. Every time I saw him, he was dolled up and had makeup on, the whole nine. I knew Ivy had told me that Travis hated his lifestyle and that his own mother even talked trash about him with the way he lived. Now, all of his glam had been washed away, and he looked almost unrecognizable. He looked like a man and, ironically, not like himself at all.

Looking at him laying on this metal table, I actually felt grateful to him. He saved Ivy. If it wasn't for him and even that nigga, Travis, she might not be here now. I knew I was doing the right thing by taking care of Kyan's arrangements.

"Do you need a minute, son?" the director asked, extending a box of tissues to me.

Was I crying? I didn't even realize it until I saw my reflection in the mirror above the drawer. I wasn't crying over Kyan because I barely knew him, but the more that I looked at him, the more that it reminded me that it could have easily been Ivy. And just like it was my fault for his death, it would have been my fault, and I wouldn't have never been able to forgive myself. Fuck! I didn't know who to be mad at. My entire life was turned upside down.

"I'm straight," I told the man.

This was starting to creep me out the way he was studying me. If this was the movie Get Out, now would be the time the nigga would be saying "run".

"Look, I need to get up out of here," I told him. "You gonna have to get somebody else to help you."

"It's fine, son," he smiled again. "I understand."

We started walking back to the office, and he was telling me everything that would happen from that point on.

"After the funeral, Ms. Summers will have to sign off on the paperwork, and we'll be able to have the young man cremated. From that point, his body will be ready within about a week."

"Aight," I said as we entered his office.

I heard him, but an image of Ivy crying at the funeral entered my mind. Would anybody be there to comfort her? Would anybody be there to mourn him? I wondered how she was coping. I just wanted to fix it. Maybe I could hit her up on Facebook. What would it hurt?

I suddenly had an idea of how to make it right.

I hoped she liked it.

"You look like you have something on your mind," Mr. Ross said, sitting back in his chair.

"Well, yeah, I do."

I gave him the idea that popped in my head. I knew there was a way to give Ivy a great memory of her cousin. The funeral director took all of the information, and within a couple of minutes, I was ready to go. Being in there was fucking with my head. I needed to talk to my pops quick. At this point, he was the only person that I felt like would understand where I was coming from.

"You take care, Mr. Valentine," the director said as I got ready to walk out of the door.

I turned and looked at him again and his eyes were already fixated on me. What the hell was it with this dude?

"You didn't need my help, did you?" I asked.

"No," he smiled. "But I knew that you needed mine."

I walked out and headed to my pops, trying to figure out what the hell that meant. Somehow, I had a feeling that I would find out sooner than later.

CHAPTER EIGHT
STEVE VALENTINE

"So, is she safe?" I asked into the phone.

"Yes. I haven't really noticed anything out of the ordinary so, I guess that's a good thing."

"All right good," I said. "How she holding up?"

"As good as can be expected, I guess, for somebody that's lost her family and man," he told me.

"Well, just keep an eye on her."

"Will do. You just make sure that you keep that son of yours safe and away from that girl," he warned.

"I got it under control." I assured him.

"You're really going to try to go after Theo?" he asked.

"Yep." I answered. "Soon as Keys gets here, we on the way to pop up on that snitch Trouble that set him up. He thinks Keys is dead. So, we gonna show up and catch his ass off guard."

"I can't believe he's still trying to destroy you," he said. "It's been going on for years."

"I know," I agreed.

"Well, if you gonna do this, stop him for good."

He was right about that. If Theodore didn't want to leave on his own, then I was going to *make* him leave.

"Aight, I gotta go," I announced. "If anything changes, make sure you call me."

"Of course."

I hung up the phone and poured myself a glass of scotch, taking a long swig. I enjoyed the burn as the alcohol took the edge off.

The way that I saw this going between me and Theodore, one of us was going to end up dead. And if I knew Theodore, his ass wasn't going to go down without a fight. Neither was I. He had put my family through enough. It was time for him to get some of that pain back that he had caused.

I thought about Bridget. Seeing her hurting like that the last time that she was in Chicago and having to treat her so horrible killed me. She didn't deserve it. She had been a good woman. Initially, I had left because she was starting to question the fact that I wasn't aging. I would have rather left her and allowed her to grow old with a human that loved her than to make her watch me live in perfection while she aged or died from disease. I hadn't been able to visit since Theodore resurfaced, and I missed Bridget and my mortal kids. But now that Theodore was on the prowl, I had to keep my distance. I didn't know if he knew that I was back in Chicago yet, but he was a smart metahuman, the oldest of us all. He would find out and when he did, his terror would begin again, and his first attack would be on my mortal family. I couldn't allow that. So, for now, I had to keep my distance. It felt good being around my boys, but I longed for the day that I could have all of my kids together without fear of my own damn family trying to harm them or worse.

My phone rang, and I looked to see Reese calling.

"Hey, son. Everything okay?" I asked.

"N-not really." I didn't like he was being timid and stumbling over his words. "Bridget isn't doing too good. She's sick."

"What do you mean she's sick?" I asked concerned. "She was fine when I saw her a few weeks ago."

At least from what I remembered, she was. I had rushed her away so fast so as not to put her in harm's way that I didn't really notice. But she'd seemed okay.

"Pop..." He hesitated.

"Spit it out," I urged.

"She got Cancer," he said.

What the fuck? How the hell could this happen to her? I was ashamed. This woman had come looking for me begging me to come home and all I did was turn her away. Did she know she had it when she came to find me? If she did, I would never forgive myself.

I definitely had to get rid of Theodore now. Even though I didn't feel any physical pain, my heart definitely felt pain knowing I could lose her still.

"Pops, you all right?" Reese asked.

"Yeah," I managed. "Look... uh...just keep an eye on her the best that you can. And if she needs anything–"

"Yeah, I know," he said stopping me. "I got you. What's going on there?"

"About to set things in motion," I told him. "Waiting on your brother to get here so that we can go drop in on Trouble."

"Well, let me know if y'all need me. It's nothing for me to come up there," he offered.

"No," I told him. "It's better that you be there looking after Bridget and the kids."

"Aight," he said.

I hung up the phone and poured another drink. This had to work. Evil could no longer prevail.

"All right, Theodore," I said taking a sip of my drink. "I'm coming for you."

DREAM FRANKLIN

Since Keys was back and obviously not near death, I had started looking at dresses and was ready to get this wedding on the way. I was going to be Mrs. Valentine, and I needed to stunt on these hoes.

"Baby, what you think about having our wedding in the summer?" I asked him.

He was slouched on the couch in the living room playing video games while I was in the recliner on the computer looking at venues.

"This summer?" he asked. "You know it's June, right? Yo', why you trying to rush it?"

"Well..." I smiled. "I just wanna hurry up and be Mrs. Valentine, that's all. I mean, you finally got your shit together and proposed, so I wanna make sure that I get my man to that altar."

I probably shouldn't have said it like that, but, hell, I was being honest. I didn't wanna risk having some long ass engagement and then this nigga change his mind. Not after all I had been through and the bullshit that I dealt with when it came to his ass.

"I don't know," he said slightly frowning. He hadn't even looked up at me. "I'm not trying to rush. Let's just be engaged for a little while."

"At some point, you're gonna have to go from engagement to marriage, Keys," I said. "So why are you trying to have a long engagement?"

He was getting on my nerves with his bipolar attitude. One minute, he acted like things were good, and then the next, he was distant and pissy.

When he didn't have anything to say, when he only gave me a blank expression, I jumped to my feet, mumbling, "Whatever."

He just sat there playing that damn game like nothing was bothering him. I heard his phone ring and listened to see who he was talking to as I went to the kitchen.

"What up, Pops?" I heard him answer as I went in the frig. "Oh word? Okay cool. I'll be there in a minute."

I rolled my eyes. Ever since his daddy popped up in his life, he jumped every time his father called. I got that his mother had lied and hid his father from him all of his life, but I didn't like how it was seeming as if his father's sudden appearance was bringing more bad than good. Nothing bad was happening with Keys until his pops and brothers showed up. Since they'd popped up, he was real moody, short with me, and keeping secrets. Yes, he had proposed, and our relationship was good, but something was off with him and something wasn't right with his father and brothers.

I was going to find out what it was. I grabbed a Lime-a-Rita out the fridge and headed back into the living room.

"So, I guess you're going out?" I asked, opening the can.

"Nah, nothing like that," he said cutting the game off. "Just getting up with pops and some of my brothers. We're gonna swing by the club later. The club has been shut down the last few days, so I gotta get it back running."

"Trouble can't handle that?" I asked.

His jaw clinched tight all of a sudden, like my persistent questions were getting on his nerves. "Nah. Not like I want it done. *Dreams* is my shit. It needs to be done my way."

"I guess," I sighed. "So, you're gonna be out all night?"

"I don't know, Dream. I've been gone from the club for damn near a week," he said, putting on his shoes. "It's gonna be some work trying to get folks back to the club without them thinking the club is gonna get shot up all the time. I gotta rebrand it. It's too big of a money maker. I'ma get up with Zeek and we gon' see what's popping."

I nodded my head and tuned him out at that point. He was still talking, but I had an attitude, not that he even noticed. I was standing right there in front of him, texting Zeek, but Keys wouldn't even know because his focus was elsewhere.

Zeek and I hadn't spoken since the day we learned that Keys had gotten shot. But I knew that he wouldn't be able to say no to me.

I texted him that I was about to come see him. Keys had money to make and that was cool. But if he wasn't going to give me that attention that I needed, I'd go to the next nigga.

My phone buzzed, and I smiled seeing that Zeek had responded. But the smile faded drastically when I read that his response said to stop texting him.

Ahhh, that's cute.

Zeek was really trying to act like he didn't want this pussy. I guessed that I was going to have to remind him of what he was missing. He knew I didn't take no too kindly.

Keys stood up and walked towards me while I grabbed my keys to leave.

"Where are you going?" he asked.

"To mind my business," I answered. "But don't worry, I won't be staying out all night."

I knew that would probably piss him off. He mumbled something under his breath and walked past me. I walked out and headed to the car, driving straight over to Zeek's house. I parked down the street like I normally did and looked around to make sure the coast was clear.

Walking to the door, I could hear trap music playing inside the house. That was some of the best music to fuck to. Forget all that slow, R&B shit. Let a nigga listen to some trap music while he's hitting a blunt, and he'll tear that pussy up.

I knocked on the door and waited for him to answer. I knew he was home because his car was there.

"Open the door, Zeek!" I yelled. "You don't want me out here yelling in front of your neighbors. I'm sure they'd love to hear what? we do."

The door flung open a few seconds later, and he stared at me like I was some crazy bitch off the street.

"What the fuck do you want?" he snapped.

I smiled and pushed my way inside. He was standing in some dark jeans, shirtless, showing off his chest.

"Why aren't you answering my text messages?" I asked, ignoring his question.

"Dream, I told you I'm done dealing with yo' ass," he said. "I don't know why you ain't getting that shit. Keys is my boy and you supposed to be his fiancée."

"Yeah, yeah, yeah." I sighed. "I done heard all this shit before. Come on, Zeek. We both know that you're done when I say you done. And you ain't done, nigga."

I trailed my finger down his bare chest, admiring him. He snatched my wrist and pushed me away.

"Yo', what the fuck is wrong with you?" he growled. "You on some real bullshit. I'm seriously starting to think that your ass is bipolar or some shit. You the only bitch that will cheat on her nigga when he trying to wife your hoe ass. Then you on his homeboy dick like it's cool."

I laughed at his little good boy routine. "If you didn't wanna fuck, you wouldn't have dicked me down in the first place," I pointed out, pressing against him and flicking my tongue on his chest. "So, you can miss me with this whole peer pressure after school special shit. Now come on. Let's get it in real quick before Keys comes to get you."

"What?" he asked.

"I said let's get it in real quick before he comes to get you. He said he was gonna hit you up and come scoop you in a little bit so that he can talk about rebranding the club," I rattled off.

"See that's what I'm talking about," he snapped, stepping back. "He could show up any fucking minute. How the fuck am I going to explain your ass standing here in my gawd damn living room grabbing at my dick?"

"Well, if you would just give me what I want, I can be long gone." I smiled. "Come on, Zeek, you know how good it is."

I started moving towards him, and he actually looked shook.

"Man, you are psychotic," he said. "Real shit, you need to fall back. I'm not gonna fuck you. Get that through your head, Dream! Me and you? We're done. No more popping up at the crib. No more fuckin' at the club. None of that. Yeah, I messed up by fucking my boy's girl. But I'm not gonna keep doing it."

This nigga was sounding like a straight bitch right now.

"So, now you just want to stop?" I huffed looking at him in disbelief.

His eyes bucked at me, and he laughed sarcastically. He shook his head as if I was the biggest disappointment of his life. "I've *been* wanting to stop, bitch, but your crazy ass kept coming at me."

"Yeah and you kept giving it to me," I clapped back. "Now what?"

"Look, I said what I had to say. We done," he said moving further away.

I shrugged, tauntingly, threatening smile spreading across my matte lipstick lips. "I guess I'll just have to have a conversation with Keys."

"About what?" he asked with a cocky look on his face.

"About how his boy is trying to fuck on the low." My smile grew even more wicked. "You know I can get that nigga to believe anything I say."

"Wow. Yeah, your ass really is delusional," he observed. "So, you wanna make it seem like I came after you? Okay. Cool. Go ahead. Tell him. I don't give a fuck."

I wasn't expecting him to actually call my bluff. I guess my face gave off my shock because he smirked, pleasingly.

"That's what I thought," he said. "Yo', you're poison. Your soul is gone. Get the fuck up out my house."

He walked over to his door and opened it to let me out. I laughed to myself at his demeanor as I walked past and out the door before he slammed it in my face. Zeek had no clue what I was capable of. But he would soon learn. I could be a total bitch when I didn't get my way. And he had just released the beast.

CHAPTER TEN

IVY SUMMERS

I took a long, deep breath, readying myself to do this. Then I spoke into the mic, "It feels good to see so many people here to say goodbye to Kyan."

I stood at the pulpit and looked out into the congregation as Kyan's body lay in his casket. Despite my worries, there were a lot of people that came to pay their respects and say their goodbyes to him. Oddly enough, I even saw Travis' mother, Renee, sitting in one of the seats. That shocked the hell out of me because she didn't even know my cousin. All she knew was that her son didn't like me hanging around my closest, gay cousin because of his lifestyle.

I guess she was more thoughtful than I thought.

I kind of wished Keys could have been here with me. Even though I was being strong in front of everyone, I really wished he could be there to comfort me physically, instead of through his contribution.

I had come to the funeral home to bring clothes for Kyan to be buried in when to my surprise, Mr. Ross told me that his entire service had been paid for. I knew who had paid for it, without the funeral director even telling me. The only person that I knew that was capable of doing something like that would be Keys. I appreciated him for what he did. It did take some stress off, but now the hardest part of it all was happening, standing here in front of everyone, giving Kyan's eulogy, and I was alone.

"If you knew Kyan, then you know he had the most electric personality," I continued. "Kyan was the type of person that could make you laugh when you were having the most messed up day. And he was infamous for creating and designing some crazy looks."

A few people in the congregation laughed and smiled as I struggled to speak about my cousin. But for the most part, there were mostly tears of sadness.

"As crazy as he was, he had a whole other side to him," I said. "Kyan had this... spirit about him. He knew how to bring the best out of any person. He had a lot of demons that he was dealing with..."

I couldn't help but to look at my Aunt Catherine, who was sitting in the congregation and hadn't said so much as a word. She had this stone-faced expression, but at least she was there. Yet, I couldn't tell if she was there because she loved Kyan or if her presence was just for show.

"But the good thing about Kyan is that no matter what he was going through, he never let you see it. There were plenty of times where he and I would have conversations about things that he wanted to do in life and I would listen in amazement. He had so many dreams outside of living in Chicago." I paused and took a couple of deep breaths to stop the oncoming tears, ignited by the memories of what was supposed to be our last day living in Chicago. "It's no secret how Kyan was killed. He was gunned down for trying to make sure that I was safe. And although it was something that neither one of us saw coming, that guilt is something that I'm going to have to carry with me for the rest of my life. And even though it's hard knowing that he's no longer with us physically, I know that he died doing what Kyan does; being that protector and looking out for his cousin."

I didn't know how much longer I could go without breaking down. It was getting harder for me to talk, looking at Kyan in front of me in his casket. There were so many emotions going through my head. But I had to fight through this.

Kyan did, however, look beautiful as he lay there. Even in death, he was serving these bitches. I had made sure that one of his friends did his make-up. I had dressed him in one of the latest Moschino outfits that he had gotten from Saks that still had the tags on it.

He was flawless.

"It hurts because we were supposed to start over together. We were supposed to start this new life and it all just fell apart in a matter of minutes," I went on. "I know there's so many people here that were affected by his passing and that had memories of him. So, at this time, I want to invite you to say a few words. If Kyan meant anything to you, then please, come and speak. Kyan would want to remember the fun times."

I turned to walk back to my seat, and the pastor helped me down the steps. People stood up and walked towards the podium to speak on their memories. I tried to just walk to my seat without taking another glimpse at Kyan, but I couldn't help it. I turned, looked, and I just broke down. I couldn't control nor contain the tears anymore. I cried out for God, and Renee came and wrapped her arms around me.

"It's okay, baby," she whispered. "You just let it out."

I cried and shook as this woman comforted me. I couldn't hear what people were saying because I was crying so loud and it set off a ripple effect of tears. I watched as everybody walked past the casket trying to hold it together. It wasn't until his mother got up and walked over to the casket that I even saw somewhat of a human side from her. She leaned over, and for a second, I think I actually saw her crying. I guess it literally took his passing for her to show emotion.

Thankfully, Renee was by my side through the remainder of the service.

At the end of the service, I promised her that I would call her, even though I didn't want to worry her since she had to get ready to bury her own son. I made the announcement that Kyan's body was going to be cremated so there would be no burial and stomached through the repass. I tried to speak to my Aunt Catherine, because I was genuinely concerned, but she managed to avoid me, so I left and headed back to my hotel to lay down. It had been a really hard day for me, and I just wanted to try to get some much-needed sleep.

THE CAUSE AND CURE IS YOU 2
by *Jessica N. Watkins*

While riding in my Uber, I thought about Keys. It had been easy to push him to the back of my mind while preparing for Kyan's funeral, but now thoughts of him were flooding my mind.

Why did I ever have to meet him? Why did I get in that car that night? I should have just kept walking. Why did I have to be the one to love somebody that I couldn't have?

I thought about his gesture of paying for Kyan's funeral and decided to reach out to him. To prevent myself from ever calling him again, two days ago, I had deleted his number from my contacts and changed my number. So, I had to hit him up on Facebook. I had deleted him from my friend's list too, but I figured I would hit him in his inbox at least to thank him for helping out with Kyan.

I went to his page. I smiled seeing the profile picture of him. He was standing in all black with those broad shoulders of his and that large frame. I remembered how good he felt holding me.

God, I miss him.

I had to let him know how I felt. I needed to see him before I left for Dallas, if just for one more time.

Those thoughts soon faded, however, when I saw a picture that his little bitch had tagged him in of her kissing him and showing off her ring. The post read: *Guess who's about to be Mrs. Valentine? He liked it, so he put a ring on it. "Valentine's Day" is coming this summer! #RoadtoValentine #ImGettingMarried #HesAllMine #IGotTheKeys.*

My heart sank. Seeing that just made me so damn mad. Don't get me wrong, I knew that he had proposed, but seeing it and seeing him smiling with her just killed me.

"Miss, we're at your destination."

I was so caught up on the post that I hadn't realized that the Uber driver had already pulled up to my hotel.

"Oh, thank you," I said.

I closed the app without inboxing Keys. Then I got out of the car and headed to my room.

The last thing I needed was for anybody to see me break down. Of course, my face was already stained with tears from the funeral, but now I had another reason to add to my tears.

Once in my room, I stared back at his page at that picture. Then I unfriended him and blocked him. I had to let him go. I couldn't keep holding on.

I laid down on the bed, and just stared at the ceiling. I could hear Kyan telling me, "Fuck him, girl. Move the hell on! You wanna kill the nigga? You already killed me, so let him go and let him have that bird ass bitch." That's exactly what he would say, and he would be right.

CHAPTER ELEVEN
ANTONIO 'KEYS' VALENTINE

"Yo', this nigga 'bout to piss his pants when he sees me walk through the door," I told my pops.

We were pulling up to the club and about to confront Trouble. I was ready to get at his ass and do some damage.

"You just make sure that you don't get too ahead of yourself," Pops warned me.

"Man, I told you I'm good," I reiterated.

He was so worried about me fucking Trouble up. I wasn't going to kill him right away. I knew that it was something bigger at hand that we had to handle first, so I had to be patient. But I was going to enjoy watching his ass squirm the first chance I got.

To think, I trusted his bitch ass. This motherfucka managed to get right up under me and play me. One thing I don't tolerate is a motherfucka that I once trusted to cross me. Once you do that, you're a dead.

Pops parked the car and pulled out a flask, taking a swig. He offered me some, and I declined.

"All right, let's get in here," he said with a frown and wince as the alcohol burned his chest.

We both hopped out the car and headed to the back door. It was still early in the day, so not much of the staff was there yet. There were two cars in the parking lot, one of whom was Trouble's. I opened the door and walked in with my pops right next to me.

As soon as we entered the club, we ran right into Trouble, in the hallway. I damn near burst out laughing at the look of awe on his face. He looked like he wanted to shit bricks. He also looked like he was seeing a ghost for the first time in his life.

"K-K-Keys?" he stammered.

I gave him a wicked and taunting grin. "Hey, what's up, bruh?"

"Boss!" I heard behind me. I spun around to see one of my bartenders, Jesse. "We thought you was gone!"

"Nah, man, why you think that?" I asked, playing dumb.

He started to fidget nervously. The guilt was all over him. "Man, they said you was inside the club when it got shot up," he told me.

I studied Trouble, who looked beyond uncomfortable. I swear his punk ass was about to cry.

I looked over him and asked, "You good, Trouble?"

"It's... uh...I mean...uh...what's good, my nigga?" he said, walking cautiously over to me and dapping me up.

This motherfucka actually dapped me up like shit was sweet! I wanted to put his ass through the brick wall in front of us, but lucky for him, there were other employees nearby taking stock of the bar, so I had to be cool.

He cautiously looked around. Then he leaned into me and whispered, "Man, I thought you were—"

"Dead?" I finished his sentence, getting close to him so that only he could hear. "Yeah, I can see how you could think that since you were the bitch ass nigga that set me up."

"Nah, man, it wasn't even like that. I swear to God, it wasn't," he started rambling. "Just let me explain. See, it wasn't like you thought."

"Why don't we go to your office then?" Pops suggested, placing his hand on my shoulder to stop me from doing something crazy.

"Yeah. Let's do that," I agreed.

Trouble looked at my pops, then at me. I just knew he was about to do something that was gonna make me want to put a bullet in his head before I was supposed to.

"I would be real careful right now, if I was you," I whispered. "Don't try shit. 'Cause I will put a bullet in your motherfucking head before you can make a move."

"Yeah, son, let's go talk about this little *mix up*," Pops said loudly, letting Trouble know to play it cool.

"Glad to see you aight, boss man!" Jesse yelled out.

"'Preciate that, bruh," I said over my shoulder as we headed to the office.

We walked Trouble to the office, and I could practically hear his heart beating out of his chest. As soon as we got in and I closed the door, I slammed his body against the wall. The building shook. As I could hear the employees screeching outside of the door, Pops gave me a knowing look.

"Issa earthquake!" I heard one of the other bartender's shout.

I ignored the chaos outside and growled at Trouble, "So, what's up, motherfucka? Where the fuck is Theodore?"

My grip was so damn tight around his neck that I had him dangling above the floor.

He gripped my wrists with the fear of God in his eyes. "Man, what the fuck are you motherfuckers?" He was trembling. This wasn't fear of me, this was fear of the unknown.

Trouble started struggling. He was trying to break free, but I was much stronger than he was. "Man, let me go! Come on, Keys," he begged. "Look, man, I'm sorry. I didn't pull the trigger, though. I ain't wanna do that shit! That old man made me! I didn't have a choice!"

"The fuck you didn't!" I gritted. "I ain't trying to hear shit you gotta say! Now where the fuck is Theodore?"

"I don't know," he choked out.

"Put him down," Pops ordered.

I wasn't trying to hear Pops right now. I wanted to murk this bitch so bad.

"*Now*, Keys," Pops urged.

I dropped Trouble's ass, and before I knew what was happening, Pops had kicked him in his head, knocking him completely to the ground, and putting his foot on his neck.

"Where is Theodore?" Pops asked calmly.

"Man, I'm telling you, I don't know," Trouble winced.

"Wrong answer." Pops pulled out his gun, attached the silencer, and knelt down, putting it to Trouble's head. "Now, you can tell us where the fuck he is, or your brains can be splattered all over this gawd damn floor."

"Okay, man!" Trouble caved as he started shaking like a stripper.

"Start talking!" I barked.

"Look, man, Theodore is my connect that I met like a year ago," he started explaining. "I heard this other hustler had pure product for dirt cheap. I paid him to get me a meeting with his connect. His connect wound up being Theodore. Business was booming for me after that, but then when I tried to reup a few weeks ago, Theodore told me that he wasn't going to sell to me no more, unless I brought him to you. I didn't know why, though."

Gripping his bottom lip with his teeth and nose flaring, Pops pressed down harder on his neck, and Trouble started sputtering and coughing for air.

"Look!" Trouble pleaded. "I swear to God, I didn't know he wanted to kill you. I even told him that you weren't in the game no more and that you went legit," he strained with wild eyes. "But he started threatening to kill me and my family if I didn't bring him to you!"

"So, you just sold me the fuck out?" I asked through gritted teeth.

"I didn't know that it was gonna go down like that," he pleaded.

The Cause and Cure Is You 2
by *Jessica N. Watkins*

I slammed my fist into his face, instantly breaking his nose. Blood started spewing, and he started crying like a little bitch.

"The fuck you mean you didn't know shit was going to go down like that when you're the one that killed me?!"

"Keys, I swear!" he pleaded. "I ain't know, man. Once you told me that you were on your way to the club, he said I had to be the one to pull the trigger to prove that I wouldn't say anything about what went down. Otherwise, he would kill me too! I had to do it!"

I was gripping my fists so hard that my knuckles were turning white. I was ready to kill his ass. Fuck the plan. My pops still had the gun to Trouble's head, while this punk started crying like a fucking baby.

"Come on, man," he sniffed. "Please? Just let me go. I swear to God! I'll get my family and we'll leave. Just please don't kill me, man."

"Was you begging for my life, motherfucka?" I sneered.

I grabbed Pops' gun, pressed it to his temple, and he started blubbering. "Come on, Keys. Don't do this shit," he pleaded over and over. "Please?"

"Nigga, shut the fuck up and take this shit like a motherfuckin' man!" I growled. "You was a man when you was gun toting in this bitch! And you're fronting like you was oblivious to shit, but who killed Kyan?" I asked.

When he looked away, I had my answer. I knew his bitch ass was the one that killed Kyan. Theodore and his crew were metahumans. They wouldn't have needed to use a gun to kill Kyan. They could have killed him with their bare hands.

"Look, man, it wasn't on no personal shit," he rambled. "He was just screaming, and Theodore told me to shut him up. He *made* me do it!"

I nodded my head slowly. I looked at the gun and Trouble's eyes grew wide.

"Come on, man, what the fuck you doin'?!" Trouble screamed.

"Shut the fuck up!" Pops ordered. Then he looked around, grabbed a rag that was on my desk, and shoved it into Trouble's mouth. I aimed that gun at his foot and pulled the trigger.

"Arrrrrgh!" he muffled a scream.

"Stand the fuck up!" I ordered.

Pops waited a few minutes before he took the gag out of his mouth.

"Aaaargh, my foot! Fuck!" Trouble spat with spit flailing from his mouth as he struggled to stand on one leg.

"Better your foot than your brain," Pops pointed out as he yanked him up.

I knew that wasn't enough justice for Kyan, but that would soon come. Oddly enough, I could imagine Ivy's face when she saw the excruciating pain that Kyan was in. A part of me was doing this for her. I was going to make Trouble suffer. Ivy, Kyan, and even Travis would get their vengeance with Trouble's death, but I needed him alive for right now.

"That was just to show you that I ain't bullshitting. I'm not gonna kill you, motherfucker," I said. "That would be too easy. Instead, you gonna give me what I want; Theodore. You're gonna take me to him."

His eyes widen again, and he started shaking his head vigorously.

"Yeah." I nodded. "The same way that you brought me to him, you're gonna take me to him."

"Keys, I can't do that. That motherfucka is crazy! He'll kill me and my whole damn family!" Trouble whined.

"You said that shit like you got a fuckin' choice," I told him. "I don't give a fuck about him being crazy! You gon' take me to his ass."

"Man, he gon' kill me," he rambled.

"If he don't, I will," I threatened, raising the gun at him again. "The way I look at it, you help me find this motherfucka, and I might let your bitch ass live. If you don't, I'll blow your fuckin' head off right here. Your choice, bitch."

The minute my finger started to hug the trigger, he buckled.

"Okay!" he gave in. "Okay."

"That's what I thought." I slid one of the chairs over and kicked it into him. "Sit down."

As Trouble slumped down in the chair, Pops asked, "How do you get in contact with Theodore?"

"I always meet him at the trap that's closest to the club, when it's time to reup. I'm supposed to be meeting him in a couple of days," he confessed. "He's supposed to be giving me some more now that things have died down and the cops stopped sniffing around."

I had heard on the news that the murders had been classified a robbery homicide with no leads, since all the security cameras had been turned off during the incident. Trouble's entire family had alibied him. They had no idea that I had even been there, since my brothers had cleaned all of my blood from the scene.

"Where?" Pops pushed.

Trouble hesitated, and I aimed at his knee, tired of dealing with his hesitation.

"All right!" he mumbled.

He started talking and telling us what we needed to know.

Finally, we had our way in, and I was headed back into the game. But this time, I was going for blood, not money.

THEODORE JONES

"Hey, boss. You got company."

I don't know why these niggas want to bother me while I'm getting pussy.

Smooth was about to get himself shot knocking on my gawd damn door when he knew I was busy with a bitch.

I kept stroking into this wet mouth while I spat, "Tell whoever it is to come back later! I'm busy right now, damn it!" Feeling this hoe start to deep throat my dick, I coached her, "Yeah, that's it. Just like that, baby g–"

"It's Trouble," Smooth called through the door. "He said that it's urgent."

"Motherfucker, didn't you hear me?! I don't care how urgent it is!" I yelled. "Tell that bitch I said he can wait. I got this bitch in here. And if y'all got a problem with understanding what the fuck I'm saying, we gonna have a bigger problem!"

I didn't give a fuck about Trouble right now. He was days early for his meeting. All I wanted to do in that moment was bust my nut in this hoe's mouth.

I was at one of my traps in the back room, and I had a bad ass chick on her knees sucking my dick while I relaxed smoking on my Cohiba. I wasn't trying to hear anything Trouble had to say right now. That bitch ass nigga had been blowing up my phone, talking about he needed to get out of town and how the cops was on his ass. I had been watching the news closely, and little did Trouble know, I had a friend in the homicide division, so I knew damn well the cops weren't looking for him. Something had spooked his stupid ass.

My dick was getting soft. This nigga had fucked up my nut.

"Get up!" I barked, pushing the hoe back.

She stood up, agitated, and crossed her arms across her perky, 34 C's.

"What the fuck?" she asked, sucking her teeth with slob dripping from the creases of her lips. "I wasn't done."

"You can't even keep my dick hard," I groaned.

"It ain't me that's the problem," she mumbled.

My eyes squinted at her audacity to get smart. "What the fuck did you say?"

I snatched her by her hair suddenly, dragging her down to the ground. She cried out in pain, and I pulled harder.

"I didn't say anything," she whimpered.

"Yeah, that's what I thought," I said, letting her go with a jolt. "Get the fuck outta here."

She hurried to the door in her little feelings. She fixed her clothes, adjusting her shirt and pulling her skirt back down, and walked out without saying a word. I zipped my pants up and snatched the door open. Smooth stood on the other side with the fear of God in his eyes.

"Bring that motherfucka back here," I ordered.

Relieved that my anger wasn't aimed at him, he disappeared up the hall with the hoe behind him.

I walked back into the room, preparing myself to deal with this punk motherfucker.

Since the 1970's, I had spent every day making sure that I was the only metahuman left on this earth. Once my brother, Frederick, and I started a war, I made it my mission to be the only person in the world with these abilities. That way, I would never have to fear any man. I would always run everything and have my way. I'd never had kids and had killed much of Jones' clans for that reason. Those that I hadn't killed, had vanished, choosing to live regular lives over living in fear of my reign. Many of our offspring, and even Fredrick, had been stupid enough to allow love to kill them, so I had been able to get rid of them with ease. But no pussy would have ever been good enough for me to choose it over life.

When I overheard Trouble talking about his business owner being shot and then being up and walking so fast, I knew that he had to be an offspring of Fredricks. Then when I would get him to talk about Keys, and he went on and on about his inhumane strength, it was confirmed. Many of the Valentines' I had killed or were in hiding because they knew my mission to rid the world of every metahuman, except myself. And from the sounds of it, Keys had no idea of what he was. But he had to go before he'd figured it out.

Within seconds, Smooth was returning with Trouble moping behind him. I could tell by looking at this bitch,

Trouble, that he had done some foul shit. He just looked like he was guilty.

"What are you doing here? You better have a good reason for fuckin up my pussy," I growled as he and Smooth stepping inside. I motioned to Smooth for him to come in and close the door behind him. "I was 'bout to bust a few nuts, and you fuckin' shit up."

"Look, man, my bad," he apologized. "I know we were supposed to meet up in a few days, but I need to get the hell up out of here. Theo, it's cops crawling everywhere. They at the club trying to shut it down. Then they talkin' about they got witnesses," he complained.

I watched him questionably. "The news said that there were no leads."

"They still got witnesses, and you know how the police get down. They can make those witnesses say anything, if they want to."

"Sounds like you can't handle your shit like you supposed to," I snapped. "Otherwise, it wouldn't be nobody walking around this bitch talking about witnesses. So, who the fuck is the witness?"

"Man, I don't know," he said with a sappy shrug. "But I know I wasn't the only motherfucka in there and I'm not trying to go down for this."

"You sound like a real bitch right now." I laughed. I could smell the fear on him.

"Look, man—" he started.

THE CAUSE AND CURE IS YOU 2
by *Jessica N. Watkins*

I ran up on him and snatched him before he could finish his sentence. "I don't know who the fuck you think you talking to," I said, pulling a piece and pressing it against his head. "But you better watch what the fuck you say. I'll murk your ass before your body can hit the ground."

He looked like he was ready to piss himself.

"I ain't even trying to come at you like that," he replied slowly, the gun still at his head. "I swear. I'm just saying, shit is crazy right now. If people find out that I shot Keys, I'm dead."

Wait a fucking minute...

I didn't like how he'd said that. He said he'd *shot* Keys... not *killed* Keys. I had lived for countless years, which had given me limitless wisdom.

So, I was far from stupid.

My eyebrow rose slowly. "So... he ain't dead?"

Instantly, Smooth covered his face in fear for Trouble and shook his head.

When Trouble's eyes started darting, I already knew the answer. That bastard had lived. That doused a gallon of gasoline on my fiery rage.

Reaching back, I lunged forward and caved Trouble's jaw in. I could hear his jaw break as he dropped to the floor.

"You mean to tell me this motherfucka lived?!" My voice roared to levels that shook the walls around us. "And your bitch ass coming up in my set talking about you tryin' to get out of town?"

133

He lay on the floor gripping his jaw, squirming in agony.

"Get this bitch ass nigga up!" I snapped at Smooth.

Smooth hurriedly snatched him up, standing him in front of me, limp.

"I knew you were on some bullshit," I said. "Where the fuck is he at!?"

"Theo, I swear I don't know what you talkin' about," he gritted.

I caved the other side of his face in, and he dropped to the ground again.

"Nigga, don't fuckin' lie to me! Do I look stupid to you?! Where the fuck is he?!"

At this point he could barely speak, but I didn't care. Smooth snatched his ass up, and I punched him several more times until he collapsed on the floor coughing up blood. I pulled my gun out and shoved it in his mouth.

"Since you want to act like a bitch, I'm gon' treat you like a bitch and make you suck this like you're one of these hoes. Now where the fuck is he?"

He lifted his hands in surrender. So, I slowly took the gun from his mouth, and, lucky for him, he started to tell the truth. "He showed up at the club a few days ago. But I swear to God, I don't know where he is. I just know that he's alive."

"What did you tell him?" I asked.

He started shaking his head and stammering. "Come on, Theo," he pleaded. "I didn't say nothing about you. He doesn't remember that you were there. All he knows is that somebody killed his people!"

"Don't insult my motherfuckin' intelligence!" I barked. "I already know that your bitch ass told him everything. I can smell the bitch on you. Now open wider."

I shoved the gun into his mouth, pushing past teeth that I knocked out along the way, down his throat, and his eyes got wide as he started to gag on the gun.

"Yeah, get to suckin', bitch," I laughed.

I knew Trouble had already given Keys all the information that he needed, otherwise he wouldn't have been so eager to get out of town. Which meant that Keys was going to be looking for me. But it was fine. He could look for me all he wanted to. Hell, he could even find me. There was no way that he could beat me. He might have been a metahuman like me, but I was too strong for him. I had been on this earth much longer than him, honing my abilities.

Tired of watching Trouble play himself, I removed the gun from his throat. He gasped for air with tears running down his face as he begged, "Look, man, I swear I didn't say shit. Just let me go. Come on. Please?"

I looked at him and laughed. "Damn, at least die like a motherfuckin' man."

Then I knelt down and looked him in the eye. "I told your ass that it was either you or him," I reminded him. "So, what I'm about to do is get rid of your bitch ass. Then I'ma go fuck that little bitch of yours. Yeah, she can get to fill a real nigga before I plug one in the bitch."

I stood back up and looked down at him as the color left his face. The look on a man's face that knew he was about to die was probably the sorriest shit I had ever seen in all my hundreds of years of living.

"It's a shame, Trouble," I taunted him. "I really liked you. Now, I got to kill both you and Keys." Then I looked at Smooth. "Leave us alone. I got this."

CHAPTER TWELVE
DREAM FRANKLIN

"So, I see Keys proposed to your trifling ass," my sister, Fancy, said, pointing at my ring.

"Yep," I smiled wide, admiring this big ass rock on my finger.

I had come over to my mama's house to tell her about my engagement and to get something to eat. I had asked her to cook some food for me, so I could take it back to the house and make Keys think that I had cooked it. I could have learned how to cook and did this myself, but for what? It wasn't like my mama was doing anything.

"So, when are you going to tell your little *fiancé* that you got four kids?" Fancy nagged.

I swear this bitch gets on my damn nerves. She was always trying to throw shade at me, with her uppity ass.

"Why you so worried about what the hell I'm doing?!" I snapped.

"Y'all, stop that," my mama fussed, putting food into plasticware.

"I didn't even start it," I argued. "That was her, always running her mouth 'cause she jealous."

"Jealous of what?" she sneered with a disgusted frown. "You?"

"Hell yeah. Jealous 'cause I got everything you want," I said, rubbing my ring in her face.

She started laughing, clapping her hands. "Yeah," she replied, rolling her eyes and smirking. "I'm real jealous of the fact that you keep spreading your legs, making all these babies that you ain't taking care of. I'm real jealous that you're hoeing your body out to the highest bidder. Yeah, that's something really to be jealous over, Dream. I'm jealous that you're lying to your fiancé pretty much about everything that you are and got your mama over here cooking dinner for you to take to your man, so you can lie *again*." She threw her head back and started cracking up. "Yo', that is the dumbest shit I've ever heard in my life." She shifted her weight in the chair and leaned forward, her smile quickly vanishing and turning into a sneer. "Bitch, ain't nobody jealous of you," she snapped. "And I don't want shit you got. I got a good job. I don't have all these kids running around here. What I want you to do is step up and take care of your damn kids. Mama don't need to be taking care of them. She's getting old, and she's sick of running after their bad asses."

"Well, then since you know so much, why don't you help her then?" I clapped back.

"What the fuck you think I been doing?!" she grunted. "They ain't my responsibility though! You was the one out here spreading your legs to these niggas, so you should be the one taking care of your kids!"

THE CAUSE AND CURE IS YOU 2
by *Jessica N. Watkins*

I sucked my teeth and rolled my eyes. "Girl, whatever. You act like you're better than me 'cause you got a job or whatever." I sighed. "I make more money than you, doing nothing."

"Oh, you do something! Fucking *is* something!"

"Whatever. Mama is the one that said that she was going to take care of them for me so that I can finish school." I huffed.

"You never finished! You've been out of school for a long time, Dream! You should have been handling your responsibilities a long time ago!"

"All right now, that's enough," Mama interrupted as she walked over and sat down. "Look, my head hurts, and I don't want to hear a bunch of yelling back and forth. Y'all are sisters, and you need to act like it. Dream, baby, I know you all excited and everything over this engagement, and mama is so happy for you," she smiled. "I wish I could meet him, though, seeing as how he's about to be marrying one of my daughters."

I sighed in frustration. *Why the hell do she got to meet him? It ain't like he is marrying her.*

"Mama, I know. I'm sorry. He's just been busy a lot," I told her, rattling off some bullshit.

Truth is, I didn't want him knowing anything about my life before him. Because then he may find out about my secrets that I had worked hard on hiding, and I wanted to keep my lies locked far away.

Mama just nodded her head. I could tell she was disappointed, but this was my fiancé and my life. If I didn't want them to meet, then that's just what it was!

"Well, I know the kids will be happy to have a new father figure," she said.

Tuh! Those kids would never meet Keys! I had to keep the lie alive.

"Just like they glad to have all them damn uncles," my sister mumbled.

"You know what, Fancy? Fuck you!" I spat at her.

Her nose turned up as she shook her head. "Sorry, I don't want *everybody's* sloppy seconds."

"See? This is exactly why I don't come over here," I stressed. "Every time I come over here, y'all comin' for me."

"Baby, ain't nobody coming for you," mama sighed. "I think your sister's just a little frustrated is all. Look, mama don't mind helping you. But I'm getting old, and you know it's getting harder for me to keep moving around. The kids...they uh, well, they're getting a little out of control."

"Okay, well, whoop they asses or something," I told her with a shrug.

"Now you know they too quick for that," she said. "They're practically taking over the house. And, baby, I need some help."

"Fine, Mama," I huffed reaching for my purse.

I handed her a stack of money and stood up.

"Thank you, baby. That's sweet, but it's not just about the money," she continued. "I appreciate you helping us pay the bills and everything. But I'm not going to be around forever. And these kids need to be with their mama."

"Well, then, why would you say that you were going to take care of them for me, if you knew you was going to turn around and throw it in my face?" I pushed.

I was getting real sick of this.

"Dream, nobody is trying to throw anything in your face," she said. "I'm just saying that now you're in a position to take care of your own kids."

"Yeah, but you don't have anything to say when I'm giving you money every month," I pointed out.

"That's the least you could do," my sister cut in. "Look around, Dream. The house is barely standing. Your kids tear every damn thing up. They're eating everything up in the house. Mama can't keep everything up by herself. So, yes, the least you could do is reach in your little high-priced bag and give your mama some money, since she's taking care of your children that your own fucking fiancé don't know you have."

"You know what? Keys is *my* man. I got this," I hissed.

"Yeah okay," she said. "I'll believe it when I see it."

"Look, I ain't got time for this," I said standing up. "I gotta go. Mama, I'll send you something extra to help with repairs for the house, okay? And I'll put some money in there for you to get the kids some clothes."

At least I was trying to help her with that.

"All right, baby," she said with a sigh.

She was visibly frustrated, but I didn't know what she wanted me to do. There was no way that I could take those kids home. I don't know what the fuck my sister's problem was. My mama complained every now and then, but she still took care of them.

I had kept this a secret for three years. There was no turning back now. Hell, those kids barely knew me anyway.

IVY SUMMERS

"Ladies and gentlemen, welcome to Texas! At this time, we are about twenty minutes outside of Dallas-Fort Worth Airport. The temperature is currently seventy-two degrees with a ten-percent chance of rain. If you have any trash, flight attendants are currently coming around with bags. Other than that, please make sure that your trays are in their upright position. At this time, we ask all passengers to remain seated with your seat belts fastened. We hope that you enjoyed your flight and thank you for flying Southwest Airlines. Attendants, please prepare for landing."

I took a deep breath and looked out the window at the beautiful blue skies. The sky was so clear. I felt like it was a sign that I was moving in the right direction. The day that I left Chicago, I left all of that hurt from Keys behind. It hurt to leave the city that I'd grew up in, but I needed to do this for me.

I had stopped at Aunt Christine's house to tell her goodbye, despite our last conversation, and even though she showed no emotion, I think she was happy for me.

The entire plane ride, I just thought about how my life had started to change for the better. I went from being the fiancée of a possessive and controlling man that was too afraid to lose me, so kept me under lock and key, and now after losing him and my cousin, I was picking up the pieces and putting them together somewhere else. But, deep down,

The Cause and Cure Is You 2
by *Jessica N. Watkins*

I still missed Keys. He was on my mind heavy, no matter how hard I tried to forget about him.

The plane finally landed, and I went through the hustle and bustle of baggage claim. The hospital had sent a car service to pick me up and take me to the apartment that they had set up for me. I felt like I was a superstar. I could get used to this! I listened to the driver aimlessly talk about the city while he drove us through the hectic traffic.

When we arrived at the condos, I was floored. This place was amazing! If this was how I was going to be living for the next twelve weeks, then I never wanted to go back to Chicago. The place was fully furnished and decorated with colors of turquoise and brown.

"I take it you find everything to your liking?" the doorman asked as I stood looking in awe.

"Yes," I said smiling. "It's perfect."

He nodded, setting my things down, and I gave him a tip so that he could leave. I didn't have much time to relax because I actually had a meeting with the director of human resources of the department that I would be working in that afternoon.

I began to unpack and get settled when a phone rang in the kitchen, making me damn near jump out my skin.

I rushed over to catch it.

"Hello?" I answered.

"Yes, hi, Ms. Summers. This is the concierge downstairs. We're calling to let you know that you have a package that was just delivered for you. Our doorman should be bringing it up to you now," he spoke.

"Ooookay," I said curiously. "Thank you."

I didn't know what it could be. I had literally just touched down in Dallas not even a few hours ago, and I hadn't ordered anything. I headed to the kitchen to grab something to drink out of the refrigerator and looked at the view from the large windows. I could see Wolfgang Puck's restaurant, 560, in the distance. I promised myself that as soon as I got the opportunity, I was going to go.

There was a light tap at the door, and I walked over to see the door man holding a box.

"Ms. Summers," he said handing it to me.

"Thank you," I replied, taking it and closing the door.

I sat down on the couch and opened the box to find a smaller, white box inside with my name written on it. The handwriting looked somewhat familiar. I saw the yellow envelope at the bottom and curious, I opened it. My heart started to pound when I saw that it was from Keys.

I know that this will probably never make up for you losing Kyan. It's not a day that goes by that I don't think about you. I miss your smile. I miss your voice. I know you felt like you did what was best by leaving, and I have to remind myself that you deserve better than me. You deserve a man that is going to love you and be with you day in and day out. This is just a small token to let you know that I do love you. You are my soulmate. I hate that you pushed me away, but I know that you were doing it to protect me. Neither of us wants to see each other hurting. Neither of us wants to see each other in any pain. But I'm hurting for you every single day. I hope this pendant gives you some comfort while being in Dallas by yourself.

I hope you don't think that I was stalking you or anything, but I got your address from the funeral director and thought maybe that I would have Kyan sent to you. I hope that this makes you feel better. I know it won't bring him back, but at least now he'll always be with you.

Love, Keys.

By the time that I was done reading his note, tears were streaming down my face. This all felt like a dream. I couldn't be with the man that I loved, not because he was an awful person, but because he was a metahuman... A metahuman? Was that even possible?

I shook my head at the confusion that still clouded my brain. Keys had proven to me that he had the ability to heal on his own. I had seen it with my own eyes. But it all still felt so unbelievably unreal.

I looked at the pendant through my tears. It was beautiful. He had Kyan's name engraved on it, and looking at it, I fell in love with Keys all over again. I held it tight, feeling as if I was holding Kyan's hand, since I knew that his ashes were inside.

The Cause and Cure Is You 2
by *Jessica N. Watkins*

I didn't know how I was going to keep dealing with the hurt of losing both him and Kyan, but it looked like it wouldn't be stopping any time soon. I just had to come to the realization that no matter how much I wanted to forget about Keys, I would never be able to. You can never forget the one that you really truly love. Keys had proven that.

I walked to one of the mirrors and put the necklace on, admiring it in the mirror. Keys had done good, and he was right. I did feel that much closer to Kyan.

Now, I had two things to thank Keys for. He deserved for me to push past my hurt and jealousy and at least do that. He had gone out of his way to be there for me, so I had to do the same.

I logged on to my Facebook again, flopping down onto the couch. I went to his page and inboxed him, letting him know that I was appreciative of the gift and that I missed him as well. I wasn't expecting him to respond so fast, but when I heard the ding on my phone and saw that he had messaged me back, I felt those butterflies in my stomach fluttering around with such might that it was hard to breathe as my eyes fell on his message that read, ***Are you okay? Do you need anything?***

Damn. Now why did he have to ask that? I needed him, but I couldn't tell him that. I started wondering if talking to him would put him in harm's way. I remembered him explaining to me about the whole immortality thing, but I didn't think it would hurt just talking to him through

Facebook. Besides, I was all the way in Dallas, and he was back in Chicago. I didn't think I would need to worry.

> ***Ivy***: *I'm okay.*
> ***Keys: You sure?***
> ***Ivy: Yes.***

I wanted to say something more, so much more. Suddenly, I felt like this had been a mistake... a huge fucking mistake. A simple sentence from him was tugging at my heart and making the ability to live without him impossible. I fought the tears as I watched another message from him pop up.

> ***Keys: I wish things were different.***
> ***Ivy: Don't do that. Don't drag this on with sweet nothings. Just let me move on.***

Thankfully, my phone rang, interrupting our conversation. As I answered, I took a deep breath, trying to bring myself down from the high that Keys always put me on.

On the phone was the driver, letting me know that the car service had arrived to take me to the hospital.

After hanging up, I sent Keys a quick message.

> ***Ivy: I'll keep in touch.***

THE CAUSE AND CURE IS YOU 2
by *Jessica N. Watkins*

I could at least do that. We couldn't be together, but I couldn't imagine not knowing if he were okay and vice versa.

Then I closed the app before he could say anything else. Just talking to him had eased my mind, and I felt a little bit better about the choice that I had made to leave. This had to be done if I wanted him to live. And I loved him so much that I would rather have him live without me than experience his death because he was with me.

I hurriedly changed into a black sheath dress that fell a little under my knees. Then I took my black flats out of my suitcase. I left my locs in the updo and put on minimal jewelry. Then I rushed out of the condo, to the elevator and out of the building to the waiting car.

Heading to the hospital, I took in the city sights and thought about how I would make this place home, making a mental note of everything that I needed to do. By the time I got to the hospital, I was a bit jet lagged, but sleep was something I would have to get later.

A young white girl that couldn't have been more than a hundred pounds soaking wet met me at the greeter's desk.

"Hi, you must be Ivy," she smiled.

I nodded shaking her hand. "Yes."

"Well, welcome to Dallas. I hope you got everything settled in okay," she said as I followed her. "We're going to be starting the meeting in about fifteen minutes. You'll get a tour of the hospital later, but we just want you to kind of get updated on as much information as possible. Oh, and you'll be meeting with the Director of Human Resources, Timothy James."

"Okay," I replied.

We went up the elevator to one of the conference rooms. Once inside, I sat down. I was starting to get nervous. I had butterflies in my stomach. This would be my first job in a very long time. I hoped that I wasn't rusty.

Things were starting to get real. I had come a long way and lost a lot along the way, but out of all the hurt and tragedy, something was finally going right.

The door opened and in walked a tall, black man that appeared to be in his late twenties. *Damn, he is fine.* He reminded me of Khalil Khan. He had this pretty, caramel skin, and he smiled at me, flashing some beautiful, white teeth. He wasn't as wide and brawny as Keys was, but I could tell that he was healthy enough to at least work out on regular basis. But, damn, his smile was captivating.

"Ms. Summers," he said, extending his hand to me. "It's a pleasure to meet you."

I felt myself blushing. "Yes, you as well," I managed to get out, standing up.

"Are you okay?" he asked. "You look a little flushed."

Fuck!

"Yes. Yeah. Just got a little warm for a second," I told him.

Damn, why in the hell was he so fine? Skin was all pretty, and he was tall and stocky. And damn if he didn't smell all good.

"Well, welcome to Baylor Hospital," he replied. "We heard about your family's passing. So sorry to hear about your loss. Glad that you're here. If you'll take a seat, the nurse supervisor should be here in a minute."

I smiled. "Okay."

I could already tell that it was about to be rough trying to focus during this meeting. I couldn't keep my eyes off this man. Maybe leaving Keys behind wasn't such a bad thing. I did need to move on. I needed something to take my mind off of Keys. And Timothy was a hell of a start!

CHAPTER THIRTEEN
ANTONIO 'KEYS' VALENTINE

"Uh, why you acting like you don't hear me talking to you?"

Dream was standing behind me, nagging. She was standing so close behind me that I could smell the Gucci Bamboo that she had sprayed on her neck this morning. I could also imagine the smirk she most likely had on her banana-colored coated face.

Her attitude was starting to get on my nerves. She was constantly whining and nagging about every little thing. I was trying to make things work like my pops said, trying to put my all into it, but Dream was being a fucking nightmare.

"I know you hear me, Keys!" she snapped.

"Damn, I hear you, aight? The whole gawd damn block hears you," I said, turning to her.

Yeah, I was right. She had the same ugly smirk on her face that she always had when she was grilling me.

"Okay, then answer my question. Why are you leaving so early?" she asked.

"'Cause I got business to handle Did you forget that people got shot up and died in my club? I gotta make sure all the staff is on point, so we don't get shut the fuck down. Zeek and I gotta make sure this new security team that we hired is on point."

The Cause and Cure Is You 2
by Jessica N. Watkins

I *was* going to the club, but I had to go holla at Pops first. Trouble had disappeared since giving us that bogus information. Since he was nowhere to be found, I figured he had run. For now, I would let him. Theodore was number one on my hit list.

We had started to hit him hard already. With the info that Trouble had given us, we had taken out one of Trouble's trap houses, killing everyone inside and taking all of the product. The plan was to cause so much static in his organization that he had no more product or buyers and would be forced to leave Chicago. We hoped that, with his dealings in the game, he wouldn't even suspect that it was us.

For now, we were allowing Trouble to live because we needed all of the info he had on Theodore's organization.

"Well, what time are you coming back home?" she questioned.

"When the club closes, what you think?" I pushed. "Yo', what the hell is wrong with you?"

"Ain't shit wrong with me," she replied with an attitude, crossing her arms across her chest. "I'm just trying to figure out why you've been ignoring me. Between you being in your phone all the time and going to the club, you've barely said two words to me." She then shifted all of her weight to one hip, which made it poke out. Looking at her, I wished that she could have been my soulmate so that all of this would have been easier. Dream was gorgeous. She was built to perfection. Her creamy skin was flawlessly kissable.

But besides all of that, the only thing that came from her was ugliness… But I had created that monster, so I was willing to deal with it, if I couldn't have Ivy.

"Dream, do you just wake up and figure out how to fuck with me?" I stressed. "It ain't been but a couple of days. You act like I'm just going to fuck off or something."

"How about I don't want you to go to the damn club and get shot at again?" she spat.

"All the more reason for me to be there to make sure that security is tight," I told her. "Me and Zeek got everything under control."

"Zeek?" she huffed. "I don't trust him."

I just shook my head in disbelief. Lately, Dream would start tripping every time I said Zeek's name. Zeek had been around since I met Dream, and now all of a sudden, it was like she hated him.

Seeing that I wasn't giving in, she shrugged and said, "Well, I guess I'll just go out with my homegirls then."

"Okay." I shrugged, turning back around and walking into my closet to finish getting dressed.

I didn't give a damn what the hell she did. I had other things to worry about besides her little temper tantrums and trying to make me jealous. I was thinking about taking out Theodore's next trap. We needed to make it impossible for him to survive in this city so that we could run him out. We had already taken out one trap house that involved two major levels of Theodore's organization, and tomorrow, we were gonna take out a couple more.

After throwing on a black Supreme fitted shirt, which my sleeve tattoos oozed out of, and matching jeans, I left the closet. "All right. I'm out."

Dream didn't even look at me from the bed as she muttered, "See you later."

I grabbed my keys and walked out the door before Dream could say anything else. I really didn't give a shit about her attitude. I know Pops said to try to get back to as normal as possible, but the only thing that I really cared about was in Dallas living her life. So, I had to put all my focus on getting my club back up and running and getting Theodore out of Chicago so that I could live as close to a normal life as I could now that I had lost Ivy.

Lucky for me, I still had a lot of connects on the street that I had hustled with that was more than glad to help me and my pops take Theodore down. I wasn't the only person that wanted Theodore out of this city. A lot of hustlers on the street was tired of how he was brutally running and destroying the game.

Once in my ride, I called my Pops on the way to the club.

"What's up, son?" he answered.

I laughed and shook my head. This old man was a cool motherfucker.

"Hey, where you at right now? I'm on my way to the club."

"I'm already here," he told me. "You need to get here ASAP."

"I'll be there in five minutes," I said before hanging up.

****

When I pulled up, Pops was in his car parked behind the building. He hopped out, as I did, and looked around.

"What's going on?" I asked as we met between our cars.

"Check the trunk," he told me.

I stared at the way that he was cautiously looking around nervously. "What's going on?"

"Check the trunk," he repeated.

I walked over to the trunk of his car and, when he popped it open, was shocked to see Trouble's body in there twisted like a pretzel.

"Damn." I cringed as I took in his mangled body. He had been beaten savagely. His face was so swollen from broken bones and bruised that he was almost unrecognizable. His limbs were barely attached to his torso. It looked like animals had torn him apart. But no animal had done this. Nor had any human.

I shook my head as I tore my eyes away from his remains. "I bet he went back to Theodore and told him I was alive." My eyes tightened as I bit my bottom lip with frustration. "He had to. Why else would they kill him?"

"Which means he is going to come back for you again," Pops mentioned.

"Yeah, but Ivy's in Dallas, so clearly whatever he does do can't hurt me," I said.

Pops raised a bushy eyebrow. "You think he can't find out where she is as easily as you did?"

"Fuck!" I hissed. "You shouldn't have let Trouble go."

"If we didn't let him go, it would've raised suspicion with Theodore," he reminded me as he looked down on Trouble's body. "Damn, he got fucked up real bad. Metahumans did this," he observed.

"How the hell did he end up in your trunk, though?" I asked, confused. "Where did you find him?"

"Nah, more like his ass found me," he said. "I pulled up, and when I got ready to go in the club, I looked over and saw his legs hanging out of the trash can. So, I put him in the trunk of my car 'cause I didn't know if anybody else was going to pull up before you got here."

"Zeek's supposed to be here in about an hour, so good thing you showed up first."

"Well, one thing's for sure, this was definitely a message," he added, pulling out a cigar, lighting it, and taking a few puffs. "He killed this motherfucka and dropped him off at the doorstep of your club."

Theodore had definitely sent a message. He knew I was alive. He had to go. He was destroying everything that I had worked too fucking hard for.

The Cause and Cure Is You 2
by *Jessica N. Watkins*

I wasn't trying to go back into the streets hustling. I was trying to stay legit. I couldn't afford to have my livelihood shut down. Not again. Especially after I had proposed to Dream, and she was going crazy with the wedding planning.

But knowing her, she wouldn't care if I had to go back in the streets.

"Man, I'm done playing these fuckin' games," I spat. "This motherfucka ain't scaring me. I don't care how many bodies he drops at my door. He ain't running me out, and he ain't gon' take me down."

Pops took another puff of his Cuban. "Trust, I'm sure Theodore is starting to worry a little. See? He all muscle. He's too busy playing checkers. But we're playing chess," he smiled.

"Yeah, well, it's about to be checkmate on his ass," I said, looking at Trouble's mangled up frame. "Look, we gotta get rid of this body before somebody sees it."

"Don't worry about it. You just handle your business with Zeek," Pops told me. "I think I know where I can get rid of the body."

"Where?" I asked curiously.

"No questions. I got it handled," he assured me. "Get things right here and get your club in order."

"Aight," I said, walking to the back door.

"By the way, how's it going with you and Dream?" I heard Pops ask.

158

"Man, she's bugging the fuck out." I sighed in frustration as I turned back around to face him. "She wants me to be up under her every minute of the day. Since I have been sneaking around since Theodore showed up, she doesn't trust me. She thinks I'm with another woman."

"What else did you do?" he pressed curiously.

A guilty smile spread across my face. "Why I had to do something?"

He just gave me this knowing look, and I sighed and confessed, "Ivy hit me up a couple of days ago. So I haven't really been paying Dream no mind. My mind has been on Ivy."

Pops shook his head and smirked. "Why are you playing with that girl? Leave Ivy be."

"I'm not trying to play with her," I argued. "We're both dealing with missing each other. Plus, it ain't like we around each other. She all the way in Dallas."

"Keys, son, that girl walked away from you for a reason," he fussed. "She's trying to protect you. She's trying to save you. You got to think about how she's feeling. She's never going to be able to let you go if you're popping in and out of her life like that. Now, if you're going to be with her, like I said, there's nothing wrong with that. But you're gonna have to be careful and know what you're risking. If you're not going to be with her, then you've got to leave that girl alone and let her live her life. She loved you and cared enough about you to walk away. So, if you love and care about her enough, you've got to do the same."

I didn't want to hear it. But I knew he was right.

"As long as you got her in your life, you're never going to be able to focus on what you got with Dream," he continued. "I know she ain't the one that you really want to be with but make it easy on yourself. 'Cause stringing two women along? Oh, that can be dangerous as hell." He started laughing as he took another puff. "And you know Dream is the type of broad that'll end up on an episode of Snapped, the news, or trying to get you locked up or some crazy shit like that. So, you got to be careful," he warned.

"Yeah, but, Pops, what can it hurt just talking to Ivy? Why can't we just be cool?"

He threw his hands up in surrender. "Okay," he said. "Clearly, you're going to learn the hard way. Go ahead. But when it blows up in your face, don't say I didn't warn you."

"That's 'cause it won't," I assured him. "'Cause I'm not doing anything other than talking to the girl."

"Yeah, okay," he laughed getting in his car. "I tried to tell you."

I watched him drive off and dismissed his warning while walking in the club.

THEODORE JONES

"Yeah. Suck that dick. Stop trying to be all cute with it."

I looked down at this broad, Regina. Everybody called her, Tiny, though, on account of how short she was. But, damn, she knew how to make a nigga feel good with that mouth. She was taking all ten inches of it too.

"Nah, don't grab it. Put your hands down," I told her when she tried to grab a hold of my dick. "I wanna see what everybody's talking about."

She opened her eyes, looking up at me from where she was kneeling on my floor. I guess bringing up how she had been passed around had made her feel some kinda way, but I didn't give a fuck. She was still gon' fuck with me no matter how mad she was.

Tiny was a slut that we tossed around the crew. Her initial interest was in me, but I had never been the type of man that settled down. She wanted me so bad that she did what I said, however. So, when I told her to please any member of my crew, she did, as long as she would have another turn with me sooner or later.

I was towering over her, practically ramming my dick down her throat. Tiny was bad as hell. She was right under five feet tall and a pretty red bone. Her hips were wide, and her ass was something that looked like it needed to be on the cover of King Magazine. Not to mention that her titties were bigger than two cantaloupes sitting in the middle of her chest. She had all those damn tattoos, though, and that irritated the hell out of me. I couldn't stand a woman that had tattoos all over her body. It was hard to really admire a woman's body when it was covered up in ink. But even with all that, Tiny was still bad as shit.

In all my years of being alive, Tiny was one of few bitches that knew how to make a nigga weak. I had fucked a lot of broads, and I mean a lot. I was born in 1801. I had lived for two-hundred and sixteen years, had visited damn near every city in the United States and hundreds of countries. I had fucked a woman of damn near every race. I had fucked thousands of women. But from what I could count, only a handful of them had made me bust so damn fast from head. Tiny was one of them. She took directions well, and she did everything with passion. Tiny was my go-to for a good nut. I had fucked every hole on her.

Not a lot of women could take my frame, considering that I'm damn near twice her height and three times her size. I was two-hundred and sixteen years old, but I had the body of a young nigga. And this young nigga was putting in work on her ass.

"Oh my God, daddy, you taste so good," she moaned.

"Well, shut the fuck up and keep tasting it then," I told her.

I knew talking to her like that was going to make her cream. I watched her play with her clit while she slurped on my dick. I felt my dick jumping in her mouth.

Taking my balls in her mouth, she started humming and massaging them, and I was ready to fuck her brains out in the middle of her small apartment.

"Daddy, I want you to fuck this pussy so bad," she begged.

I snatched her by the back of her head and shut her up, making her gag on my dick.

"Open your mouth wide," I ordered.

She did what I'd said, and I could feel the tip of my dick hitting the back of her throat. Tears were forming in her eyes, but she kept going.

"Fuck!" I groaned.

Between her gagging on my dick and moaning, she was about to get an entire day care of kids shot down her throat. It's no wonder there were so many guys that had fucked with her. Any man would get caught up in this. I damn near wanted to stake my claim to keep any more of my crew from ever experiencing this magnificent mouth again.

I fucked a lot of bitches, but I never got close enough to anybody to fall in love. Every broad I messed with, I made sure it was just sex. I would fuck with them for a little bit, and then kick them right onto the curb. It kept me safe from ever falling for my soulmate, whoever she might be.

I snatched her up and pushed her to her small bed, laying down on my back. My feet were hanging off the motherfucker.

"Come hop on this dick," I told her.

She jumped up fast and slid her small frame down on my dick. That pussy of hers was like a sand trap. It was so wet and warm, and I sank in deep.

"Shit!" she hissed.

She was taking her damn time trying to sit down on my dick, so I pushed her all the way down.

"Ooo shit!" she screamed. "Ooo, fuck! Your dick is *so* big. Shit, daddy, I *love* this dick!"

"Oh, you love this dick, huh?" I grunted, pushing deeper inside her.

"Yes, daddy!" she screamed.

I swear I loved these young hoes. They stroked my ego and made me feel real good. Tiny was barely twenty-five, but she was very experienced.

I started pumping her harder, making her scream and run.

"Nah, you gon' take this dick," I told her. "You wanted it. Ain't that what you said?"

"Yes, daddy!" she screamed.

"Who pussy is this?" I growled, smacking her ass.

"Ah!!" she yelped. "It's yours!"

I smacked her ass hard again, and she hissed.

"You gonna give this pussy to anybody else?"

The Cause and Cure Is You 2
by *Jessica N. Watkins*

"No, baby!" she answered as her milky titties bounced up and down. The sight made my dick hard as steel.

"You better not, you hear me?" I threatened.

"Yes, daddy! It's yours! Oh God, it's yours!"

I scooped her up and flipped her over, making her get on her hands and knees.

"Spread them cheeks," I told her.

"Yes, baby," she smiled, rushing to do what I asked. "Ooo, daddy, fuck me in my ass."

I smacked her ass with so much force, that she cried, collapsing onto the bed.

"Shut the fuck up! You take this dick the way I tell you to take this dick," I growled.

I spread her cheeks wide and slid in her walls that were dripping wet as I pumped her long and deep. Then quickly pulled out and slid into her tight ass. That drove her crazy as I went back and forth between the two, making her cum all over my dick.

"Daddy, I'm cummin!" she moaned.

I shoved her down into the pillows and started plowing her harder. I was going to fuck this bitch so good, she wasn't going to have any walls left. I was going to stretch everything out, and every stroke I made, I signed my name to that motherfucker.

"Oh fuck! I'm cummin! I'm cummin!" she screamed.

I felt her pussy clench my dick as she squirted all over the place.

"Theoooooooo!" she screamed.

I gripped her shoulders and kept banging her, not stopping for shit.

"Oh fuck, I'm cummin again!" she screeched.

I was digging in her pussy so hard, I thought my dick was going to come flying out of her stomach. The more that I grinded, the harder that she came. Soon, I started to shake, and I pulled my dick out, turning her around and making her put her mouth to work.

I jacked my dick and busted my nut all over her face and this nasty bitch licked it all, spitting it back on to my dick and sucking it again.

"Gawd daaaaamn!" I growled.

I let out every drop, and she swallowed every last one. Then both of us collapsed onto the bed, and she curled up under me. I pushed her ass away. I wasn't with that affection shit. Not with no hoe anyway.

"It's too hot for that shit. Move," I grunted.

She moved over without saying a word. I lay there catching my breath for a few minutes before I sat up, saying, "I gotta get ready to roll out."

I wasn't about to be laying up under her. I had business to handle. I had lost three major crew members. One of my trap houses had gotten jacked a few days ago, and we'd found them pumped full of bullets.

I would have thought that it was Keys retaliating, but him alone couldn't have pulled off nothing like that. It was one of these other hustlers, trying to get to my pure product, and I had to make the streets bleed for this shit.

"You comin' back later on?" she asked, interrupting my thoughts.

"I don't know yet," I told her. "I gotta see what shit looking like."

"Well, I'm probably going to go check out this club with my homegirl," she yawned.

"What club?" I asked.

"Umm, it's this joint called *Dreams*," she told me. "I've been trying to get up in there, but they've been shut down because of some shooting."

Her going to the club might not be a bad idea. I needed a pretty, young thang.

"Aight. Just don't forget that that shit is mine and mine only," I said pointing to her pussy. "Don't be in there trying to embarrass me, fuckin' with some other niggas."

She giggled and covered herself with a blanket. "You so damn possessive," she laughed.

"I'm not fucking playing," I seethed with a stone-cold face. Her laugh faded, and fear replaced her humor as she stared at my eyes turning cold. "Trust me, you don't wanna get on my bad side."

CHAPTER FOURTEEN
DREAM FRANKLIN

"Oh my God, why is this line not moving?"

My feet were already hurting in my Balenciaga pumps, and I hadn't even made it into the club yet. I was standing outside of the SLR bar with my homegirl, Sky, waiting to get into the club.

When Sky smacked her lips, I knew she was about to start complaining. "Why can't we just go to your nigga's spot like we normally do?" she asked, whining.

"Because, girl, I'm not trying to be in there tonight." I sighed. "Every time we go in there, I got eyes watching me. Keys is trying to keep me on a leash and act like I'm supposed to be jumping through loops for his ass." I rolled my eyes, but unbeknownst to Sky, I was making that frustrated motion at myself. I was lying through my teeth. Keys wasn't studding my ass.

"Well, you the one got the ring, so you better be jumping," she laughed. "For a rock like that, I'd be asking how high and where he wants me to jump."

I just shook my head. Sky was my girl, but she was simple as hell. She wasn't my first option of chicks to kick it with, but I needed to get out of the house bad. And I needed a change of scenery, so I did not want to sit in *Dreams*. I had found out about this club through my homegirl, Jazz. She would come kick it sometimes when her baby daddy was acting up. She was supposed to be meeting us there but had flaked at the last minute. So, I was stuck with Sky.

Even from the outside looking in, I could tell that this spot wasn't hot like *Dreams* though.

I ran *Dreams*. Everybody there knew me and knew I was Keys' woman. But I couldn't meet any new dick there, and that was the problem.

Every time I tried to get at Zeek, he kept bitching about how it was wrong and how I was Keys' woman and all that bull. I was literally throwing the pussy at him, and he would curve me for some other chick. He wanted to act like he didn't want me, and was all up under them basic bitches, so fuck him. I could easily get me a new dick. Which was why we were at this new spot.

Chicago was full of fine ass men. A lot of ballers and celebrities hung out at this club and the crew from the Black Ink Crew Chicago was supposed to be there tonight. Shit, let me get Ryan Henry's fine ass one good time! If we could ever get out this long ass line.

"We might as well just go to *Dreams* where we actually can get in!" Sky whined.

"I told you I'm not trying to be in there tonight. Plus, I'm tired of seeing the same motherfuckas."

"Well, bitch are you tired of the free drinks too?" she asked. "'Cause I ain't got no money, and we ain't got no hookups here like we do there."

"That's cause *we* ain't got the hook ups. *I* do," I corrected her. "And since when have we ever paid for a damn drink? You know any club we ever went to, we ain't got to worry about that."

"I'm just saying, we've been standing out here for damn near an hour," she complained.

"And we're gonna get in," I said. "Just wait. Watch me work."

It was time for me to stunt on these hoes. I stepped out the line and sashayed past a bunch of regular broads and dudes tossing out comments as I headed to the front of the line. I saw a few bouncers standing around gradually letting people in. One of the bouncers who looked easier to bait stood out. He was about Keys' size, which was surprising because Keys was bigger than most. To top it off, he had this olive skin tone and these long locs. He had some sexy hazel eyes, like he could be mixed with something. He had on a basic black Under Armour muscle shirt and some black jeans with a skull cap, his locs flowing out. He was standing with this stone-cold expression until he saw me walk up.

I could see him looking me up and down, while I tried not to laugh. This shit was about to be real easy.

"Excuse me," I greeted him smiling.

"What's up?" he asked.

"Um... me and my homegirl was trying to find our other friend and she just texted me that she's inside already," I lied. "You think you can just let us in?"

THE CAUSE AND CURE IS YOU 2
by *Jessica N. Watkins*

"Now, why would I let you and your homegirl roll through ahead of everybody else?" he asked still eyeing me.

I smiled flirtatiously, licking my glossed, full lips. "'Cause you like what you see."

"I like a lot of what I see out here, yo'," he shrugged, looking away. "Besides, we almost at capacity."

"But it's only 10:30," I said.

"Free 'til midnight," he told me.

"So, you mean to tell me that you can't let me and my homegirl in? Just this one time?"

I stepped back so he could once again look at my entire frame. I pretended to look at something behind me quickly so that he could get a good view of this ass. When I turned back around, he was looking at me like I was a snack. My ass alone was the whole damn buffet!

"I mean… if I let you in, you gon' have all these broads out here trying to get in without waiting," he said.

"And?" I pressed, biting my bottom lip sexually. "They don't have to know. You could've been looking our name up on the list or something."

"I might be able to do something. But what you gon' do for me?" he smiled.

Typical nigga. But I got his ass.

"Well, that depends," I said giving him a sexy look. "What you want?"

He was fine as shit and had no idea who I was, which was even better.

"Where your homegirl at?" he asked.

I pointed behind me. "She still over there in line."

"Aight. Go get her."

"Okay." I smiled.

"Aye, but hold up," he said, walking up on me. "You didn't tell me your name."

He was so close, and my body was screaming for him to touch it. He was about to get it. The way he was looking at me, he was about to have me bend it like Beckham right there!

"Love," I smiled with my answer.

He chuckled and gave an intrigued look. "That ain't your name."

I giggled, "Yes, it is."

I didn't want to tell him my real name in case he knew Keys. That's the last thing I needed.

"So, what's yours?" I returned.

Now, he was smiling flirtatiously. "They call me Horse."

The biggest grin formed on my face. Looking at him, I could see why! I played it cool, though. I nodded like it was no big deal.

"So, you gon' give me your number?" he asked.

Some the women in line were giving me stank faces. I just smiled, taunting them, as I rambled off my number and he put it in his phone.

I then called Sky and she happily jogged to the front of the line. "Horse" let us right in. It was hilarious watching all the bitches out there sucking their teeth, all pissed off. I was used to it. It wasn't my fault that these hoes couldn't get the VIP treatment like me.

"Aye," I heard "Horse" call behind me.

I turned around with a smile that met his. *Damn, he's fine.*

"My name is Reggie."

I playfully pouted. "Damn, I like horses."

He shook his head and I giggled. Then I turned back around and followed Sky into the club, making sure that I switched slow and hard along the way, because I knew Reggie was still watching.

We walked inside, and it was wall-to-wall packed.

Looking around, it was a lot of men in the building, but most of them looked broke as hell. It was a *few* ballers that I spotted, but not any that had more money than my man.

When my eyes found Sky again, I spotted her entertaining some bum who had on some knock off Gucci.

"Girl, come on, so we can go get some liquor in our system," I said.

I drug her away from his low budget ass and over to the bar. We ordered a few drinks, and I opened the tab with one of Keys' credit cards.

He might as well foot the bill for the night.

After lingering at the bar for a bit, and several shots, we were ready to hit the dance floor. Soon as I hit the floor, I heard Cardi B's *No Limit* come on, and the DJ was doing a crazy mix.

THE CAUSE AND CURE IS YOU 2
by Jessica N. Watkins

"Oh shit!" me and Sky screamed.

We started twerking on the dance floor, and I threw my hands up quick.

> *"Fuck him then I get some money. Fuck him then I get some money*
> *Fuck him then I get some money. Fuck him then I get some money.*
> *I need tongue. I need face. Give me brain, concentrate*
> *Apple phone, Prada case, Kill a weave, rock a lace."*

We were on the dance floor rapping all the lyrics like we were Cardi B herself. I didn't even realize that I had niggas watching me shake my ass, but I wasn't surprised. I *always* got attention.

****

We spent song after song getting it on the dance floor, and before I knew it, the club was closing down. I pulled my phone out from my bra and saw that Reggie had texted me, giving me his number as well. I shot him a text back, letting him know that I was locking his number in.

Me and Sky managed to get to the exit without getting grabbed by the desperate niggas that was trying to shoot their last shots before security kicked them out. I looked to see Reggie watching me from by the door, and he motioned for me to check my phone. I opened it to see that he had sent me a dick pic. Damn, his dick was huge! It was beautiful and flawless. Surprisingly, it was bigger than Keys, so big that it looked like it would hurt. But I was never the type to run from a challenge.

The message along with the pic read: *Now what am I going to get for making sure you got in and had a good time tonight?*

"Where we on our way to now?" I heard Sky ask.

Behind her, I rolled my eyes to the sky. She was so irritating. "To drop you off."

I heard her smack her lips. "Noooo, let's go to the after hour."

I looked back at Reggie and smiled, "Nah, boo, I got something to do."

Tonight, I didn't have a fiancé. This pussy was about to get some much-needed attention. Call me Rhianna 'cause I was about to werk, werk, werk, werk, werk, werk!

IVY SUMMERS

Every part of my body was aching. I practically crawled to the couch when I got home. All I wanted to do was lay down and go to sleep. I had just got off of work, and I was exhausted. Working at Baylor for the past week was definitely an experience, but, man, was it draining. I'd been working day in and day out crazy hours, and even though I loved it, I needed a break.

Tomorrow was going to be my first day off since I got to Dallas, and I planned on sleeping in late, and then going out to do some much-needed sightseeing and shopping. A few of my co-workers had offered to show me around, but I wanted to explore it on my own. I was in desperate need of some retail therapy.

The good thing is, with the hours that I was working, it was keeping me from being so focused on what I left behind in Chicago, mainly Keys. I had started to feel normal again. Being in Dallas had been a huge help. Day by day, it was becoming easier and easier to move on. I still thought of Kyan and Keys daily, even Travis. I had been wearing Kyan's necklace every day. Wearing that necklace daily, in a way, I felt like I wasn't alone in Dallas.

Settling on the couch, I kicked off my crocs. I laid back and just closed my eyes to enjoy the silence. I never thought that I would like work so much, but I did. I had great co-workers and had already grown attached to a few of my patients.

I lay there for several minutes catching my breath before forcing myself up to my sore feet and padding into the bedroom.

Stripping out of my clothes, I climbed into my bed. I logged on Facebook on my phone, and scrolled my timeline, looking at the usual pettiness and drama. I stopped at a picture of Keys that a bartender at *Dreams* had tagged him in and tried to ignore how much I missed him. I had ignored a few of his inboxes because I was trying to put more distance between us so that I could move on. I couldn't keep holding on to him emotionally like I had been.

I hadn't really had an opportunity to talk to him much since I started working anyway. Those twelve-hour shifts kept me busy and getting back acquainted to the nurse life was mind consuming. I was always in a meeting or dealing with patients. The last time he and I talked was the night after I'd arrived in Dallas and he was telling me that he was stressed out from everything that had happened at the club. From looking at the pictures lately though, it seemed like everything was a whole lot better for him.

I shot him a quick reply in his inbox letting him know that he had crossed my mind, that I was doing fine in Dallas, and wishing him well. I was finding it easier to not think about him as much, but it wasn't enough. He was still on my mind more than I could handle for me to function without sadness or heartbreak. What my ass needed to do was what I told him I was going to do, leave him the hell alone.

My phone rang, and I looked to see a number I didn't recognize.

"Hello?" I yawned, answering the phone.

"Hey, Ivy. H—how are you?" I heard a deep voice hesitate.

I straightened up while my expression turned with curiosity. "Who is this?"

"I'm sorry. This is Timothy," he announced.

What the hell? I thought as a smile crept across my face.

Since my first day, it was hard to deny how fine he was, but I told myself to stay focused on work and healing from the last fine man that had fucked my head up. I thought I had caught him staring at me a few times, but I talked myself out of it.

I perked up quick and sat up in the bed.

I smiled and tried to sound as sexy as possible as I said, "Timothy. Hi."

"Hi. Look, I apologize for catching you off guard. I know it's extremely unprofessional of me, but I got your number out of your file. I needed to talk to you," he told me.

"Okay," I replied confused. "Is everything okay?"

Oh shit! Am I about to be fired?

"Yeah. Everything is good," he assured me.

I was so scared that my heart was racing.

THE CAUSE AND CURE IS YOU 2
by Jessica N. Watkins

"Listen, Ivy, I know I sound real crazy, and I could potentially lose my job for this, but I feel like we have an attraction to each other. Well, at least I know I'm attracted to you," he paused. "I know you probably have a lot of guys that try to get your attention, and I hope that I don't sound too forward, but I was wondering if maybe you would be interested in going out."

I was so glad that he couldn't see the big ass grin on my face. I looked like a kid in a candy store. This explained so much. Somehow, over the past week, he had found some form that he had "forgot" to have me sign every other day, so I had been in his office a lot. And every time that I was, I found myself mistakenly in there for twenty minutes because he kept talking to me about everything, except work, like where I was from, what moved me to Dallas, which I hadn't told him all the details of.

"That was really sweet," I told him. "And no, you're not wrong. I'm attracted to you too. I just didn't want to say anything. I felt like I needed to focus on being in a new city and my new job."

"I understand," he replied. "So, would you be interested in going out?"

"Sure, I would like that," I confessed. "But are you sure it won't get either one of us in trouble or anything?"

"Not at all," he said. "I promise."

It didn't sound bad at all. And he was over human resources, so if anybody would know, it would be him.

"Maybe we can just start off small. Go out for coffee or something and then go from there," he suggested.

What could it hurt? What other options did I really have? Keys? He was all the way in Chicago, and if I went anywhere near him, he could die. Besides, Keys was not the last man on the planet. Why the hell was I still waiting around like there would ever be a chance for me and Keys? I had somebody right here in Dallas who was fine, made good money, and was interested in me... and he had no fiancée.

"Yes," I finally said, "I would like that."

"Great. So... how about tomorrow?" he asked.

"That's actually perfect because I'm off," I informed him.

"Oh, okay, well that's great," he chuckled. "So, I'll pick you up around noon?"

"Sure," I agreed. "Is this your cell number?"

"Yeah."

"Okay. I'll text you my address in the morning."

"No need. I got it in the file," he laughed. "I'll see you tomorrow, Ivy. Good night."

"Good night." I smiled and hung up.

I laid back on the bed and could not stop smiling. For the first time, I felt like I'd made the right choice breaking it off with Keys. I deserved happiness. I didn't know if Timothy was going to be the one, but I was damn sure going to find out.

****

The Cause and Cure Is You 2
by *Jessica N. Watkins*

The next morning, I got up, ransacking my entire closet trying to find something that was sexy but still conservative. Timothy wasn't like the other guys that I had dated. Travis and Keys were street dudes. From what I knew of Timothy, he was a college dude that had gotten this cushy job straight out of graduate school. So, I wanted to look the part, especially since he was used to seeing me in scrubs.

I eyed the maxi dresses that would have been my usual go to. Dallas was scorching in the damn winter, so it was like being in fucking hell in the dead of summer. I longed to have the wind blowing through all of my sweat soaked crevices through that dress, but I didn't want all my curves, lumps and bumps jiggling everywhere, and it was too gawd damn hot for spanx.

I finally settled on some high waist jeans from Fashion Nova that hugged my ass just right and gave it a nice little lift. I matched it with a cute, white keyhole top that showed a small hint of cleavage. I twisted my locs into an up-do and applied light make up, giving me that naturally beat look like Kyan taught me.

As soon as I was satisfied with how I looked, the intercom buzzed, and the doorman let me know that Timothy was downstairs. I took one final look in the mirror, smiling at my reflection and headed downstairs to meet him.

I nervously fidgeted with my top as I rode the elevator down to the lobby. It's crazy how as women, no matter how many dates we go on, the first one with a guy is always nerve wrecking. I just couldn't help but to think about all that I had been through with Travis and Keys, and how I so desperately finally wanted something with a guy to go smoothly.

When the elevator doors opened on the lobby floor, my eyes met Timothy's, slowly and electrifying, like a movie. I swallowed hard as I took in his overbearing presence and stepped slowly off of the elevator, taking every step cautiously to make sure that I didn't fall in my five-inch heels.

"Wow. You look amazing," he admired as I approached him.

I blushed and smiled. "Thank you. You look good yourself," I complimented.

He had on some khaki colored slacks with an olive green casual shirt. Both were slightly fitted, so showed off how in shape his large frame was. I could smell his cologne as I walked closer. He gave me a hug, and I wanted to be like Whitney Houston and exhale all on him.

"Did you have a particular place in mind?" I asked as we headed out of the door.

"Yeah… it's a coffee shop not too far from here that I go to sometimes," he told me.

"Oh okay," I agreed.

We walked to his car, and I admired the beautiful 2018, red, Land Rover. It was beautiful. Like a gentleman, he opened the door for me. He seemed a little shy and almost

THE CAUSE AND CURE IS YOU 2
by *Jessica N. Watkins*

anxious, but I found that cute. I felt like he was the one out of my league, but he was more nervous than I was.

As he drove us to the coffee shop, he actually rode with the music low and asked me all of the getting-to-know-you questions that he hadn't managed to ask during the many times I had been in his office. That conversation flowed into the coffee shop once we got there, and we spent the next couple of hours getting to know each other better.

I didn't have a bad thing to say about Timothy. I had to admit, it was a good feeling. He was single, thirty years old, with no kids... and single. Did I mention that he was single? He had no baby-mama, no fiancé, nothing.

If only things had been this easy with Keys.

CHAPTER FIFTEEN
ANTONIO 'KEYS' VALENTINE

"Uh unh. Nah, don't run. Where you going?"

"Ooo shit! Keys!" Dream moaned. "Baby, I can't take it. I can't take it!"

I was fucking her from the back, while she was trying to run off the bed, screaming and hollering. With so much on my mind, the last thing I wanted to be doing right now was fucking her. But she had been adding to so much of my stress with her bitchie attitude. But I knew she just wanted this dick, some attention. That's all her ass wanted was for me to fuck her real good like I used to, and she would chill the fuck out.

Though she was getting on my nerves, I was trying not to trip because I was in fact hiding a lot from her. Not only was I hiding who I truly was, but I was indeed being secretive and vague about my comings and goings because there was no way that I could explain why I was back in the streets.

We had taken out two more of Theodore's trap houses. He was a hard man to find. He was ducked off like El Chapo, but we were closing in on Theodore's bitch ass. It was only a matter of time before I could get to him. In the meantime, I told myself that I was going to give Dream more time and attention because she *was* right, my head hadn't been in this relationship in a long time. I was going to take her shopping later, which, of course, she was ready for, but first a nigga needed to get his dick wet... Even though Ivy was in the back of my mind the entire time. Thoughts swam in my mind of her because I wished I could be knee deep inside of her instead. She had been gone two weeks, and every day that I thought it would be easier to front like I was with the woman I loved, it became harder and harder.

"Keys, baby, slow down!" she begged.

I plowed into her harder, ignoring her request.

"You wanted this dick now you 'bout to fucking take it," I growled pushing deeper into her.

"Fuck!" she cried out.

Her ass was bouncing up and challenging me to dig deeper into her walls.

"That's what you was wanting, huh?" I panted. "You was wanting daddy to dick you down real good so you can act right?"

"Yes, baby," she whimpered.

"You gone stop tripping and be good for daddy?"

"Yes, baby, I'm gonna be goo- Oh fuuuuuuuck! I'm cumming!" she yelled as she came on my dick.

I squeezed her ass, watching her shake. "You better."

One thing that I would never deny was that Dream had some bomb ass pussy. She rode my nerves, but she could take some dick just as good. She was throwing it back on my dick so damn good, she had me ready to bust. I could feel my dick throbbing.

"Shit."

"Oh God, baby, I'm about to cum again!" she said.

"Hell yeah," I groaned, about to bust my damn self. "Go ahead and cum on that dick."

She turned into the Tazmanian devil and started throwing it back on me like she was possessed. Her ass was bouncing so damn fast, it looked like Jell-O.

"Shit!" she screamed.

I grabbed her hips, pulling her into me, shoving her face down into the bed, fucking her as fast and as hard as I could.

Before long, both of us were sweating, and my dick was covered in her cream as she shook and shuttered, cumming over and over again all over it.

"Ooo! Gawd damn, baby, I love this dick!" she hissed.

Suddenly, Ivy's face flashed before my eyes. I slowed up and reminisced on how good she felt. I would never fuck her the way I did Dream. With Ivy, it was love making. Damn, I missed how she felt. Dream had some good pussy, but Ivy's was literally my kryptonite. She was my weakness. I remembered how it felt being inside of her sugary walls and how she gripped my back, clawing at me with her fingernails. Ivy would make this purring noise whenever I entered her. I was gentle because I always thought I would break her when I would enter her.

Dream barely even flinched when I would slide in. She was only into it when I got rough with her. She got off on shit like that. I could choke her, smack her ass around, and she'd be cumming all on my dick. But with Ivy, the sex was intense. Kissing her and touching her would damn near make me bust. I thought about the taste of her lips, and how they felt around my dick.

"Fuck."

I was fucking Dream, but in my mind, I was making love to Ivy. I had forgotten that Dream was even there until I heard her moan that she was cumming again. I opened my eyes, reminding myself that I was with Dream, and after a few more strokes, I finally came.

"Oh fuck!" She yelped, collapsing onto the bed giggling. "Damn, baby. I missed that dick."

"Yeah, well, now maybe you can chill the hell out," I huffed as I laid down to catch my breath.

She curled up next to me laying on my chest. "I'm sorry babe," she apologized. "You know you be at the club a lot, and it just seems like you don't want to be with me anymore."

Damn. Hearing her say that really fucked with my head. I felt like shit. Dream hadn't done anything wrong. I was just taking my frustrations of Ivy being gone and this shit with Theodore out on her. She didn't deserve for me to keep fucking up. She wasn't like Ivy, but she loved the hell out of me.

"I know," I admitted putting my arm around her. "Look, now that things are starting to get back to normal with the club and everything, and the cops ain't up our asses anymore, I'm going to be around more. And don't be talkin' 'bout I don't wanna be with you," I added. "You done been with a nigga through everything. That's why I'm making you wifey."

It sounded good saying it, but I knew it was bullshit. She wasn't meant to be my wife; she had gotten the title by default.

"Well, you can make it up to me tomorrow when we hit them stores," she giggled and reached to kiss my cheek. "I love you," she purred.

I felt bad that I inwardly cringed when I replied, "I love you too."

I shook my head and held her tight. When she was like this, I was good. If only she could just stay this way.

"You so damn spoiled."

"Shit, after dealing with you, I should be," she said.

I laughed and nodded. "I got you."

"I'ma go take a shower," she said wiggling from my grip. "I'm all sweaty and stuff."

"Aight."

I let her go, and she got up, heading to the bathroom. I turned over to go to sleep. I was worn out after all the work I'd been putting in.

I groaned as my phone started vibrating on the nightstand. I grabbed it, unlocked it and saw that it was a Facebook notification. I picked it up and looked to see that it was just some folks tagging me in pictures from the club. I scanned them and went through the rest of my timeline.

THE CAUSE AND CURE IS YOU 2
by *Jessica N. Watkins*

Curious, I went to Ivy's page. I hadn't really talked to her lately. The last conversation that we had, she was telling me that she had started working and had insane hours. I couldn't get mad at her distance, but I did miss her like crazy. I wondered how she was doing. Looking at her pictures, I felt this numbness. She was so beautiful. I missed her smile. I missed her being in my arms. I wondered if she had met anybody. I wondered if she missed me like I missed her. I started scrolling through pictures that she had taken in the last couple days. She looked radiant. She had the pendant on that I had given her. I smiled, wondering if she thought of me, in addition to Kyan, when she was wearing it.

Damn man. This shit hurt like hell. How could I be so in love with a woman but not able to be with her?

"Wow. So, you're really looking at pictures of this fat bitch after you just got done fucking me?!"

I jumped and turned over to see Dream standing on the other side of the bed with a towel wrapped around her. As she glared at me, anger churned in her eyes. The shower water was still running, so I hadn't heard her come in.

"Huh?" I asked, closing out of the Facebook app.

"Nigga, don't play stupid with me!" she snapped, snatching up a pillow and hurling it at me. As I caught it, she seethed, "You scrolling through pictures of this bitch after you just got through fucking me? Wow, my nigga!"

I sighed. "Come on, don't start that bullshit."

Her eyes bulged dramatically. "Don't start?!" she replied. "You are the one starting shit! You the one over here looking at her pictures, looking like a sad ass puppy, but just a few minutes ago, you were telling me that you love me! If you wanna be with her ass so bad, go be with the bitch!"

I sat up, saying, "Dream, calm down. I don't wanna be with her." I was lying through my teeth, but I had to say whatever to make her feel better. I felt bad that she had caught me red handed. "I was checking on her 'cause her people was shot in my club. That don't mean I'm trying to be with her. I'm with you. Ain't I?"

"Yeah, you here, but your mind is clearly elsewhere. Like why can't you just let this chick go? What the fuck is it with this broad?" Her voice cracked, and her eyes filled with tears.

"Baby, stop," I said, going over to that side of the bed. I pulled her to me as I told her, "Ain't nothing going on with me and her, okay? She don't even live here no more. She all the way in Dallas."

Why the fuck did I say that? I thought as her eyes narrowed.

"What?" she hissed. "How do you know where she lives? You've been talking to her?!"

I cringed but smoothly lied, "She posted it on her profile, babe."

She eyeballed me as the tears flowed from her eyes. She hardly ever cried. When she did, I knew she was at her breaking point. And how could I blame her? She had caught me.

"I don't know what's going on with you, Keys," she said as she shook her head slowly. "But this shit with you and this chick is getting old," she snapped. "I refuse to be with a nigga that's already thinking 'bout the next bitch. I am too good a woman for that shit, and I am tired of going through this shit with you."

As bad as it hurt to know that I couldn't be with Ivy, I didn't want to hurt Dream either. I had done enough of that. I had proposed to her. I was the one that decided to stay with her and make it work after Ivy walked away.

It was time to do what my pops said. I had to let Ivy go. I knew whatever I did to make it up to Dream it was going to be big. To have her crying? This was an epic fuck up. I was going to have to break the bank to get her to forgive me.

"I'm sorry, baby, okay?" I apologized as I pulled her down on the bed with me.

When her butt landed on the bed, she pouted and folded her arms as she scooted away from me. "You need to unfriend her," she sniffed.

I nodded in agreement. "Okay." I figured that was coming.

"You need to unfriend her and then block that bitch," she ordered. "I'm not playing, Keys. If I find out that you're still talking to this bitch, I don't care if she's in Dallas or not, I'm out. I refuse to be with you through yet another bitch."

"You won't. I promise," I told her.

I leaned in to kiss her and she pulled back. "Uh unh. Do it now," she ordered.

"Huh?" I asked.

She folded her arms across her chest and glared at me with eyes that had creased to narrow slits. "Unfriend the bitch and block her *now*."

I wanted to tell her to chill with the name calling. Every time she did it, my blood boiled, but I knew that was only gonna make it worse, so I picked up my phone and got on Facebook. I went to Ivy's profile and tried not to hesitate as I unfriended her and blocked her. We were still friends on Instagram, which Dream didn't know that I had. Hopefully, I could explain the situation to Ivy there. Damn. I had just told myself to let Ivy go, and I was already thinking about how I could talk to her.

"See? Done," I told Dream, putting the phone back down.

She just looked at me and walked back to the bathroom.

Yeah, this was going to be a serious break the bank moment. That was the only way I saw myself getting out of this.

THEODORE JONES

"Oh God, that was amazing," Tiny moaned as she collapsed on my bed next to me.

Tiny had just finished screaming out in pleasure for dear life. I had let her come to the crib finally after making her wait. She had been blowing my phone up begging for the dick as usual, so I let her suffer for a while. She was the only broad I had had at my house in a minute. I usually only got my dick wet at the spots to ensure that no one could ever find out where I lived. She had been running her mouth about her and her little hoe friends going to *Dreams*, so I knew I could easily get information from her if I let her come over and feel that much more comfortable.

Come to find out, Keys is not the only metahuman in town. Steve and his sons were here as well. I knew because once Tiny told me that the owner of the club was always there with his brothers and father, I told her to show me a picture of them. She pulled up Keys' Facebook page and, when she showed me a photo, I knew that I was looking at metahumans. At first, I thought that some of the young hustlers were robbing me, gunning for me. But the way my traps were getting hit, Steve's name was written all over it. He was trying to run me out of Chicago, knowing that if I couldn't make any money here, I would have to go elsewhere. But I was smarter than that motherfucker.

THE CAUSE AND CURE IS YOU 2
by *Jessica N. Watkins*

I was untouchable. He could never get to me. I was always two steps ahead. That's how I had run his ass out of Chicago the first time. I knew all his tricks. Too bad the nigga didn't know all mine. I was going to take everything from him. I was going to find out where that wife and mortal kids were, fuck his bitch and then kill her and those damn kids too.

But first I was going to finish off Keys. I had gotten wind that Ivy had gone to Dallas for a job, and I had connections everywhere. It was nothing for me to get her back to Chicago and kill them both. I saw how dumb he was over her. That's the problem with niggas. They let bitches fuck they mental up. I didn't have that problem though.

I cringed as Tiny curled up next to me. "What I say 'bout that cuddling shit?" I snapped, pushing her off me. "It's too fucking hot for that."

"Well damn," she snapped. "My bad. You act like you don't wanna touch me unless we are fucking or something."

I ignored her attitude because I wanted another round of head before I kicked her little ass out.

I got up and threw some clothes on to head to the kitchen for a glass of water. I walked past the two guards standing outside, that jumped when they heard the door open.

"Mr. Jones," one of them spoke.

I nodded and headed downstairs. I could see the guards outside the house posted up. Security at my house was tighter than Alcatraz. I started thinking about my next

194

move as I headed to the kitchen. Now that I knew that there were more metahumans in town, I had to think more strategically. But Tiny fucked up my concentration when she came bringing her ass in right behind me bouncing around in her panties and bra. She was starting to get on my damn nerves. She was one of those type of hoes that got extra clingy when they thought they had a nigga. As I walked towards the dishwasher, I made a mental note not to invite her over no more.

I looked over my shoulder to see her rifling through the refrigerator.

"So, you just walking around my house, half naked?" I asked.

"I was just getting something to drink. What's the matter?" she asked, looking confused.

"You're tramping around my gawd damn house showing your body to niggas that you don't even fuckin' know," I snapped.

"Oh my God. It ain't like they ain't seen it before," she tried to argue.

I grabbed her and pushed her ass up against the refrigerator, and she flinched.

"I don't give a fuck what these motherfuckas have seen," I growled. "You in my motherfuckin' house and got me looking stupid. Show me some damn respect and stop acting like some hoe."

"Okay," she whined. "I'm sorry."

I let her go and went back to what I was doing. She grabbed her drink and stood there pouting looking stupid. I didn't feel any sympathy for the hurt look on her face. She knew better than to try me.

I grimaced at her stupidity as I threw the dishwasher open. I reached in for a cup without looking and suddenly felt a piercing feeling shoot through my hand.

"Arrrgh!" I barked, shocked, so loud that Tiny jumped out of her skin. I snatched my hand back and looked at it, wondering what the hell that feeling was... and my heart started to beat wildly when I saw blood oozing from a wound on my hand.

I stood there frozen, in shock and pure awe.

"Boss, you all right," one the guards asked rushing inside the kitchen.

I looked towards him slowly. I could imagine how spaced out I looked as fear entered my body like a raging flood.

"Boss," he urged.

Still staring at my hand, I answered, stuttering, "I'm... I'm fine."

"You're bleeding," I heard him say.

Finally, I tore my eyes away from my blood and cut them at him. "I got it. Get lost."

He nodded and disappeared obediently.

"Are you okay?" I heard Tiny's dumbass ask.

"Didn't I just fucking say I was okay?" I spat, quickly moving away.

Why the fuck am I bleeding? I was so lost. In over two hundred years, I had never felt pain. The White man had whipped me in the fields, beat me during protests, gangsters had shot at me... and nothing. I felt absolutely nothing. None of their whips had pierced my tough skin. None of their batons had broken my ribs. No bullet had ever entered my body. I had walked away from car accidents that others had lost their lives in... And now this?

What is happening?

"Baby, you sure you good?" Tiny was on my heels. "Let me see," she said in that whiny ass voice of hers.

I spun around, ready to kick her out of my house in her panties and bra, when it hit me. *Fuck! It's this bitch!*

"What the fuck did I just say?" I barked moving towards the island to grab a paper towel.

"Damn, I just asked a question," she mumbled. "Excuse the fuck out of me."

I turned, snatched her little ass up, and threw her against the wall, not thinking about my strength at the time. "I said I was good!" I yelled.

She started crying as I walked up on her. She lay on the ground, cowering in fear. I had to get the fuck away from her.

"Get the fuck out." I ordered.

"What did I do?" she pushed speaking meekly.

"I said get the fuck out!" I roared as I pulled her up off of the floor. I tore towards the front door, her feet dangling along the way. I could see my security team peering down the hall in curiosity, but they would never interfere when I was manhandling one of my bitches.

I snatched the front door open. I let her go and she toppled out of my hands onto the porch.

"But what about my stuff?" she asked looking distraught.

Instantly, the guards outside picked her up and carried her to the gate. Of course, she tried to fight them off, but her little tiny frame was no match for them. I didn't even realize that I was holding my breath until I closed the door.

What the fuck is happening? Tiny? How?

The guards inside watched me with curled eyebrows as I tore up the stairs, towards my bedroom. I was just as baffled and confused as they were. I went inside my bedroom, spewing, "I don't want any more interruptions tonight," and slammed the door.

The curse had found its way to me and with the biggest hoe in Chicago. Luckily, there was no way that I would risk my immortality for her slutty ass. I had dodged it all this time. I was always two steps ahead. No way I saw this coming.

I looked at my hand and watched as it began to heal. The wound closed like magic. Instantly, the skin was once again perfection.

I had to get rid of her. I wasn't about to lose everlasting life. Fuck that. I would kill her first... Problem solved.

CHAPTER SIXTEEN
IVY SUMMERS

I stood smiling up into Timothy's eyes. "I had a really good time tonight."

Timothy had just walked me to the door after another date.

"Me too," he replied as he squeezed my hand slightly and leaned in to kiss me.

My knees buckled, and I felt a flutter in my stomach. I loved kissing Timothy since the first time he'd done it after our date at the coffee shop. Anytime he put his lips against mine, the room would spin. And he had been doing that a lot. We had gone out so many times by now that I didn't know what number date it was, but with each date, his kisses got longer and longer.

I wrapped my arms around his large frame and got swept away. He stood at 6'4" and was around two-hundred and thirty pounds. He wore these glasses that made him look nerdy in a sexy way. His voice was so deep that every time he spoke, I shuddered. When you looked at him, you would never think that his voice could be that deep, but it was. Every time he spoke, I felt the rumbles in my stomach.

We haven't had sex yet, but I knew when we did, I was going to need to stretch in preparation because there were quite a few times where we would be hugged up, and that thing would be poking at me. Not to mention he wore a size fifteen shoe.

I had learned so much about him and had grown to like him a lot. He had gotten married when he was eighteen because his girl was pregnant, so he worked and put himself through school while she stayed at home. They had been married for over a year when he got into a freak accident and the doctor revealed to him that he was sterile and couldn't make children. He confronted his girl about it, and they ended up doing a DNA test. When he found out it wasn't his, he filed for divorce.

After he left her, he got another job and kept working his way through school. Even now, he still helped her out with the little girl every now and then because he had such a close bond with her. I found that admirable. Most men would have become bitter and jaded and took it out on any woman that they met. But he was the exact opposite.

His eyes were so dark that it was almost scary, but you could see his desire in them. He was the epitome of the perfect guy. But I was only going to be able to hold on to my self-respect but for so long. I was fighting not to throw myself at him all the time. If he kept kissing me like he was now, he was gonna get it. I knew he was anxious too. I had caught him staring at my ass a lot and he would tell me that I looked like I tasted delicious. I was trying, but he wasn't making it easy at all.

He had this quiet nature about him, but it's what made him so sexy. He wasn't out there trying to fuck a bunch of different broads. His physique was one that caught attention, but it didn't seem like he was too worried about it when other women would stare. He had started to pay me more attention at work. Other staff had started to talk, but he acted like it didn't faze him.

Everything was going good in life. I'd been working for the hospital for two months now and was doing a really good job. A lot of the directors in charge complimented me on how good I was doing. I'd even gotten offered a permanent position that would give me the opportunity to stay in Dallas. I would have to give up the condo, but for the amount of money that I was making, I could afford my own place...finally. Although I would miss some of the perks, and of course the free rent, the idea of starting over officially was great. Especially if I had Timothy's sexy ass to entertain me.

We finally broke away, and he grinned, flashing those pretty, white teeth.

"I need to get up out of here," he whispered in my ear. "Before I end up tossing you over my shoulder caveman style and taking you upstairs."

I giggled as he motioned towards the elevator and squeezed my ass.

I shivered in his touch. "Well, in that case..." I stood on my tiptoes to kiss him again. We locked lips for what seemed like an eternity before he broke away. I could hear this rumbling noise deep in his throat, and I smiled.

"You are making this really hard," he told me, pressing his dick up against my thigh.

My eyes grew wide, and I blushed. "Oh really?" I answered innocently.

He stared into my eyes, asking, "Woman, what are you doing to me?"

"Nothing yet," I purred. "But if you don't quit messing with me, I'm going to do something to you that might be more than what you can handle."

He chuckled evilly and shook his head, saying, "That's it."

He grabbed my waist, and literally scooped me up. I squealed in shock, completely caught off guard.

"What are you doing?" I squealed.

"Don't try to act all innocent now," he replied as he walked through the lobby. "I told you that if you didn't stop enticing me I was going to take you."

"Oh my god, baby! Put me down!" I squealed.

"I will when I get you upstairs," he said.

He hit the button on the elevator and I giggled as the doorman watched, amused.

"Okay, seriously, Timothy, put me down. I'm too heavy," I fussed.

"Woman, hush," he ordered... and I creamed.

The elevator door opened, and he rushed inside, pressing the number to my floor.

"Okay, you can put me down now," I said as soon as the door closed.

"Nah, if I let you down now, we won't make it off the elevator."

"Fuuuuuck," I mouthed as I felt myself cream again.

Luckily, within seconds, the elevator door was opening. As soon as he stepped off, he let me down and pounced on me. His dick was screaming to be freed from the pants that were binding it. I let out a soft moan and grabbed it in my hand.

"God, I want you so bad," he whispered in between trailing his tongue down my neck biting me.

I walked him towards my condo and hurriedly keyed my way in with Timothy behind me, raping my neck with his tongue. Once the door was open, I rushed towards the couch and pulled him on top of me.

Then all of a sudden... something changed in me. I felt him on top of me, ripping at my clothes, and I got scared. I thought, *This is how Travis and I started. This is how me and Keys started.* And after those thoughts, I realized how Travis and I had ended, how Keys and I had ended. I stopped kissing back. I stopped touching back. I suddenly got tense.

I pulled away from him, and he gave me a puzzled look.

"Is everything okay?" he asked. "What's wrong?"

I sighed and straightened up. I grimaced. That fucking Keys. I had this gorgeous, educated, established, *single* man in front of me, and I was still thinking about Keys.

"Come on, talk to me," he urged, scooting closer to me. "I can tell it's something."

I looked at my hands to avoid looking at him. How could I be thinking about another man who was miles away right now when I had a man that wanted me right here?

"I'm sorry," I apologized. "It's just... I really wanted this to happen. Honestly, I've been thinking about it for a while. I just...I don't know why, but I'm just afraid that I'm going to open up to you and end up having a situation like I did with ..."

I couldn't even bring myself to say his name. I felt stupid even bringing up another man during a moment like this, but I was feeling so emotional that I needed to talk to somebody, anybody.

"Your ex?" Timothy finished for me.

"Something like that," I told him.

During our many conversations, I had told Timothy about Travis, but he knew that my most recent heartbreak was created by Keys. I had only told him that Keys couldn't be with me because of things that he was dealing with in Chicago. I couldn't tell him every single detail as to why Keys and I weren't together. He would look at me like I was bat shit crazy if I'd did that.

I sighed, feeling so defeated. "I guess I'm not as ready as I thought I was." This wasn't fair. I doubted that Keys was having an issue having sex with his bitch.

Timothy smiled and cupped my chin turning me to him. "Baby, you have nothing to worry about," he told me. "If he chose anything over you, then he's insane. I'm feeling you. I like you. I didn't think I could ever really get involved with another woman like that until I met you. It wasn't even in my plans."

He looked at me with those gorgeous eyes of his, and I melted.

"I know it's only been a few weeks, but I really care about you, Ivy. I don't want you to feel like I'm playing you. We can go as slow as you want. I'm going to show you that there's good men out here."

I believed him. I felt so stupid for even stopping our flow because of Keys. I was still caught up on this nigga when I shouldn't have been.

"I hope you're not upset or mad or anything," I pouted.

"Nope," he smiled. "Ivy, I can smash anybody I want to. But I'm not just trying to be with you physically. I'm trying to be with you. I'm trying to make you forget everything about all those niggas that was stupid enough to break your heart."

God, he is amazing.

"Has anybody ever told you how sexy you are when you get all sweet?" I smiled.

He licked his lips, eyes boring into mine. "Nobody that mattered."

This man was nothing short of incredible.

I had made the right decision walking away from Keys. So why couldn't I let go?

ANTONIO 'KEYS' VALENTINE

"Bruh, you look like the damn penguin from Happy Feet," Zeek laughed.

"Fuck outta here with that," I grunted with a half laugh.

We were inside a tuxedo shop, getting fitted for tuxes for the wedding. Time had been flying by, and this damn wedding was right around the corner. I really wasn't trying to get married so soon, but after everything Dream had dealt with, I knew it would make her happy.

The only thing that would make *me* happy would be finding Theodore. He had gone underground or something. We'd taken out damn near his entire operation, but we couldn't get to him. I was pissed. As long as Theodore was in Chicago, we were all at risk.

I had to distract myself for the time being.

"So, you ready to get married?" my best friend asked.

"Man..." I said shaking my head. "Bruh. Dream is killing me with this wedding. She done turned into one of them damn bridezillas. She's snappy all the damn time and going off on everybody."

She had been a nightmare. Every time I turned around, she was bitching about something; her bridesmaids were too fat, her mother didn't want to wear the dress that she'd picked out, the menu for the reception wasn't right.

"Well, you know it ain't too late to back out," he shrugged. "I'm just saying. You know you're wifing the wrong one... You talk to her lately?"

I knew he was talking about Ivy.

"I talked to her a couple days ago in the DM. But we really didn't say much. She's been working," I told him.

She'd become a lot more distant lately. I had a feeling that she had met a nigga down there or something because whenever I would hit her up, it would take her days to respond. I had to be careful contacting her because Dream was always on my ass. Even though I deleted her from Facebook, I had started sending her DM's on Instagram. I told her about what happened, and she'd even took days to respond to that.

I really fucking missed her man. Why couldn't it be Ivy that I was saying I do to? Instead, I was about to marry a girl who didn't do nothing but complain and spend money like water.

"Man, you might have to make a trip down to Texas, bruh," he suggested.

"Man, heeeell nah," I said shaking my head. "You know Dream would kill me. I need to focus on Dream. She's the one I'm gonna marry."

Zeek busted out laughing, clapping his hands bent over.

"*You* didn't even believe what you just said." Zeek was cracking up like he was watching a Kevin Hart stand up. He was right, though. I didn't want to marry Dream. I was marrying her because I felt like it was the right thing to do, because I felt like I owed her. She would make any hood nigga happy and if I had never met Ivy, then we would have been somewhat happily ever after. But you know what they say, if you can't be with the one you love, love the one you with.

I ignored Zeek's retarded ass and started to take off the tuxedo. He eventually stopped laughing and cleared his throat.

"Nah, but seriously, bruh. Are you really trying to marry her?" he pressed. "Like is this really what you wanna do? Marriage is forever, my nigga. I hope you know what you're doing."

"Why you keep asking me that?" I asked.

"I know you're still thinking about Ivy," he replied. "And it's one thing to fuck around on somebody when she's just your girl. It's some other shit when she is your wife. Didn't you say she peeped you talking to her on Facebook?"

"Yeah." I nodded, trying on a new pair of pants.

"Bruh, come on," he said. "You know Dream ain't that submissive, leave it to Beaver type chic. She liable to fuck up all your shit if you get caught talking to Ivy again."

"Yeah," I agreed.

She had made that clear. Ray Charles could see that shit. But I was really going to try to do right by her. And from the looks of it, conversations with me and Ivy were becoming so scarce that they will eventually be extinct.

"Our shit been rocky, but Dream's a good woman," I told Zeek. "She's been down for me since day one. She's a rider."

"I'm not saying she's not," he replied. "I'm just saying be careful. 'Cause if you know that she ain't where you really trying to be, she gone see it sooner or later."

"Damn, bro, you gon' counsel me or try on these tuxes?" I pressed.

I laughed. "Dawg, I'm just being real with you. You know you still want that girl."

I did miss Ivy. I did want to be with her. I was willing to risk my life to go to Texas just to hold her one more time.

"It don't matter. Me and Ivy ain't gone work my nigga," I said, shaking away the thought.

Zeek rolled his eyes and started looking at the rack the tailor had just brought in.

He had my mind wandering right now. Dream deserved this wedding. She really did. But Ivy's face was the one embedded in my mind every time I thought about walking down that aisle. She made me want the perfection that I felt whenever I was with her.

"It's crazy, Z. When I sit back and think about getting old and having kids, I see Ivy's face," I admitted. "I don't know if I can have that with Dream."

Zeek's eyes bucked as he chuckled sarcastically. "Then why the fuck are you still with her? Real talk, bro, her ass ain't the type of chick you need to be with no damn way.

I'm not trying to sound like a hater, but I wouldn't trust her. Why is she trying to rush you to the altar?"

"She is rushing me, but I am just doing what I gotta do to make her happy."

Zeek shook his head slowly. "I ain't saying be done with her, but you ain't gotta marry the girl either," he advised.

I wished that I could break it down for him to understand. If I could, I would tell him that it ain't just loyalty that's making me stay with Dream. I wished that I could tell him that being with Ivy was lethal. Even if it wasn't Dream, I would never be fully happy because I knew Ivy was the one. It was just easier to make it work with Dream rather than starting over with a new chick.

I knew Zeek wouldn't understand.

"Like I said, bruh, I know what I'm doing," I told him. "Trust me, I've let Ivy go. We're just cool. Even if I want to be with her, it's better for both of us that I don't. Too many problems. Trust."

"Aight," he nodded. "Just don't let me see you on Snapped or Fatal Attraction."

"Man, come on now, you're starting to sound like Dr. Phil." I laughed trying to lighten the mood.

He lifted his hands slightly. "My bad, bruh. Just trying to look out for my boy."

"That's why I got you for the best man," I said.

He nodded. "You know I got you a hundred bands."

CHAPTER SEVENTEEN
IVY SUMMERS

"I'm gonna head in," Timothy said as he started putting on his clothes. "I'll try to leave there around noon so that we can go check some of those places out."

"Okay," I yawned.

I was watching him get ready for work. It was eight in the morning, and I was supposed to be going to look at a couple of places to rent later that day. We had both taken the day off, but he got called in for an emergency meeting.

"I'll call you when I'm on the way back, okay?" he said leaning down to kiss me on the forehead.

I puckered my lips and he jumped back laughing.

"Nah, no lips. I'ma need you to go brush those teeth. Your shit is wreaking," he joked.

I flipped him the finger and curled back up under the covers. He left, and I lay there trying to motivate myself to get up. I was exhausted. I had put off looking for an apartment for the last couple of days because I was so drained. But I had to start looking and soon because I only had a couple of weeks left in the condo before I would need to move.

Ugh. Why can I not get up?

I was trying to figure out what it was exactly that I had been doing that was making me so tired lately. I hadn't switched up my routine at all, but lately I had been completely drained.

I picked my phone up off the nightstand and scrolled through my Facebook. It had been two months, and it was becoming easier to live with the fact that Keys and I wouldn't be. But I still kept tabs on him. I couldn't help it. It was like I was addicted to finding out what was going on with he and Dream. Since I was blocked from his Facebook page, I followed him through Dream's page, which was public, and it seemed as if she made sure that every post that she made was public. So I was pretty much able to see anything that they did.

As usual, all her posts were about the wedding. As time went by, it was a bit easier to stomach watching her be so happy to marry him. Timothy had a lot to do with that.

I checked my Instagram to see if Keys had messaged me.

We didn't really talk as much, because I was with Timothy, and I wanted to focus on him since I finally seemingly had a good guy that was all mine. I had somebody that actually wanted to be with me. So, I told myself that I would just make sure that our conversations were light. I still missed him. I still loved him. But letting him know that wasn't going to change anything.

I saw that I had a new message from him, and my heart tore seeing him say how he missed me. I shot him back a quick message letting him know he was on my mind and hoping he was well and finally managed to drag my ass out the bed. The minute I got up, the room started spinning, and I felt nauseous. I belted to the bathroom, barely making it before throwing up into the toilet.

"Oh God." I coughed. "What the hell did I eat that is making me so damn sick?"

I looked at myself in the mirror as I brushed my teeth, and I could practically hear Kyan screaming, "Bitch, you pregnaaaaaant!"

My heart started pounding as I slowly came to the realization. I started thinking back to when the last time I had a period. Fuck. It had been a minute. I was so stressed with work and everything that I hadn't even thought about it. I ran back to my room and looked on my phone to look at my calendar. I hadn't had a period in two months.

Fuuuuck!

I couldn't be pregnant. Not now. Things were going too good. I had a good job. I had a man that I was really interested in. I just couldn't be pregnant. Not right now. Maybe I was tripping.

I looked at the clock on the wall for the time and saw that it was almost 8:30. I threw on a T-shirt and jeans to run down the street. There was a drug store nearby that was in walking distance, so I figured I would go and get a test just to be sure. I was probably making a big deal out of nothing.

I headed downstairs and made my way to the store, already coming up with reasons in my mind for my illness. Maybe I had been drinking too much with Timothy. Maybe my blood pressure was up.

Fifteen minutes later, I was back in the condo and taking the test. Not chancing anything, I had bought two different brands to be sure. The entire time my heart was racing. What if I *was* pregnant? What the fuck was I going to do? Was I going to keep it? Could I raise this baby by myself? I knew that the baby wasn't Timothy's because he couldn't have kids. And even though we'd had sex finally, even if there was a small possibility that he could make kids, we'd been using condoms. This was Keys' baby. He hadn't worn a condom the last time that we had sex, the night that I told him to leave me alone. How could I be pregnant by a man that I couldn't even fucking be around or else I would kill him? That was about to marry another woman? While I was boo'd up with a guy that I had just met?

The thoughts had me hyperventilating to the point that the room was spinning as I waited for the results to pop up on the sticks.

I was pacing the floor. Those sixty seconds were a damn eternity. When it was time for me to look at the sticks, my hands were literally shaking. Sure enough, both tests showed that I was pregnant. That Clear Blue flashing 'PREGNANT' before my eyes was like a danger, warning sign.

I broke all the way down. I wasn't ready to take care of a baby by myself. There was no way in hell that I could tell Keys that I was pregnant. I knew the minute that I did, he would want to do the right thing and would be in Dallas on the next thing smoking. I couldn't do that to him. I couldn't risk him knowing that I was carrying his child. That would be the perfect opportunity for that psycho that was after him to finish what he started, including killing me!

If I did keep this baby, then I would have to raise it alone. Keys had too much to lose. On top of already knowing that I was basically his kryptonite, he was about to be married. That bitch would flip her wig if she found out that I was pregnant by him. I knew he didn't tell her that we slept together. Otherwise, I would have seen her on CNN or some shit.

How the hell was I going to tell Timothy? After everything he had been through with his ex-wife, how could I go to him and tell him that I was pregnant by a man that wasn't even mine to begin with, and expect him to still want to be with me? How would I explain not having Keys around this baby? I felt like my only option was for me to have an abortion. But what if this was my only chance at being a mother?

I went to my bed, laid down, and started to cry. This was hard. I wanted a family. I wanted kids, eventually. But not like this.

I continued to cry, wondering why things had to be like this. If I was his soulmate, it was supposed to be easy. The one is supposed to make things better, not worse.

I cried, praying to God for some type of answer. I loved Keys too much to let him lose his life because of me. Ultimately, I knew that I had only two choices. I had to raise this baby by myself or get an abortion. Either way, I could never tell Keys about this baby.

I crawled back under the covers, clutching them tight, wishing that I could just start the day over. Maybe if I had gone to sleep, I'd wake up and this would have all just been a bad dream. I closed my eyes and tried to clear my head. I didn't even realize I had dozed off until my phone ringing snapped me out of my sleep. I looked to see that it was Timothy.

"Shit!" I jumped up praying he wasn't too close.

"Hey," I answered.

"Hey, gorgeous," he replied. "I know your butt didn't go back to sleep."

"No." I lied quickly.

"Good. Listen I hope you don't get too mad, but I'm going to have to cancel on you this afternoon. I'm not going to be able to make it back no time soon," he told me. "We're short-staffed today, and they need me to finish payroll."

"It's okay," I responded.

"Oh okay. Well we can always go look at places in a couple of days," he offered.

"Yeah, that's fine. I'll talk to you in a little bit," I said rushing him off the phone.

"Okay, babe."

I hung up and sighed. I was going to the hospital, but it wasn't going to be for work. I needed to make sure that I was actually pregnant. Even though I had taken a couple of tests, those things could be wrong. I wasn't going to believe it until I saw a blood test.

I tried to make myself look somewhat presentable and then headed out the door to go to the hospital. I went straight to Keisha's department. We had met in the cafeteria during my first week of working here. She was new as well, so we agreed to lunch together so that we wouldn't be alone. She worked in the lab, as a phlebotomist, so I knew that she could get a blood test done a lot quicker than I could.

"Hey, girl. What are you doing here?" she asked as I walked into the lab. There were a few patients in the seating area that looked at me as if I was skipping the line when I walked straight to Keisha's cubicle. "I thought you were off today."

"Yeah, I was," I told her. "But I came up here because I really need you to do me a favor, and I couldn't ask over the phone."

"What?" she asked, looking as if her mouth was salivating.

"Keisha, you can't tell nobody."

"Who would I tell?" she said, rolling her eyes. I wouldn't let up, so she smacked her lips. "Okay, I won't say anything. So, what's up?"

"I need you to do a blood test."

She looked at me crazy and frowned. "A blood test for what?" she pried.

"To see if I'm pregnant." I told her.

Her mouth dropped open. "Already? Damn, you and Timothy haven't even been together that long!"

I sighed. "I know." I damn sure wasn't going to tell her that it wasn't his baby.

"Look, Keisha, please don't say anything. I wanna tell him in my own way so don't you open your mouth."

"Girl, you ain't got nothing to worry about," she said. "I won't. You lucky that you came in when you did though. Long as you get your blood drawn by one o'clock, I can get same-day results."

"Okay cool," I told her.

I sat done, and she prepped me to draw my blood, while aimlessly talking to me about some gossip. I hadn't befriended many people since starting at the hospital. I was cool with a few of the nurses, but Keisha's bubbly, talkative ass had made friends in the last two months. She was not making me feel at ease about telling her I might be pregnant.

Luckily, a few minutes later, everything was done.

"All right, I should hear something within the next couple of hours," she told me, eyeing my anxiety. "You okay?"

"Yeah," I replied. But I wasn't. I wanted to crawl into a hole and just die. I needed to get the hell out of there.

"All right, girl, I appreciate it," I said. "Just give me a call."

"No problem," she smiled. "Good luck. Hope y'all get a girl."

I gave her a half smile and rushed out the door. I was ready to go back home already. I headed back to the condo, and let my mind wander once again. As strange as it sounded, a part of me wanted to have this baby so that, if I couldn't have him, I would always have a piece of him. But that wasn't a good enough reason to keep a baby. Plus, I didn't know how this whole situation would work. Will the baby be different like him? Would it have some type of super human strength? Would that affect my pregnancy? I didn't know *what* to think.

For now, I was just going to act like it didn't exist. I was going to sleep my problems away. After some crazy traffic, I made it back to the condo and headed straight for the bed. I laid down, pulling the covers over my head and tried to black out everything that happened in the last few hours. This was my only way to escape.

That escape didn't last long because a few hours later, I woke up to Timothy shaking me. Because of my odd hours, I had given him a key so that hooking up would be easier.

"Ivy," he called out.

"Huh?" I said opening my eyes.

He was standing over me, with a pissed off look on his face.

"When in the hell were you going to tell me that you're pregnant?!"

CHAPTER EIGHTEEN
STEVE VALENTINE

"I don't understand. Why can't you just come home?"

"Bridget, we've been through this," I told her as I groaned inwardly. "I can't be with you."

"But you don't understand," she sniffed through tears. "I *need you.*"

"No... you don't," I urged, fighting the guilt.

This was eating me up. I knew that she didn't understand why I had grown so distant so suddenly.

Bridget had been crying to me on the phone for the past ten minutes. Hearing her distraught made me feel like less of a man. I knew that it would be a mistake calling her, but after talking to Reese and finding out that her condition had gotten worse, I at least wanted to hear her voice one more time.

I wanted to be there for her, but I knew that as soon as I got there, Theodore would kill her and even my kids to get to me. As far as I knew, he didn't know where they were, so I had to keep my distance until Theodore was handled.

"Steve, it's something I have to tell you," she whimpered.

I already knew what she was going to say. I still wasn't ready to acknowledge it, though.

"I'm dying, Steve..." She paused before she spoke again. "They said I only have a couple of months left to live. I was diagnosed with breast cancer a couple of months ago, and I was trying to do the chemotherapy and everything. But it's just gotten worse. Now the cancer has spread to my brain and I don't have that much time left. Baby, I have maybe a couple of weeks left."

She broke down in tears as soon as she got the words out. I was trying to hold it together because hearing her actually say it broke my tough heart into a million pieces. I didn't want to speak because I didn't want her to know how bad it was hurting me.

"Hello?" she said into the phone after several moments of silence.

"I'm here," I forced myself to say through the pressure in my throat. "There's nothing they can do? Did you get a second opinion?"

"No," she whispered. "It's too late for all of that. There's nothing that they can do. All they said was that I could try to do radiation to give me a little more time, but I'm not trying to be living the rest of my days feeling like a mutant because the medicine is making me worse than the damn disease," she said. "And I don't want to live the last days hooked up to a bunch of machines, nauseous, and losing my hair. I already went through that with the chemo. And I just..." She stopped talking, and I heard her begin to cry again.

THE CAUSE AND CURE IS YOU 2
by *Jessica N. Watkins*

I really wanted to just go to her, grab her, hold her, and tell her that I was sorry. But there was so much more to lose if I did. I knew she probably thought I was the biggest asshole on the planet. Truthfully, I was. I was being a coward by hiding. I was being a bitch by staying away from her in her time of need. The woman I loved was going to die alone. She may not have been my soulmate, but I loved her, and she meant the world to me.

My kids would resent me. The bad thing was, it wouldn't be the first time.

"Look, Steve, I don't know what I did," she spoke. "But I just...I really need you right now. Can you *please* come home?"

I sighed and leaned back into the chair, looking at a bottle of Dusse that sat next to me. I reached for it, opening it and took a drink straight from the bottle. This was the only comfort I had at the moment.

"Bridget, it's not that I don't want to," I told her after the burning sensation in my chest went away. "And I'm not saying that I don't care—"

"But that's what it seems like Steve!" she interrupted. "You just left! You didn't give me any reason. You act like you don't give a fuck about me or this family anymore. You hurt me. And now I'm sitting here begging you to come home because I'm dying, and you won't even come. So how else am I supposed to feel?"

I didn't know what to say. I had lived long enough to know that nothing I could say would make it right, unless I risked her even earlier demise and death of my children by flying down there.

"Come home," I heard her plead. "Please?"

I took a long drink from the bottle and swallowed hard.

"Steven!" she cried out.

Her desperateness pulled at my heartstrings. This wasn't fair to her or me. I hadn't asked for immortality, nor had she asked to fall in love with a man that would end up having to watch her die. But I had married her, allowed her to fall in love with me, had kids with her knowing that eventually I would have to walk away, no matter me hoping that that day would never come. That *was* my fault. And no matter Theodore's threat on our lives, I had to be a man.

"Okay," I answered finally. "I'll come home."

She sighed in so much relief. "I love you. I just want to make the last days that I have happy. Whatever was wrong, I'm sure we can fix it." My eyes squeezed together, feeling sorry for her because I knew that no matter how much she tried, she couldn't change who I was. "But I just want to make sure that I can die knowing that my husband loves his family and loves me."

"I do," I assured her. "Nothing's going to stop that. Nothing's going to change that. So, stop crying. I'll be home soon."

"Okay. Thank you." When she said that so sincerely, I felt like less of a man. She shouldn't have had to thank me for being there during her demise. I should have been able to be there with no uncertainty or hesitation. And for this Theodore had to be banished to the farthest, darkest corner of the earth.

"You don't have to thank me for being there for you. See you soon." I hung up and took another swig of the Dusse, picked up my phone, and dialed the number, hoping that I could get a favor.

"Hello?"

"Hey, what's happening? It's me. I need your help...*again*," I gruffed.

"What else is new?" he chuckled.

"I know. Look," I started. "I need to go home to Florida. She's dying. I can't let her die alone. I need to be there for her."

"If he finds out that you're there, you know he's going to come for her and the kids," he warned.

"I know," I acknowledged. "But some things are just worth the risk."

"Okay," he said.

"Maurice, I really need you," I reminded him.

"All right," he agreed. "Just come by the office."

"Thanks."

Then Maurice taunted, "What are brothers for?"

DREAM FRANKLIN

"Damn, baby girl, who the hell is that that keep calling your phone?"

I shrugged, leaning against him on the couch as I let him finish watching his little basketball game before I got me some. Reggie and I had been fucking since that night that I had met him. He had been the perfect Zeek replacement.

"I don't know," I groaned without looking at the phone.

It was most likely Fancy, though. She had been blowing my phone up since I got to Reggie's place, and I had been ignoring her.

"You good," he told me. "Go ahead and answer if you need to."

"No," I insisted. "It's probably my sister calling back. She don't want nothing."

His perfect lips formed into a big smile at the sound of that. "Oh word? You got a sister?"

I giggled and shook my head. "Relax, homie, it ain't even like that. Trust me, she's not your type anyway."

Looking down on me, his smile faded into his mouth as he seductively licked his lips. "Oh, so you got all the looks, huh?"

Damn, he's fine. And he got a big dick too? He is a fucking unicorn.

"Yep," I said, feeling my clit pulsating in my panties.

I grabbed his face softly. Fuck this basketball game. I was ready to get it in. I leaned in and was happy that he wasn't fighting this kiss... and then my fucking phone rang again!

"What the fuck!" I snapped as Reggie laughed. "It's not funny."

I picked up the phone and answered with a serious attitude.

This shit better not be about those gawd damn kids, I thought as I answered, "Hello!"

"Dream, what the hell?" I heard my sister hiss. "I've been trying to reach you."

"Yeah, I can see that. I'm busy. So, what the hell do you want?"

"Mama is in the hospital. You need to get here *now*," she rushed.

"What happened?"

"I don't know, but it's not looking good," she told me. "You need to get up to the hospital now."

I groaned out in frustration. Knowing Fancy, she was probably overreacting.

"Aight," I agreed just to get her the hell off my phone. "Just text me the info, and I'll be there when I can."

I hung up before she could reply and got back to Reggie and those lips.

"Everything good?" Reggie asked.

I nodded hurriedly. "Yeah. It's going to be as soon as you get up in this pussy."

****

Three hours later, I was walking through the hospital. I had decided to just ignore the rest of Fancy's calls until I got that good-good.

Fancy had sent me her location in the hospital in a text message, so I hurried towards the area that she said she was in. I found her in the waiting room with the kids, who were all over the place. She was pacing back and forth while on her phone. My phone was ringing yet again so I knew she was calling me.

"Damn, Dream!" she snapped when she saw me walking in. "It takes you three hours to get to the fucking hospital?!"

"I told you that I was busy," I dismissed her as I walked past my oldest and plopped down in a seat.

"Too busy to check on your mama who is in the damn hospital?" she popped.

"*You're* here with her," I snapped with a shrug.

Her eyes bulged as if she couldn't believe my audacity. "*You* should have been here too! Especially with your bad ass kids!" she said through gritted teeth.

"Whatever, with your dramatic ass. Just tell me what happened to mama," I huffed.

She plopped down in the seat next to me. I rolled my eyes as I noticed the AKA cropped top that she was wearing.
Boogie ass.

"Dream, mama had a stroke."

"She what?"

"She fell out at home and the kids called 9-1-1. When they got here, luckily my neicy-poo was smart enough to give the police my cell phone number when they got here." She sat there smiling at my oldest, Andrea, who was eight years old... I still didn't know who the hell her daddy was, and the lil' heifer acted like she didn't like me.

"She's alive," Fancy added. "But she hasn't awakened from the surgery yet... And they're saying that when she does, it's a possibility that she might be brain dead." My heart dropped as she went on, "They just told me thirty minutes ago."

I was in shock. I didn't fuck with my sister, but my mama...that was my girl. She was my savior. She had my back. And no matter what, she never let my sister judge me. I wasn't too inconsiderate or self-centered to know that.

"Dream, they're saying that it's not looking too good," she continued. "So, we got to figure out what we're going to do."

"Let's not even worry about it until we see what the doctor says," I said.

"I'm not talking about that," she corrected me. "I'm talking about the kids."

"What you mean?" I asked her.

"Dream, I gotta work! I'm up for this promotion, and I can't risk losing it because I gotta watch your kids," she huffed. "And Mama can't do it no more. Hell, they probably the reason why she had the damn stroke in the first place."

My eyes narrowed as I looked her up and down. "Wow. You really gonna try to put her having a stroke on the kids?!" I snapped. "Did it ever occur to you that mama's just old and with that high blood pressure, that's why she had a stroke? Old people have strokes."

Fancy shook her head. "And why did she have high blood pressure, Dream? Chasing after the kids *you made* all day," she shot back. "All the more reason why she shouldn't be taking care of them now...*if* she makes it. Dream, it's time that you come out of this little fantasy world that you're living in and take care of your responsibilities. *You* made them kids. Not mama. She shouldn't be raising your kids."

I started to hyperventilate. How in the hell was I gonna take these kids home to Keys? I had *finally* gotten a ring, and he would take it away from me as soon as he found out that I had been hiding four kids from him.

No fucking way.

"Okay, so why don't you just take care of them for a while?" I stressed in desperation. "I can pay you. I gave mama money all the time."

Her eyes bucked even wider, and she laughed. "You can't just buy me, Dream. I already have a job, and it's not being a mother to kids that I didn't birth."

Now, I was having heart palpations. I was about to be right in the bed in the room next to my mama, because I was about to die if I had to take these kids home. Fancy would not be as easy to convince as mama. I knew it. It was like she was born to fight me.

"So, you just don't give a fuck about your own nieces and nephews?" I tried to guilt her.

Now, she was cracking up. "Dream, please. That shit ain't gone work with me. Girl, bye."

"I can't take care of them right now," I snapped. "I just can't. You don't understand."

"Oh, I understand," she nodded slowly. "Your ass is selfish as hell. You really want me to take care of your kids like mama and don't see anything wrong with it. Fuck my job? Fuck my life? Just stop everything and be the mother that you don't wanna be?"

"Yes, because we family!" I interrupted.

"Then bitch act like it!" she hissed. "All you do is throw money at mama or something like we're beneath you. These are your kids, Dream. Not ours. You seriously want me to take care of your kids like it's some temporary thing. Mama been taking care of your kids since the moment you had them. It's time for *you* to be a mother."

I bit my lip, taking my anger out on it and not my sister like I wanted to because I needed her to take these fucking kids with her.

But I knew she wouldn't. Fancy wasn't going to. No money would convince her to. Her watching me suffer was worth more to her than any money.

"Well, then I guess I'mma have to give their little asses up for adoption then," I said with a shrug. I was serious as the stroke my mother had just had. There was no way that I was taking these kids home. I'd rather give them to the state.

Fancy's mouth dropped. "Bitch, are you crazy?! Are you really that fucking selfish that you're not even willing to take care of your own kids when they need you the most? Come on, Dream. The only person that they had raising them or even knew as a mother just had a stroke. She is lying in a hospital bed. She might not be able to speak or move when she wakes up... *if* she wakes up. And you would rather put them up for adoption than be a mother to them? Yo', what the fuck is wrong with you?"

"There's nothing wrong with me," I huffed. "The only thing wrong is that you don't like the fact that I'm not trying to fuck my life up. I'm not trying to be living in some ghetto for the rest of my damn life taking care of a bunch of kids not having a way out living some mediocre life. Keys is my way to a better life. If he leaves me because I lied to him, I will have nothing. I will have no way to take care of them then. So, either way, I would much rather put them up for adoption and let somebody else take care of them. Now you may think that that's selfish, but I don't have to answer to you."

"You right," Fancy nodded with a cynical stare. "You don't." She looked at me with pure disgust in her eyes. She rolled her eyes, shaking her head in disappointment. She then mumbled, "I swear to God, I wish Mama had aborted your ass."

Hearing her say that didn't faze me a bit. All I did was adjust my clothes and laugh.

"Yeah, well, she didn't," I replied. "Maybe if I had aborted *them* and not listened to Mama, I wouldn't be in the situation that I'm in now."

"She was trying to get you to see that when you lay down and act like you grown, you gotta deal with the consequences," she said. "She was trying to give you an opportunity to still get an education, Dream." Her nose flared as she went on, "Listen to yourself. You are their mother. You gave birth to them. You carried them," she snapped quietly as she pointed to them.

I watched them as they ran around that waiting room, hitting each other, arguing, annoying everybody, knocking things over...

Fuck that. No way.

"Well, now, I'm *carrying* their little asses to an adoption agency, how about that?" I spat. "And I'm done talking about it." I jumped to my feet, walked past her, and headed to my mother's room to, God forbid, say my goodbyes.

CHAPTER NINETEEN
FANCY FRANKLIN

I can't believe this girl could be so selfish. Mama spent all of those years taking care of kids that Dream had made, but it hadn't done Dream any good. She was still stupid, careless, and all about self.

I always knew that Dream was trifling, but I never thought that she could be *this* damn trifling. How could she just walk away from her own kids like that? She acted as if she was too good for them or something. How could she give them away like they were just puppies? I loved her kids because they were my family, but I wasn't the one that started having babies at fourteen. I went to college and got a degree. I'd done things right. So, why did I have to be the one stuck with them because she didn't love them enough to be a mother?

I looked at my nieces and nephews sitting in the waiting room fighting over the remote and sighed. Dream wasn't fit to be anybody's mother. She thought that I was just going to take her kids and end up like Mama? Hell no. Her kids were bad as hell, and I wasn't about to spend the rest of my life taking care of them.

One of my nurses walked past the waiting room. I shot to my feet and ran to the doorway to stop her. "Excuse me," I called. When she turned around, I asked, "Is there any update on my mother?"

When she took too long to answer and sighed, I feared the worst.

"She's still unconscious," she told me. "Honestly, you may want to go ahead and start contacting family."

Tears welled in my eyes. *Not my mama. Not now. Not like this.*

She'd spent her whole life taking care of others and being there for us. She didn't deserve to go out like this so soon.

"Is there anything that can be done?" I asked, hopeful.

"Unfortunately, no," she said. "There was a lot of swelling on her brain, and the brain is such a delicate organ in the body. It controls so much. When she had the stroke, unfortunately, she didn't receive the medical care that she needed right away. We're going to watch her for the next couple of days, but, if things don't improve, then like I said, you may want to consider taking her off of the machine."

I couldn't take it. I couldn't hear somebody tell me that my mama was only breathing because of a machine. This wasn't right!

"Is there anybody I can call for you?" the nurse asked.

"N–" I stopped suddenly when I caught a glimpse of Dream hurrying onto the elevator.

"Bitch," I muttered in disbelief as I watched her leave.

"Ma'am," I heard the nurse call.

I tore my eyes away from my sister abandoning her kids once again. I looked at the nurse with heavy, tear-soaked eyes. "No. Thank you."

The nurse nodded sadly and went on her way. I sadly turned to go back in the waiting room.

"Give it baaaaaaaaack!" my nephew, Davaughn, screamed.

"No, it's mine!" my niece, Tamika, snapped back.

"Oh gawd," I groaned. I couldn't do this. I shouldn't have had to do this.

I got on my cell phone and googled the club that Dream's fiancée owned. She had tried to keep so much about him a secret because she didn't want us to meet him. But Chicago was only so big, so I knew that he had opened up a club and named it after her.

I should have done this a long time ago, especially after the way she had dismissed the kids before, but I always felt like she would eventually do the right thing and tell her fiancé that she had kids. Clearly, I was wrong.

Once I found the number, I stepped out of the waiting room, called the club, and waited for someone to answer.

"Dreams," someone answered with a deep voice.

"Hi, I need to speak to the owner," I said.

"Who is this?" the guy on the other end pressed.

"My name is Fancy. I'm his fiancée's sister. It's important," I urged.

"Hold on." Then I heard him call out, "Hey, boss. Some chick named Fancy on the phone," he yelled. "She's calling about your girl."

I could hear somebody talking in the background. Then a rough voice came on the line, "Yo', this Keys."

"My name is Fancy. I know you don't know me, but I'm calling you about Dream. I know you probably don't know what's going on, but I've got something that you need to know…"

IVY SUMMERS

"Ms. Summers, your break is over, isn't it?"

My skin crawled as I met his narrowing eyes, looking at me with judgement. It took everything in me to be civil, but I had to since I was in the staff's lounge and everyone was watching.

"My apologies," I gritted as I left the chair where I was browsing Snapchat and walked by him.

"Don't let it happen again," he warned, looking at his phone.

Wow, he was unbelievable. I instantly stopped walking. I turned back, darting my eyes at him, ready to curse him the fuck out.

"Are you just going to stand there or are you going to get to your patients?" he asked.

I sighed and had to tell myself not to go off on this motherfucker so that I could keep my job.

Ever since he'd found out that I was pregnant, he had been acting like a total asshole.

I was shocked to see that Keisha was in the doorway as I walked out of it. She looked at me with so much sympathy as she followed me into the hall.

"Fuck him," she told me. "Don't pay him no mind."

"I'm trying not to."

"You're doing a good job. Lunch later?" she asked as we approached the elevator.

"Yeah," I said with a smile.

The smile that she returned was still full of sympathy as we separated.

I had sworn that she was the one that told Timothy about my pregnancy when Timothy woke me up out of my sleep that day. But he said that he'd seen the tests in the garbage while using the bathroom before waking me up.

He'd walked out on me that day, without even giving me a chance to explain. I had explained via text message, but there had been no reply. And when I got back to work, every time I saw him, he treated me like this.

He acted like I'd done this on purpose! I had gotten pregnant *before* I even met him. I knew that it was hard for him to deal with, but he had only known me for a few weeks. I had to deal with this for the rest of my life! I didn't ask for this.

I headed to my patients' rooms and took care of them. I was tired and feeling sick to my stomach. I'd been sick every day since I found out that I was pregnant. But I welcomed the sickness because I had finally decided to have this baby. Despite the circumstances, I was going to give life. I had been surrounded by way too much death lately to kill another soul. So, it was going to be me and this baby from here on out.

I had considered calling Keys to tell him that he was going to be a father, but I knew the minute that I did, he would want to come to Dallas and to be with me. And I wasn't going to let him risk losing his life, let alone my babies. I didn't know how I was going to do it, but I was going to be a mother to this child. More than my own had been to me.

I knew it was wrong not to tell Keys but telling him that I was pregnant would open a floodgate of problems. He was days away from getting married and this psycho, Theo was still trying to kill him. I already knew that the minute that I was around Keys, death would follow all of us. As much as I loved Keys, I had to think about my baby's wellbeing more than I did Keys' from now on.

****

About three hours later, I was finishing up with my last patient on my round and headed towards the breakroom. My morning sickness had once again kicked in, and I needed to settle my stomach. I grabbed a ginger ale from the vending machine and sat down. I was alone inside of the room... until Timothy walked in. Instantly, I gave him a dismissive look.

"Excuse me," he said curtly.

I wasn't about to let him stress me. He could carry his ass right on out the door and into traffic in front of a fuck bus for all I gave a good gawd damn.

"I don't appreciate you trying to embarrass me in front of everybody," I spat.

"Excuse me?" he asked as if I had some nerve.

"I didn't stutter," I replied. "You tried to embarrass me because you're upset about what happened."

"Don't try to make this personal," he argued. "I was just telling you to do your job."

"No, you were trying to throw your weight around to make yourself feel better," I corrected him.

"Feel better about what? I'm fine," he shrugged, fronting.

"No, you're not," I said folding my arms tightly across my chest. "You're punishing me like I knew that I was pregnant when I met you. I didn't know! And if I did, I would have never gotten involved with you. After all that I have been through, this was the *last* thing that I wanted to deal with. I was finally content. I care about you. I really wanted things to progress with us. But this happened before I even met you. You act like I knew I was pregnant this entire time or something. You didn't even give me the chance to tell you. You went through my trash, and then the next thing I know, you're walking out. And now you're mad at me. You don't think I'm mad about this shit?! You don't have a right to be mad."

"I don't know what you want from me," he said softly. "You're going to have another man's baby, but you expect to stay with me and I be happy about it?"

"I didn't say that!" I spat. "I understand how you feel, Timothy. I do. But what isn't fair is you taking your frustrations out on me. I'm sorry if it hurt you. But I didn't plan this."

"Okay, so you didn't plan this," he shrugged. "Now what?"

My eyebrows curled in confusion. "What do you mean?"

"Now that you know that you're pregnant, what are you gonna do?"

I shrugged, frowning at my continued confusion with the question. "Be a fucking mother."

Timothy shook his head and chuckled. "You'd much rather have a baby with a nigga that chose another chick over you?" he pushed. "This man basically told you that he didn't want to be with you, and ain't so much as called you. And on top of that, the nigga is getting married to the chick he chose over you. Are you really that pathetic to hold on to his baby that he probably don't even want?"

My eyes bulged. "Wow," I said, looking at him with complete disgust. I was seeing Timothy for who he really was. "I can't believe that you would actually come out of your mouth and say something like that."

Granted, I hadn't told Timothy the whole story, so, of course he had no idea what he was talking about. But I had thought that he was at least smart enough to know that I wasn't pathetic.

I couldn't believe that I had allowed myself to get caught up in the hype. I really thought I was with a good guy. Guess I had been fooled...again.

"You know," I said, walking up on him. "The funny thing is, you don't even mean what you're saying. You're just mad because once again, it's another chick that you were feeling that's having a baby that ain't yours."

That definitely struck a nerve. His haughty disposition disappeared, he glared at my audacity to throw his past in his face.

Good.

I walked out that room and left him standing there looking stupid. In a sense, I felt better, but at the end of the day, I knew that I was still about to go through this alone. Completely alone. I just hoped that I could handle it.

I put my hands on my stomach and rubbed my belly as I walked back towards my unit. I was going to take care of this baby my way. I didn't need Timothy or Keys or anybody. I was tired of letting men control me.

"We don't need any of them, baby," I told my baby as I continued to rub my stomach. "Mama got you."

ANTONIO 'KEYS' VALENTINE

"Yo', dawg, you all right?" Zeek was staring at me concerned, waiting on an answer, as I hung up the phone.

"Bruh, I just got a phone call from Dream's sister, some chick named Fancy," I told him.

His eyes got wide with disbelief. "She got a sister?"

"Apparently," I shrugged as I slowly sat in a bar stool. "But there's more to it than that."

"What's up?" he asked.

"She said that Dream got like four kids."

Zeek's eyes got wider as he slowly asked, "Woooord?"

"Yeah," I told him still in shock. I rested my elbow on the bar and held my head. This shit was wild.

"I don't know, man," he hesitated. "You think it's true?"

"I mean, why would somebody call and make up some shit like that?" I asked.

"Well," he said trying to reason. "Maybe it was just a jealous female or some shit. I mean, y'all got like a week before the wedding and you know how your girl is. She's been going around telling everybody that she's marrying you and how she's about to be Mrs. Valentine and queen of the streets and all that shit. Females are petty. I can see one of them calling you on bullshit."

"Yeah, but why would she make up their mother being in the hospital?"

Zeek froze and asked, "She what?"

"She said that she was calling to tell me about the kids because their mother had been taking care of the kids all this time but just had a stroke. She said that Dream had left them on her because she didn't want to bring them home to me since I knew nothing about them."

Zeek's blink was slow as hell. "Sounds like you need to go holla at your girl, fam."

I nodded. "Oh, I am. I'll holla at you later. I got to go head to the crib."

"Aight, fam. Call me if you need me."

"Yeah, I got you," I told him as we shook up.

As I drove home, all I could think about was that phone call. Something was telling me that Fancy just wasn't some woman hating on Dream.

Who the fuck was this woman that I was supposed to be marrying? How the hell could she have a whole family that I knew nothing about? I remembered asking her about her family and she said that her parents were dead and that she didn't want to have kids with just anybody. Now I'm finding out not only did she have a mother *and* a sister in the same damn city, but she had kids too. There was no way that I could marry this broad.

I knew I had done my dirt and I wasn't 100% innocent because I had a past, but keeping something this big from me was something that I couldn't look past. If she lie about this, who knew what the fuck she was lying about. Any broad that could lie about having kids is fucked up in the head.

I pulled up in my driveway and saw her car parked. She hadn't been home as much lately, and I had figured that it was because of the wedding. But, hell, now I was thinking that maybe she was with her kids. Either way, I was about to find out.

When I walked through the door, she was laughing and giggling on the phone, but hung up quick when she heard me walk through the door.

"Hey, baby," she greeted.

"What up?" I grunted, tossing my keys on the table.

"You okay?" she asked.

"Nah," I admitted. "I just got a real fucked up phone call."

"Oh okay," she said as she started looking in her phone as she walked by me. "I got to head out in a minute. I'm supposed to be finalizing this seating chart."

"Hold up a second," I told her, grabbing her by the arm. "I gotta holla at you about something."

She winced and pulled away from me. "What's up?"

"The phone call that I just got was from your sister, Fancy..."

I watched her choke on her own spit, which let me know that this Fancy chick was telling the truth.

She began to stutter and fumble over her words. "Wh-what are you talking about? I-I-I don't have a sister."

"Dream, don't fucking play with me right now," I warned. "Your sister called me at the club and told me that you got four motherfucking kids that your mother has been taking care of." When she tried to avoid my eyes, I followed them, standing dead in her fucking face. "I thought your parents were dead, Dream?"

She laughed nervously and shook her head, but she still avoided my eyes as she obviously lied, "Clearly, you're stupid enough to believe anything somebody tells you. 'Cause I ain't got no fuckin' kids."

"Wow," I said shaking my head. "You are insane. You know I used to think that that little crazy shit you did was sexy, but I really think there's something actually really wrong with you. You had four kids and family right here in the motherfucking city and didn't tell me. We been together for three years and you ain't said shit the entire time!"

"Okay!" she screamed as she started to pace nervously. "So, I have kids. Yes," she confessed. "Yes, I kept it from you. I don't consider it lying to you because I just didn't know how to tell you. I was going to tell you when we first got together, but—"

"Shut the fuck up!" I stopped her. "Ain't no fuckin excuse as to why the fuck you couldn't tell me in all of these gawd damn years that we've been together, 'Hey, baby, I got a mother and a sister. Oh and I got four *fucking* kids!'" I roared. "Ain't shit you can say that's gone make that all right!"

THE CAUSE AND CURE IS YOU 2
by *Jessica N. Watkins*

I couldn't even look at her ass right now. I turned away from her and walked towards the couch. I was blown away. I had dealt with some real shit in my years. Real, heavy, street shit. But none of it had blown my mind like this shit right here. Not even learning that I wasn't human.

"Yo', you a trifling motherfucker, you know that?" I continued. "What kind of woman can pretend like she has no kids, no mother. I can see if you had put them up for adoption, but your sister told me you see them all the time when you go *visit your mother.*"

"I'm sorry!" she apologized as she rushed towards me. She reached for me, and I swatted her hand away as I plopped down on the couch. "When we first met, I didn't want to tell a stranger that I had four kids that my mother was taking care of. Then, every time I got ready to tell you after that, it was just bad timing. When I first thought about telling you, I found out about you cheating. I didn't know if we were gonna stay together, so I figured why even say anything. Then the next time I tried to tell you—"

I held my hand up to stop her. She was not about to spin this. "Don't do that shit," I said. "What the fuck I did then ain't got shit to do with you acknowledging the fact that you fucking lied to me from day one. You can't sit up here and try to make it seem like I'm the motherfucka that did all the dirt when you came in this motherfucka dirty. You were lying before I ever cheated on you. So, miss me with that bullshit." She got ready to speak, but I cut her off again. "I don't wanna hear nothing. I'm done. I can't be with somebody that can lie about something like that. I don't know what the fuck else you're lying about, yo'."

Her eyes grew big as she started to breathe slow and hard. "So, you are just gonna leave me after I lied about one thing, when I stayed with you through all your bullshit?!" she yelled. "Are you serious? All this that I done put up with from you?! You just gonna walk away?!"

I nodded as if I had never been so sure of something in my life, because I hadn't. "That's what the fuck I said."

"Keys, I dealt with and took a lot of shit from you too," she replied. "Okay, I hurt you. I get that. But you hurt me too. The only difference is I forgave you. I forgave you for everything that you did to me. Me having the kids was nothing compared to what you did. You cheated on me with a whole bunch of different broads. Then you're carrying on with this bitch, Ivy, that you're claiming you have nothing to do with. I'm not stupid. If I could forgive you for all of that, then why can't you forgive me?"

I stared at her tears realizing that this was the first I had ever seen her look so sincere.

"'Cause I can't trust you," I told her calmly.

"Yes, you can! Don't do this," she cried.

All the tears in the world couldn't make me love her ever again. Any love that I had for her was gone. Lying about bitches was one thing. Lying about kids, a mother, a sister, a family... that shit was just sick.

"Keys, we're supposed to be getting married," she sniffed. "We've got a week until our wedding. Don't do this. I'm sorry!"

She took a few steps towards me, but I gave her a look that let it be known I would knock the hell out of her and she stopped in her tracks.

"Well, you might as well tell Facebook that the wedding is off, since you tell it everything else."

Her jaw dropped. "Please! I know I fucked up," she wept. "I know that I was wrong keeping that from you. But I didn't know how to tell you. And I thought that once I told you that you would leave me. Like you're trying to do now."

"You had plenty of opportunity to tell me the truth." I told her unfazed, by her emotions. "But you carried on a lie. Your sister called me out the blue and told me that they're about to pull the plug on your mother, and that all you did was walk out because you don't want to take care of *your* kids. I can't marry no bitch like that!"

"How many times did I forgive you after you cheated on me, huh?"

I laughed at her. She was like a dog with a bone with this shit. I calmly straightened my clothes and got comfortable on the couch. "You need to get the fuck outta my house."

"What?!" she gasped, caught off guard.

"I didn't fucking stutter," I gritted. "Get the fuck out. I'll send you your shit later."

Her mouth dropped open and tears started flowing from her face. "Keys, you love me," she whined as if she was trying to remind me. "I love you. Don't do this. Please don't end it like this."

I had had enough. I jumped up from the couch and she jumped back. But I walked past her, through the living room to the door and opened it.

"This gon' be the *last* time I ask you to leave," I warned.

She walked slowly towards the door and stared at me with more longing in her eyes than I'd seen in them since we first started fucking around. She was humble than a motherfucker now.

"Keys, I'm sorry," she whispered.

"You can keep the ring," I told her. "That's all you gave a fuck about anyway."

She looked at me, and her attitude went from sadness to this psychotic ass laugh.

"You know what? Fine," she spat. "If you don't want to be with me, cool. It's a ton of niggas out there that'll be glad to have a bitch like me that's down for them."

I laughed. "There she go! That's the Dream I know."

She sneered at me mocking her as she hissed, "I held you down through everything. I was there for you when you were on the streets hustling, when you decided to go legit and open up that fuckin' club. Every bitch that you fucked around on me with, I was there. If you can't recognize a real

250

bitch when she's staring at you right in your face, then fuck you."

She stomped off the porch before she turned around.

"Oh, but you wasn't the only one out here. I cheated too," she smirked. "I was givin' this pussy to another motherfucka. Just ask your boy, Zeek."

CHAPTER TWENTY

DREAM FRANKLIN

I sped to my mama's house because I knew Fancy would be there. I had planned to come back that weekend, when I knew Keys would be busy with the club, to take the kids to the adoption agency. But this hoe had stepped in and cost me everything! Now, she had to pay.

I pulled up to my mama's house, and, of course, Fancy's car was there. I could hear the kids inside screaming and crying. I walked right through the front door and didn't even pay attention to the other folks in there. I was like a raging bull. I scanned the room looking for Fancy and charged right at her.

"So, you tricked on me, bitch?!" I hissed.

I lunged at her, but out of nowhere, somebody had snatched me up.

"Let me go, motherfucka!" I screamed. "Get off me!"

"Calm down," he demanded.

I didn't even know who the hell it was. I didn't give a fuck either. But if he knew what was good for him, he would let me go. He had me hemmed up against the wall, and I was fighting so hard, trying to get to Fancy that I hadn't seen who it was.

I glared at Fancy being consoled by someone. She was crying hysterically. "Nah, don't cry now, bitch!"

"Yo', Dream, you gotta calm the hell down," he said so lovingly that my anger ceased, and curiosity took over. Then I recognized his voice. I finally saw that it was my cousin, Mook.

"Mook, I'm good. Put me down," I told him. Mook was crazier than me, and he didn't condone family fighting each other. He said we fought together, not each other. So, I pumped the brakes...for now.

He hesitated before he did, but finally let me go.

"Yo', cuz on some real shit, you gotta chill out," he insisted. "Save that shit for another day. Now ain't the time."

"No, it's the perfect time for this bitch to tell me why the fuck she called my fiancé and snitched," I clapped back.

"Dream," he called. "You not hearing me."

Suddenly, I felt eyes on me. I looked around, and I finally realized that I was in a room full of people that looked like they had been crying. But now they were all looking at me like I had lost my damn mind.

"Dream," Fancy finally spoke getting my attention. "Mama's gone."

THEODORE JONES

"You mean to tell me that don't nobody know where this hoe at?!" I barked as my hand slammed on the table. "So, she just disappeared off the fucking face of the Earth?!"

Smooth, Blue, and my security detail were sitting around the table with me with no answers.

Smooth shrugged meekly. "We had men on her house. We had men on the beauty shop where she works, all the usual spots she be kicking it at. She just laying low or something."

"Maybe she left town," Blue suggested.

"Nah, she ain't left town. She right here in Chicago," I said. "She ain't never been out of Chicago before, so she don't know nothing else."

I had been trying to find out where Tiny had been since the day I threw her out of the house. I didn't have nothing to worry about, because nobody other than me knew who she was to me, other than a piece of pussy. But I wasn't taking any chances. Of all people, *she* was my kryptonite. *She* was my weakness. The thought of it fucked me up, but I wasn't about to show any signs of weakness, especially to these niggas.

I had Smooth and Blue looking for her, but these two fumbling idiots had come up empty. I had been calling her several times, and she hadn't responded. I tried to leave her messages sounding sweet and nice, but she wasn't falling for it.

"You motherfuckas got forty-eight hours to find her," I warned them.

"We got you," they both said in unison.

"I hope y'all got this shit ready for tonight and ain't handling this like y'all are handling looking for this broad," I spat.

"Nah, boss, we on it," Smooth assured me. "Trust, we got it handled. We actually 'bout to head over there now."

"Aight," I nodded. "Y'all better know what the fuck you're doing. 'Cause if y'all fuck this up, you might as well dig your grave, 'cause I'ma body both of y'all," I promised.

"We got it," Blue assured me.

Tonight, I was going to take everything away from Keys. I was going to remind him exactly what I was capable of. He had tried taking everything away from me, but let's see him survive after this. And it was going down tonight. I couldn't wait to see him crumble.

"Aight," I said reaching for a Cuban to light. "Let's load up."

ANTONIO 'KEYS' VALENTINE

"Yo', what up, bruh?" Esco answered.

My nose flared just thinking about "what was up".

"Where you at?" I asked him. "I need you to meet me at the club."

"Aye, hold on, bruh. I can barely hear you. These motherfuckers loud as hell. What you say?"

"I said meet me at the gawd damn club!" I snapped.

"Yo'... you good?"

I was weaving through traffic headed to the club. The only thing on my mind at that moment was to kill Zeek's ass. I called Esco to meet me at the club. I knew Pops was still out of town dealing with Bridget, and I didn't want to bother him. Reese was still in Florida and was supposed to come back up in a couple of days, but Esco and Lucky were still around.

"Yo, what's going on, bruh?" Esco pressed.

"This motherfucka Zeek," I said shaking my head, still in disbelief.

I was literally three minutes from the club. The likelihood that Esco was going to beat me there was slim.

"Bro, you talkin' in circles. What happened?" Esco asked.

"Maaaan," I groaned. "Dream and Zeek been fucking around."

THE CAUSE AND CURE IS YOU 2
by *Jessica N. Watkins*

"Ooooh shit," he mumbled. "Aight, sit tight. I'm on the way."

He hung up, but I was still flying to the club. Fuck sitting tight. I had called him to ensure that someone was around to keep me from doing something that would land me in jail or on the news. But I couldn't wait for him. I had to handle this shit now.

I wasn't even mad that Dream had fucked around on me. She had been a snake ass bitch for a long time. But Zeek? He had been fronting like he was my right man this whole time while smashing my bitch.

I was out the game. I been done with hustling, but it wouldn't take much for me to go back to the old me.

I whipped into the parking lot of the club, killing the engine and damn near breaking off the gear shift as I threw it in park. I didn't give a fuck who was in my path. Zeek had some explaining to do. It was still early, so it was only a few employees in the club. When I had left earlier, I didn't intend on coming back. But, of course, I didn't think that my chick would tell me that she had been fucking my homie either.

"Hey, what you doing back here?" Zeek asked seeing me walk through the door. "Did you meet your future step kids?" he joked. He was with the shits and giggles until he saw the look on my face as I charged towards him. He tried to stand and move out of my path, but it was too late; I picked him up and slammed his ass so hard against the bar that the wood broke into pieces around his falling body.

"Daaaaaaaaaaaaaaaaaaaaaaaaaaaaamn!" one of the bartenders chanted.

"You bitch ass nigga!" I gritted through my teeth holding him down.

"What the fuck, Keys?" he struggled to speak.

"You been fucking Dream this whole time?" I growled.

His eyes swelled out of his sockets. I punched him in the chest, hearing his ribs crack around my fists.

"Aargh!" he bellowed.

Employees and the few patrons inside stood around watching in awe. But they knew better than to try to stop me.

"You supposed to be my motherfuckin brother!" I heaved.

"I'm sorry," he winced. "It wasn't supposed to happen."

"Sorry?!" I bellowed. Before I knew it, I had taken all my strength and threw him across the room. I knew that I needed to stop before people realized that no man with normal strength could have done that, but I was outraged.

He hit the wall so hard that it cracked. He fell to the floor with a hard thud and he started to moan out in pain. "I'm sorry, bro."

He stood up slowly as I raced towards him and lost it. I started swinging and landing punches on his face and every part of his body. Of course, he tried to fight back, but I was much stronger and way more powerful than he was. I didn't care that my employees were watching in shock as I dismantled him. My rage was unstoppable.

Block, one of the security guards came in and rushed over trying to stop me.

"Come on, boss," he urged as he struggled to get me off of Zeek. "Come on, man, it ain't worth it. Leave him be."

I easily shook him off and went back to handling this bitch ass nigga that I once called a friend. I knew that I was beating him to death, but I couldn't stop myself. Block once again tried to pull me back with the assistance of another security guard this time.

"Come on, man," he gritted. "Calm down! They about to call the cops on you in a minute. You don't need shit else happening in this club," he said trying to reason with me. "You 'bout to kill him!"

"I don't give a fuck!" I seethed as I threw them both off of me.

They both hit the floor as I spotted Dream storming through the door. "Keys, we need to talk! I said something really stupid earlier. I didn't—" She stopped suddenly when her eyes landed on the dismantled bar, the cracked wall, and then on Zeek. She stood there motionless with eyes full of fear.

I was standing over Zeek's lifeless body, breathing heavy like a savage beast. Block gripped my arm to keep me from charging at her.

I glowered at her, "Ain't shit you got to say to me, hoe." Then I looked at Block and said, "Get these motherfuckas out of my club."

"So, after all we've been through, you're really just going to end it like this? You've done some fucked up shit too, Keys!" she cried. "The only reason I was fucking with Zeek is because you were fucking with that broad, Ivy! Ever since you met that hoe that night that's all you cared about. You think I didn't know? I'm not stupid! I know you were fucking her!"

Block stood next to me, shaking his head at Dream in disbelief. She had seen the damage that I had done and still wouldn't stop. This bitch had no off button.

"Come on, boss. I got you," Block urged. "Let's go for a walk. You don't need to be here right now."

He pushed me towards the front door, and I let him because reality had finally set in. I couldn't murder Zeek in front of witnesses. This club had enough slack as it was. His bitch ass and Dream's hoe ass wasn't going to take this club away from me.

I heard the other security guard urging Dream to leave as Block and I stepped outside.

"Keys!"

I turned around and saw that this dumbass hoe had actually followed me outside.

"Yo', you dumb as hell," Block warned her.

"Will you just talk to me?" Dream screamed running towards me.

THE CAUSE AND CURE IS YOU 2
by Jessica N. Watkins

I shook my head and kept walking. This hoe was about to make me kill her ass right in the middle of the street.

This was unbelievable. I was immortal. I had superpowers. I was a fucking metahuman... Yet, I still couldn't dodge the superpowers of a hoe.

Luckily for her, Block stepped between her and me.

"You know what? Fine!" she screamed.

Folks were standing around watching, which is just what Dream liked; an audience. She was about to put on for these fools.

"I don't give a fuck! I'm done doing this shit with you. Go chase that fat bitch! Let her deal with your whack ass dick," she snapped. "I'll go back to Zeek. At least he knows how to handle my pussy."

I don't know why I did it, but I smooth ran up and knocked the shit out of her ass. I hit her so hard that she was out before she hit the ground.

"Aw shit!" Block spat in frustration.

There were people outside with their phones out, recording and watching in shock. Just my fucking luck, a gawd damn cop was on the corner writing a ticket. The next thing I knew, he was coming towards me with his gun drawn. I stood there with my hands up. I already knew what was about to happen. My black ass was about to get locked the fuck up.

Esco pulled up and jumped out of his car as the officer was handcuffing me and reading me my rights.

"What the fuck, Keys?" Esco spat.

He looked at Dream lying on the ground with people around her trying to revive her. Then he peered into the club and saw the wreckage.

He shook his head in frustration. "What the hell did you do?"

I couldn't say shit as the officer led me to the squad car. I could have easily broken out of the cuffs, but if I didn't want the cops chasing me forever, I had to take this charge.

STEVE VALENTINE

I was in the living room playing the PlayStation with my oldest, mortal son. Bridget was in her bedroom resting. As soon as I got to Dallas, it was plainly evident that she was indeed dying. She had lost quite a bit of weight. She was so frail and weak.

I cursed my own existence, because what use was it being a supernatural being if I couldn't help the ones I love fight to live? What was the use in being mortal if I had to watch my mortal loved ones die around me.

Reese's phone rang distracting temporarily from my thoughts.

"Hey, what's up, bro?" Reese answered.

His eyebrows curled within seconds, and I looked at him concerned trying to read what was going on.

"What's going on?" I asked. "Is everything okay?"

He held up a finger and stood up walking off to listen. My gut was telling me something was going on. A few minutes later, he came back, saying, "That was Esco. So, apparently, Keys got arrested," he told me. "He found out that Dream was messing with his best friend, and he beat Zeek damn near to death."

"What?" I sighed. "I told that boy to control his temper."

"Yeah, I know," he agreed. "Esco said him and Sincere are trying to figure out how much his bail is. He said they're gonna make him stay overnight."

I shook my head. I was going to have to leave earlier than planned.

"All right. I guess I'll catch the next flight out. Just keep an eye out for your sisters and brothers, and I'll be back as soon as I can," I told him.

"No problem," he replied. "Let me know if you need anything."

"All right."

After saying goodbye to Bridget and the kids, I headed out the door and straight to the airport. After several minutes of waiting in line, I was able to catch a ten o'clock flight. I had a few hours to kill, so I got comfy in the terminal and called Esco while I waited. He filled me in on everything going on and confirmed that Keys had been arrested.

"Pops, it was bad. I'm surprised that nigga Zeek ain't dead," he admitted.

"So that means Keys probably put his powers out there for the whole world to see," I said with a grimace.

"Yeah, I know," he agreed. "But, from what everybody is saying, they've always known he was strong like that. They really don't think anything of it."

"Let's hope not," I said.

I knew that Keys was angry, but, angry or not, he couldn't be doing dumb shit like that in front of everybody. That's how Theodore had found out who he was.

"All right, I'll call you when I land," I told him.

We hung up, and I powered my phone off laying back to get comfortable.

Eventually, it was time to board the plane and after all of the safety drills, we were in the air for the three-and-a-half-hour flight.

The minute I landed, I powered my phone on and my phone began vibrating nonstop, notifying me that I had multiple voicemails and missed calls. I saw Esco's name numerous times and knew something was wrong. Calling him, I waited for an answer. After the second ring, he answered, and I could hear sirens in the background.

"What the hell is going on?" I asked standing in the middle of baggage claim.

"Pops, we got a problem!" he yelled. "Somebody blew up the club."

CHAPTER TWENTY-ONE
IVY SUMMERS

I lay in bed wide awake. My mind was racing. Even though I was secure with the plan of having this baby alone, the anxiety of doing so without telling Keys kept me up most nights. So, I did what I always did to pass the time until I finally fell asleep: started scrolling through my Facebook app. I was looking at the usual mess when I saw *Dreams* trending on Facebook.

What the hell?

Curious, I clicked on the link. and my mouth dropped open in shock.

'Explosion at Nightclub Leaves Several Dead'

"Oh my God!" I whispered in shock as I sat straight up.

My mind ran rampant with worry if Keys was alive. I logged off of the app. I needed to call Keys and started to curse myself for deleting his number. Then I remembered that everything was in the Cloud, so I logged on, and thank God, I found his number there. I called Keys for the first time since before I left Chicago.

It went straight to voicemail, so I hung up.

I placed my hand to my stomach and prayed that Keys was okay. If he was, I was going to make sure that he knew that he had a child on the way. I wasn't going to keep it from him. Not after this.

He had to be okay. I looked for him on Facebook to see if there had been any activity but then remembered he had me blocked. I tried to check his girls page, but there hadn't been any updates there either. I was trying to see if there was any type of indication that he was still alive. When folks died, Facebook was the first place people would go to express their condolences and grieve.

I had to find out something. I couldn't just sit there. The only person that I could think to call was his brother, Esco. He had given me his number before I left Detroit, in case I needed anything. This was one of those times. I just hoped that I still had his number. It took me twenty minutes to find my old phone that I had packed up, but I finally found it and charged it up enough to power it on to get his number.

I called his brother's phone, and he answered quickly. "Yeah?"

I could hear a lot of noise in his background, so I forced myself to speak loud enough for him to hear me. "Hey, Esco. Um...sorry to bother you."

"Who is this?"

"Oh. This is Ivy," I told him.

"What's up?" he asked cautiously.

"Look, I'm sorry to bother you, but I saw something online that said that the club had exploded, and people died. I tried to call Keys, but my call went straight to voicemail. I don't know what's going on. He's got me blocked on

Facebook. His fiancée's page hasn't been updated. I'm trying not to panic and everything, but this is all getting to me right now. And the last thing I need right now is any more stress, especially being so early in the second trime–"

Fuck!

"Wait, hold up," Esco said. "What did you just say?"

Good job, Ivy.

"You're pregnant?" he pressed.

'Yeah," I answered shamefully.

"Yo', what the fuck else can happen tonight?" he replied sarcastically.

"I haven't told Keys yet," I told him. "So, you can't tell him."

"Okay, look, it's a lot of shit going on right now," he said. "Keys is okay." I was so relieved that tears came to my eyes. "He wasn't at the club when it happened, so he's good. I can't really talk right now because I'm trying to handle some other shit, and this right here will just take him over the top. So just stay by your phone and I'ma give you a call in a little bit."

"Oh. Okay," I answered.

He hung up, and I tossed the phone at my side. It was only a matter of time now before Keys either called me demanding answers or was cursing me out. Either way, the cat was out of the bag, and I was a sitting mouse.

KEYS VALENTINE

"Yo', Valentine! You made bail."

"It's about fucking time," I mumbled.

After spending the night in this dirty, ass jail cell, I was ready to get to the crib. I knew Dream had probably gone and taken everything out of the damn house. I hadn't thought to change the locks before I went back to the club to confront Zeek.

I watched as the guard drug his fat ass to the cell. He took his time unlocking it and letting me out. We walked to the front, and he was running his mouth about aimless bullshit that didn't have nothing to do with me. I was ready to get the hell up out of there. I walked through the doors and saw Esco standing with Pops. I knew I was about to get a mouthful since Pops left Miami and his dying wife to come back to this hellhole.

I greeted them with a grunt. "What up?"

"What's good, man?" Esco said, walking up and dapping me up.

Pops came over and hugged me. I thought he would have been pissed, but he looked legit concerned. "You all right?" he asked.

"Yeah, I'm good," I told him. "I know you probably mad. I just... I just lost it last night man. It was so much shit going on. And that bitch, Dream, just kept poking at me. I just kept seeing them together in my head. I snapped."

He shook his head and patted me on the back as we walked out.

"Trust me, son, it's all right," he assured me. "I would be lying if I said that we all haven't had a moment like that where we snap. But, right now, we got bigger things to worry about."

"Yeah," I agreed. "I gotta go home and see what damage has been done. I know Dream done probably ransacked the whole damn house and destroyed all my shit. Knowing her, she probably went Left Eye on everything I own."

I was making a joke about it, but in the back of my mind, I was really worried as shit.

"Keys, we need to talk," Pop said as walked to the car.

Here it comes. I knew that he was pissed off.

"Look, I know what you about to say," I started, trying to smooth things over. "Pops, trust me, I wasn't going in there trying to fuck shit up like that or get locked up."

He turned to me and shook his head. "No, son, that's not it," he corrected me. "It's something else."

As we got to the car, I peeped how uncomfortable Esco looked.

"Okay, what the hell is it?" I urged.

"Last night while you were locked up, somebody bombed the club. Some people got killed."

"What?!" I roared. "What the fuck you mean people got killed? Who the fuck bombed my shit? Yo', I know this motherfucka Theo ain't behind this shit. You got to be fuckin' kidding me!" I yelled. "This bitch ass nigga did not blow up my shit. Yo', take me by the club."

"Bruh, that might not be a good idea right now." Esco warned. "It's cops everywhere."

"Dawg, I don't give a fuck!" I snapped. "This my fucking club, yo'. So, you either take me, or I'm getting the fuck out and walking to that motherfucka."

"All right," he agreed.

We got in the car, and he started driving towards the club, and all I could think about was what the hell I was going to see when I got there.

"What did the cops have to say?" I pushed.

"Police haven't released any information," Pops said.

"What time did it happen?"

"About an hour after you got arrested," he answered. "The morgue is still trying to identify all of the names of those that died in the blast."

I wished that being a metahuman meant not feeling emotional pain as well, because the guilt of anybody losing their life because of me was as bad as any bullet to the brain.

We finally pulled up on the street where *Dreams* was, and I could see police everywhere. I hopped out and ran up to see a detective taking pictures.

"Sir, you can't be here right now!" a cop urged, walking over to me.

"I'm the owner of the club," I told him, showing him my ID. "Antonio Valentine. Can somebody please tell me what the hell happened?"

"We haven't gotten any official information yet, but from what we know, there was a bomb detonated at the back of the club," he told me. "So far the body count is at five."

"Dead?" I asked in shock.

"Yes," he replied. "Where were you during the time of the incident?" I didn't like how he was eyeing me suspiciously.

"Locked up," I told him. "So, I have a *strong* alibi. I wouldn't have blown up my own fuckin club!"

"Calm down, son," Pop said walking up, seeing things getting heated.

"I'm good," I told him.

"Look, folks, like I said, we can't have y'all here right now. Mr. Valentine you should be hearing from investigators soon," he advised.

"Come on," Esco said, pulling me away.

I was trying to contain my anger as they walked me to my car that was still parked at the curb from the day before.

"I know you're mad right now," Pops tried. "But we don't need no more problems right now. *Right now*, we need to find this bastard, Theodore."

"I'm done playing games with this bitch," I announced. "His ass is going to die before the fucking sun goes down. Call everybody. Meet me at the house in an hour. We're ending this shit today."

STEVE VALENTINE

"All right look, we've all got our reasons for wanting Theo dead. He's been manipulating this family for generations. And we can't keep letting this monster take over this family. He's taken too much from us. And it's time we stop him for good."

I was looking at Sincere, Esco, Lucky, Keys, and Reese. They had all come together. Reese had flown in from Florida an hour ago. We'd been at Keys' house all day trying to find out who had died in *Dreams* and where to find Theodore. Through the course of the day, we had learned his most trusted staff had been killed in the blast and many others were injured, including Jesse and Black. Zeek had also died in the blast, and Dream had been injured.

Since the cop had arrested Keys and left, he had no idea that Zeek was nearly dead inside. Zeek had regained consciousness. Security, some staff members, and Dream were trying to get him to a hospital when the explosion happened. The last time anyone heard anything, Dream was still unconscious.

"Okay, so how the hell are we going to take this nigga down if we can't kill him?" Lucky asked.

"Right," Reese added. "Taking his street cred hasn't run him out of town, so what else can we do to stop him?"

The Cause and Cure Is You 2
by Jessica N. Watkins

"I don't know," Keys said. "But I know I won't stop trying until I see his body limp and there's no breath coming from it."

"You're all right," I sighed. "It has been too long, and it's got to stop."

"Yeah, but how?" Esco asked.

"What if we trap him somewhere and just lock him up or something?" Lucky asked.

"Come on, bro," Esco laughed. "This nigga is like us and has been that way for way longer than us. He was the first metahuman. He's strong and probably knows how to use powers that we don't even know we have. So, where are we gonna lock him up that he can't bust out of?"

The doorbell rang, and I looked at the boys' confused faces.

"Don't worry I got it," I told them.

It was time to get some outside help. I opened the door, and my brother walked in.

"Hey, brother. I really appreciate you for coming," I told him. "I know you weren't trying to be noticed and all that. But we need to end this."

"It's okay," he told me. "If it's my time to go, then so be it. I've lived a good life."

I shook my head. He was still melodramatic as always. I walked him into the room where all of the boys were seated.

"Boys. There's somebody I want you to meet," I announced. "This is Maurice. He's my brother."

I watched all of their expressions turn to confusion.

"Your brother?" Esco said, speaking up. "But...."

Keys stared at him and I could see his wheels turning.

"Yo', I know this dude from somewhere," he said.

"The funeral home," I told him.

His eyes grew wide, and he pointed to him nodding. "Yeah. You was the funeral director."

Maurice nodded and walked over to sit down.

"Yo', why are we just now finding out that you have a brother?" Reese asked me.

"Look," I said sitting down. "There's just some things that I couldn't tell you. First of all, Theodore thinks that Maurice is dead."

"And it's better to keep it that way," Maurice said cutting me off. "Once I met my soulmate, Theodore tried to kill me too. But I survived and had plastic surgery done to change my appearance so that I wouldn't be recognizable. I laid low. But I've kept an eye on things."

"So, you knew who I was that day that I came into the funeral home," Keys replied.

"Yes," he told me. "You were one of the ones that I was keeping an eye on as a favor to your dad."

"Okay, so I'm still not really understanding here." Esco interrupted. "How is this going to help?"

"Because, nephew." Maurice said. "Your father asked for my help a few days ago, and I was able to get a man into Theodore's compound."

Their doubtful expressions changed quickly, and now Maurice had their full attention. I knew it was good to have called him. I should have done so sooner.

"So, here's the game plan," I said sitting up and resting my elbows on the table. "Maurice now knows where Theodore's estate is, and he knows the layout. The estate is far out in a rural enough area where our assault shouldn't be heard. We can't kill Theodore, but tonight is the night that we run him out of Chicago. We have no other option, and neither does he. We've taken everything from him and now it's six against one. We have to leave him no choice but to run."

CHAPTER TWENTY-TWO
DREAM FRANKLIN

Oh my God, my head hurts.

What the hell was the matter with me? I tried to sit up, but my body felt like lead. I groaned, trying to focus.

"Hey," I heard a soft voice greet me.

I opened my eyes to see Fancy leaving a chair in the corner of the room and walking slowly towards me. I had to look around to figure out why the hell I was looking at her of all people. It was then that I noticed that I was wearing a hospital gown and was in a hospital room.

"What the hell am I doing in a damn hospital?" I said, trying to sit up again.

"Just relax," she urged. "Try not to move too quick."

"Lucky for you, I can't," I snapped. "I ain't forgot what the fuck you did."

She shook her head in disappointment and sucked her teeth. "Normally, I would tell you about yourself, but given the situation, I'm gonna let you slide on that one."

"What the hell are you talking about?" I asked. "What situation?"

"Do you even know why you're here in the hospital?" Fancy asked.

I sighed in confusion. The last thing that I remembered was that I'd gone to the club to try to talk to Keys, had said some dumb shit, and ended up getting knocked out. I never thought that he would actually put his hands on me. But he did. After the cops left, I went inside the club to try to calm down and the hide from embarrassment. I'd also started to drink a lot. I wanted to talk to Zeek to see what he told Keys, so I kept taking shots until they could get him up and to the hospital. But that was the last thing that I remembered.

"Did I try to drive drunk or something?" I asked.

Fancy looked so sadly at me as she sighed. "No. There was an explosion at the club, Dream."

"What?!" I whispered harshly in disbelief.

"Yeah. It was really bad. A lot of people were killed," she went on.

I clutched my chest. "Wait. Was...Keys wasn't killed, was he?"

"No," she assured me, and I exhaled loud and hard with relief. "He was in jail, but they did say that his best friend was killed."

"Oh my God," left my voice in a whisper. Tears filled my eyes. Zeek and I were far from the best of friends, but it tore at my heart to hear that he had been killed.

"He was killed instantly," Fancy added. "The police are investigating and asking everybody questions. They don't know who did it."

"This is crazy," I mumbled. "I gotta go find, Keys. He's probably losing it right now. I gotta go talk to him and make sure he's okay!" I tried to sit up again but still felt very weak.

"No," Fancy argued, lightly laying me back down. "Dream... you can't just leave."

"*Yes*, I can!" As I tossed back the covers, my eyes fell onto my lap. And when they did, I couldn't breathe.

"Dream," I heard Fancy speak slowly as I started blankly, feeling my heart bursting from my chest with disbelief. "Try not to panic."

"Fancy!"

"Calm down, Dr–"

"FANCY!" I shrieked as my eyes filled with tears. "What happened to my legs?!"

She started crying, and I lost it. "Noooooo!!!" I screamed. "No, no, no!"

"I'm so sorry, Dream," Fancy cried. "They had to amputate. There was too much damage."

"No." I cried. "This can't be happening! No, this is a bad dream. I'm going to wake up, and I'm going to be at home with Keys!" I cried as my tears turned into sobs.

Fancy looked at me with tears in her eyes, and I snapped. "What the fuck are you crying for?!" I strained. "Are you laying in the gawd damn hospital bed right now with no fucking legs? No! *I* am! *I* lost my legs, *my* fiancé broke up with me, and my mama is dead. I've lost everything in a matter of hours!"

I couldn't hold on anymore. I broke all the way down. I had been trying to live this façade that I had created for so long. But I just couldn't hold on to it anymore. I started shaking, and tears just flowed. Fancy came closer and hugged me tight.

"It's gonna be okay," she consoled me. "I'm so sorry."

"It's not fair! It's not fair!" I shrieked. "This is all my fault."

"No, it's not," Fancy dismissed. "You didn't bomb that club, Dream."

"Yeah, but Zeek getting killed is on me. If I had never been messing with him, then Keys wouldn't have reacted the way he did, and he might be alive today."

I was riddled with guilt for so much. I had been neglecting everything and everyone around me. I had been selfish all these years, ignoring my kids. I'd lost my mother, my man, and, now, my beauty. I had nothing left. What man was going to want a crippled woman? What man was going to want a woman with four kids? How did I let things get this far?

I was tired. I was tired of lying. I was tired of fighting with everybody. I was just *tired*.

"Fancy, you're right. I was selfish," I admitted.

She sat next to me on the bed and grabbed my hand. "It's okay," she stressed. "As messed up as it sounds, this happening to you gives you the opportunity to change things. I know Mama is probably beaming right now knowing that her daughter is going to get it together."

Just hearing about Mama made me break down all over again. "I never even got a chance to say goodbye," I sobbed.

I didn't have anybody to blame but myself for that either. Instead of saying my final goodbyes to my mother, I had chosen a man over my kids and family.

Karma was definitely a faithful bitch.

STEVE VALENTINE

"Okay, I count four security guards between the gate and the door," I spoke to Esco through the phone.

"I count two in the back," I heard Keys say.

We were all on three-way.

"All right. We're going to have to be quick. 'Cause the minute that Theodore senses that something is up, he's going to disappear," I said.

I took a drink from a flask, and Lucky shook his head.

"What? Why'd it get quiet?" Reese asked. He was in the car with Keys.

"Pops over here drinking like a damn fish," Lucky said.

"My bad," I apologized. "Hard to break old habits."

"Okay, well, let's save the drinking for *after* we deal with this motherfucker," Reese suggested.

"All right. Let's get everybody in position," I told them. "Esco, you take out the two at the back, me and Lucky will get the four up in the front. How many are in the house, Maurice?"

"Usually one or two," he replied from the backseat. "Most of them are on the outside."

"Good," I said.

"All right, let's get this done. We're not gonna let this nigga get away," Keys gritted.

We all went in the directions that we needed to and waited. Esco was ready and in position in a tree not far from the backyard of Theo's house. He had his AR, and it was aimed dead at the guards that worked at the back.

Lucky, Sincere, and I were going to take a different approach at the front. He was going to pull up and bring the guards closer to the front gate. Once he did that, we would take them out, and get inside before anyone noticed. Maurice was going to lie low in the car so that his identity could remain secret in case this didn't work.

"All right. Esco, you on," I ordered.

I could hear him throwing the guards off with loud noises. Of course, the guards went straight to where the noise originated, and a few seconds later, I heard two quick shots.

"We good back here," he told us.

"All right," I told him. "We're headed in. Esco, make sure to keep us covered."

Lucky sped down the street, pulling up to the front gate. Two guards walked towards us.

"Who you?" one of them asked.

"Man, I'm looking for my boy, Bones!" Lucky said with a fake, heavy southern accent.

His fitted cap was sitting low just in case there were cameras.

"Ain't no Bones here, my nigga," the guard said. "You in the wrong place."

"Oh my bad. Well, shit, can you tell a nigga where some of the hot spots is at? I'm trying to turn up while I'm here in the Chi," Lucky carried on.

"Look, motherfucka, you need to get up outta here," the guard barked as he suspiciously eyed the rest of us in the car. He walked up on the car just as I had hoped.

By the time he realized he was being set up, I already had the gun drawn on him and had pulled the trigger. Lucky reached out the window and shot the other guard who had tried to pull his piece.

"All right, there's two more at the door," I said into the phone as Lucky, Sincere, and I jumped out the car and ran towards the front door.

"I got 'em," I heard Keys say.

At this point, the other two guards had heard the shots and had come running towards us, firing from AK's. The bullets bounced off of us as we ran towards them, sparks flying as we also soared towards them. Theo's guards finally stopped firing, standing there in shock that none of the bullets had pierced our bodies. I aimed right for one of their heads and fired. His body dropped instantly, just in time for Lucky to take out the other.

"All right move quick," I whispered to Lucky and Sincere as we eased into the front door.

The boys spread out throughout the house. Esco was still outside keeping watch over the back and Maurice was planted out front.

"All right, the bedroom is supposed to be upstairs, second door on the right," Maurice said into the phone.

Keys came out of nowhere and belted up the steps, and I was right behind him. I wanted Theo as bad as Keys did, if not more. I think we were the only two that had been so personally affected by his wrath.

A guard came out of nowhere, but Sincere had him covered from behind me. I smirked as the hole appeared in his head and his brains hit the floor just as his body did.

I turned and looked at Lucky, who nodded walking down the hall to check other rooms.

We burst through the bedroom door, and there was Theo. This motherfucker actually had the audacity to be sitting back in the bed like he was lounging, with his hands behind his head. But the naked woman in bed with him was visibly shivering with fright.

She screamed, leaving the bed, trying to run, but Keys snatched her up.

Keys had the girl in front of him with a gun to her head.

Theo laughed. "You think I give a fuck about you killing this bitch? You already know the only way to get rid of me, and she ain't the one."

"Keys, let her go," I told him.

"Get the fuck out of here," Keys urged as he pushed her towards the bedroom door.

She took off running, and I stared at the man that was supposed to be my blood.

The Cause and Cure Is You 2
by Jessica N. Watkins

"I've been waiting a long time for this," I sneered.

I put my gun down and prepared to square up. Even if he couldn't die, I planned on beating him into submission. He jumped up and tried to attack me, but I was quick. I threw a punch so hard that he went through a wall, and Keys and I commenced to stomping him out. The house seemed to be collapsing around our might. One stomp to his chest had sent us all falling violently through the floor to the first floor.

As we hit the floor, debris fell around us.

I hopped to my feet, bellowing, "Get up, motherfucka!!"

He jumped to his feet in lightning speed. He charged at me again. A tornado of debris surrounded us as we attempted to demolish one another. The winds were so powerful that it tore the roof off of the house.

From my peripheral, I could see Keys, Lucky, Sincere, and Reese standing at attention, waiting to assist if I needed help. But I had years of aggression to take out on Theodore. I would accomplish the goal of making him flee. His goal had been to be the only metahuman in the world. He had picked us off one by one, but now he was against six. With every bone crushing blow, I hoped that fear of being outnumbered and alone would finally make him flee. We had taken everything from him at this point; every buyer, every pound of product, and every crew member. Now, he had nothing and no one.

THE CAUSE AND CURE IS YOU 2
by *Jessica N. Watkins*

Both of us were striking one another with everything we had and landing devastating blows that would have killed a human but affected us in no way. I was beginning to fear that we would attract the attention of the outside world before I got Theodore to surrender.

It wasn't until I smashed his face into the floor and his nose spewed blood that I saw a sign of defeat.

"Pops!" Keys called out.

He pointed to the blood that was on the floor. Theodore stood up slowly, holding his face. He and I both stood there frozen in astonishment. Theodore pulled his hand off of his face, looking at it, and realized that it was his blood. I looked back at the boys, bewildered, and they too were as confused as I was.

Even in his confusion, Keys immediately aimed his gun at Theodore, who was still frozen, staring at his blood in awe, but I stopped Keys. "That's all right, son," I said. "I got this one."

He looked at me hesitant, and I nodded my head. "It's all right." I told him. "I'm going to enjoy this."

Keys looked hesitant but nodded his head. I knew that he was a little disappointed that he couldn't be the one to end Theodore, but this had been years in the making.

"You can't get rid of me that easy, bitch," Theodore growled.

I cocked my head, staring at the blood spewing from his nose. "Looks like I can."

I dropped my gun. Shooting him wouldn't have been as fun or painful. I charged him, attacking him like a wild beast. He attempted to fight back, but, for some reason, for the first time, he was human. Blood poured out of his chest as I ripped it open with my bare hands, and I knew I had finally won. I reached in and snatched his heart from his chest, salivating at the sight of its frozen state, feeling the last beat in my hands.

I watched as he lay choking and gurgling on his own blood.

"Checkmate, bitch," I said standing over him, throwing his heart to the ground.

I turned to see the boys looking on in utter confusion.

"He's dead," Reese said in disbelief.

"Like dead dead," Lucky added.

"He is?" I heard Esco asking as he ran into what used to be the living room. He stopped dead in his tracks when he saw Theodore's lifeless body on the ground, his heart motionless next to him.

"I'm confused as fuck," Esco added.

"Me too," I said staring at him. "But we don't have time to figure this shit out. We gotta go. Start the cleanup."

"I already did that," Esco replied. "I just drug the last body to the basement."

I nodded. "All right good. Take him to the basement too and burn this bitch to the ground."

Sincere hurried towards him, easily scooped up Theodore's remains, and threw him over the shoulder. He used his powers to jump over mounds of debris as he made his way to the basement door. I watched in sympathy as Keys looked so relieved at Theodore's puddle of blood. He looked finally... free.

Then the doorbell rang, and we all froze. We all stared at one another, not knowing what the next move would be.

Lucky inched towards the door and peered through the peephole. "It's a woman," he whispered.

I motioned towards the door with a nod. "Open it."

He opened the door, and there stood a woman in her mid-twenties covered in tattoos.

Her eyes bulged as she stared at the debris, the gaping hole in the ceiling that showed the second floor, and the missing roof. She swallowed hard and blinked slow, as if she was trying to adjust her vision.

She tore her eyes away from the wreckage, staring at us as she shivered in fear. "H-h-hi," she stuttered. "I was looking for Theo. My name is Tiny."

CHAPTER TWENTY-THREE
IVY SUMMERS

"All righty. Now it's going to be a little cold, but we should be able to see this little bun in your oven." The tech stopped as she caught the tense look on my face. "Are you nervous? Is this your first ultrasound?"

I nodded. "Yes. And my first pregnancy."

"I can tell," she said, and I giggled in embarrassment.

I was at my first prenatal appointment. I felt like I was going to throw up. Of course, that was nothing new, though. Keisha was sitting next to me, and she was filming everything.

"Ooo, will we be able to tell what it is yet?" Keisha asked.

"No, it's too early. She has about two more months before we can tell the sex," the ultrasound tech said. "But we can make sure that this baby is growing healthy."

"I got a whole bunch of ideas of stuff to do for the baby shower," Keisha told me as the tech started the ultrasound. "If it's a girl, we can have little pink baby bottles filled with pink candies and pink martini glasses."

"Girl!" I laughed. "You are doing the most. I am only three months. We have a long time before we start planning a baby shower."

The nurse continued to work the ultrasound machine, and I sat nervously waiting.

THE CAUSE AND CURE IS YOU 2
by *Jessica N. Watkins*

"Here's your little nugget," she announced as she turned the screen towards me.

Keisha and I both stared with wide, Bambi-like eyes at the monitor.

"Aaawwwwww," we both sang in unison.

It was so tiny, but I could make out its head, limbs, and even its face.

"Here are... ten fingers," she pointed out, and I smiled. "Aaaaaand there's ten toes."

"Awwww, look at the little stink stink," Keisha squealed. "Okay, so I got a plan! We can do a gender reveal party, and, if it's a boy, we have a ball that explodes with like blue powder and little footballs *pop* out!"

I swear this girl got to stop watching so much damn YouTube. Me and the tech laughed as I shook my head at Keisha's antics. But I was happy to have her there with me.

"You okay?" Keisha asked me. "You're quiet."

I nodded my head in silence, still looking at the image as the nurse checked the baby's heart.

"I just can't believe I'm having a baby," I finally spoke.

"Well, believe it," she said. "You're about to be a mommy!"

This was such an amazing moment. I was really about to be someone's mother. The only thing was, I didn't know what was going on with its father. Sadness started to eat at me once again. I had spoken with Esco a couple of days ago, but I still hadn't heard anything from Keys. I'd figured that Esco had told him and Keys had decided that it was safest for him to stay away. Maybe he didn't think this child was worth risking his life for.

I could understand that decision. I wanted him to be there because *he* wanted to be there, not because he felt like he *had* to be.

Yet, because I knew the type of man that Keys was, I had expected to at least hear from him by now.

Once the ultrasound was over, the nurse gave me copies of the pictures she'd taken. Once I dressed, we headed out of the hospital. We were both off that day, and Keisha was eager to get to a dick appointment. I promised her that I would call her and headed home in my Uber. She left in an Uber going in a different direction.

I was tired, hungry, and my emotions and hormones were soaring into overload. I was crying from excitement and fear at the same time. Seeing my baby for the first time made this all so much more real for me. While I was happy, it hurt that I wasn't able to share my happiness with the man I loved and the father of my child.

"Here you are, ma'am," I heard the driver announce about fifteen minutes into our drive. I pulled myself out of my thoughts and realized that we were at my condo.

"Thank you," I said as I gathered my purse and phone and got out of the car in all kinds of feelings.

I was almost to the door when I noticed a man standing in front of the building. At first, I paid him no mind, but when I noticed him staring at me, I was forced to take him in. The closer I got, my heart started pounding as I stopped dead in my tracks, frozen in doubt.

"Keys?!" I uttered in disbelief as a slow smile spread across my face.

This has to be a dream, I thought to myself as he grinned and began to walk closer, saying, "Hey, beautiful."

ANTONIO 'KEYS' VALENTINE

She was as beautiful as ever. Standing in front of me, even though she looked petrified and confused, Ivy was still gorgeous.

"What are you doing here?" she asked nervously as I walked towards her.

"Looking for you," I told her.

My heart was racing as I finally got close enough to hold her hands.

"I...I didn't think... I'm just ...," she managed. "Wh-wh-what are you doing here?"

I chuckled nervously as I let go of one of her hands to remove a loc from her face. "Like I said, I'm here for you."

I walked closer to her and pressed her body against mine. In that moment, I exhaled like a bitch. I enjoyed finally having her in my arms again... until I noticed that her midsection was a little rounder and hard. I let go of her hands and touched her stomach with both of mine.

"You're pregnant?" I asked her.

She bashfully nodded her head slowly, biting her nails nervously.

So, now I knew what Esco was talking about.

After Pops had killed Theodore a few days ago, when we got back to Pops' crib, I had told Pops and my brothers that I wanted to go see Ivy and let her know that it was over and that we could be together. I was making the decision to be mortal just to be with her. The only person that argued with me was Lucky. Esco had told me that he had talked to Ivy when she had called to make sure that I was okay from the explosion at the club. He said that she had some life changing events happening and that I needed to be there with her.

"Wow," I whispered in shock. "H-how far along are you?" Fear had me stuttering. Instantly, I realized that this baby could possibly not even be mine. I hadn't slept with her in months.

"I'm thirteen weeks," she whispered.

I did a quick calculation in my head. That meant she'd got pregnant right before she left Chicago.

I grinned slowly. "So, you mean to tell me..." I started to put things together. This *was* my baby.

"I need to sit down," she said, suddenly walking past me in a rush.

She rushed towards her building and sat on the stoop.

I stood in front of her, stuffing my hands into my pockets. "Why didn't you tell me that I had a kid on the way?"

"Because, Keys," she started. "Why do you think? The last time we saw each other, you were telling me that you couldn't be with me because it was too dangerous. I knew that if I told you that I was pregnant, you would want to be here. I didn't want our lives in danger, so I didn't tell you."

Tears filled her eyes as her head lowered. "I'm having your baby, and I have to do it by myself, because I will hurt you."

She was breaking down. She shivered as she cried.

I walked towards her and wrapped my arms around her. Her face fell into my chest as she sobbed and wrapped her arms around me. She held on to me so tightly that I could feel her acrylic nails scraping against my skin.

"It's okay," I told her. "I'm here now, and I'm not going anywhere."

"But you can't be here," she whispered pulling away from me. She looked up at me with tear-soaked eyes. "What if he comes after you? I don't want to have to tell my baby that his daddy died because he chose me. I'd much rather you not be here. I don't want to put my baby, myself, or you through that."

"That's why I'm here, though, baby," I told her cupping her chin. "We don't have to worry about that anymore." I smiled. "Theodore is dead."

"What?" she asked, her mouth dropping open.

I filled her in on everything that had happened; how we killed Theodore and burned the house down. I told her about the girlfriend showing up to forgive him and us finding out she was the reason why he had become mortal. We made sure that she stayed while we burned the house down, to ensure that he wouldn't heal. She hadn't seen any of the bodies. We had been able to easily pay her to keep her mouth closed about us burning the house down. Plus, she was really feeling Lucky, so she was happy to keep our secrets.

I then told Ivy about everything that happened between Dream, Zeek, and me. Even though I didn't say anything to anybody, it did fuck with me to know that Zeek died in the explosion that night. I honestly had no sympathy for Dream.

"Ivy, I don't want to live a life of regret," I told her as she sat there in amazement, taking in all that I had told her. "*You* are the one thing that makes me happy. *You* are the one. I want to be with you… and now nothing is between us to stop us."

She looked at me with this innocent expression, and I saw doubt. "What if there is another guy out there like Theodore? Then what?"

"Honestly, baby, I don't know," I told her. "But I would much rather live a life where I know I got you by my side than live years not having you. You're having our child. And I don't want to miss any of that."

"Really?" she said hopeful, fresh tears in her eyes.

I stroked her face and pulled her up to her feet. I wrapped my arms around her, pressing her body into mine. "Yes. Ivy, we belong together," I said. "You are the reason I was made. I don't want eternal life if I can't have you in it. I want you. And I plan on spending the rest of my life showing you that."

Finally, her doubt washed away. Finally, she had relaxed in my arms. Finally, I was able to grab the back of her head and bring those beautiful lips to mine. Finally... I was feeding our starvation. We would no longer have to long for each other. We had the rest of our lives to love on each other... forever... however long that may be.

EPILOGUE
IVY SUMMERS

"All right, baby. Time to push one more time. I'mma count to three, and then I want you to push really good, okay?"

My eyes rolled. "Oh my God! Shut up, Keys!" I snapped. "I swear to God, I fucking hate you!" I spewed.

Keys was standing over me with a fucking smile on his face, while his son was trying to rip through my body. I had been in labor since last night. It was almost twenty-four hours later, and now he was finally ready to come.

"Oh my God, this shit hurts!" I cried.

"Come on, baby. You can do it," he encouraged, grabbing my hand.

"Don't touch me!" I growled, pushing him away.

"All right, Mrs. Valentine," the doctor spoke. "Let's give it one more good push, okay?"

"Okay," I grunted in pain.

"Now see I just said that and she told me to shut up," Keys laughed.

My head spun towards him like the exorcist. "That's because you're getting on my fuckin nerves!" I hissed with narrowed eyes.

Keys just laughed again as I prepared myself to push.

"All right, here we go," the doctor told me.

I grabbed a hold of the rails on the bed and bared down, pushing as hard as I could.

"Good push!" the nurse holding my legs encouraged me.

"Aahhhhhhh!" I screamed.

"Keep pushing! Keep pushing! Keep pushing!" the nurse chanted.

"Ooooooh my gaaaaaaaaawd," Keisha screamed with her face frowned up in disgust as she stared at my opened legs. She could barely hold the phone up to record the birth.

I bared down and gritted my teeth, continuing to push.

"Here he comes!" the doctor announced. "Here come the shoulders!"

After twenty-four hours of labor, finally, Antonio Valentine Junior made his entrance into the world, and I heard him cry. I collapsed back onto the bed, and Keys kissed me.

"Good job, wifey," he said.

I smiled, catching my breath and watching as they cleaned my beautiful son up. As they lay him on my chest, I looked down at him, and I felt a sense of pride. I had done it. I had given birth to this beautiful baby boy.

"Hello, handsome," I whispered. "Welcome to the world."

I looked at Keys who was glassy-eyed.

"He's beautiful, baby," I told him.

"The both of you are," he admired. "You did great, baby. I love you."

"I love you too," I told him. Then I squirmed with guilt. "Sorry I got a little mean."

"It's okay, baby."

We both gazed at our son, and I realized how happy I was. After all of this time, I finally had my man. After the day that he popped up on my doorstep, at first, it had been a lot of back-and-forth with Keys traveling between Dallas and Chicago. Then he decided that he was going to move to Dallas and try to open up a new club there. I wasn't too thrilled with the idea at first, but if it made him happy, then I was good. Besides, getting out of Chicago was the best thing that happened for me, and I hoped that it would be the same thing for him.

And I had become Mrs. Valentine. We decided to hold off on the big wedding until after I had Junior, but we were still able to celebrate with close friends after a quick courthouse ceremony a month ago. Keisha had even started talking to Keys' brother, Lucky, which I found hilarious. Those two were a match made in hell.

Life couldn't be any greater.

"All right, Mommy," the nurse said, coming towards me. "We're going to take him over here so that we can give him his work up."

The nurse took him from me. Keys followed her over to the bassinet where I watched as she evaluated him. I could barely feel the doctor sewing me back up. I fought to keep my eyes open, but they kept drifting closed. I welcomed the sleep, until I heard the nurse's voice. "Hmmm, that's weird."

My eyes shot open and darted towards them. Keys stood behind her, looking back and forth from me to the bassinet with wide eyes.

"What's weird?" I asked in fear. Keys' anxiety was only making mine worse. He stood there like a deer caught in headlights, not knowing what the fuck to do or say.

The nurse looked back at me with a peculiar smile. "I'm trying to give him his Vitamin K shot, but this stupid needle won't puncture his skin."

THE END

ABOUT THE AUTHOR:

Jessica N. Watkins was born April 1st in Chicago, Illinois. She obtained a Bachelors of Arts with Focus in Psychology from DePaul University and Masters of Applied Professional Studies with focus in Business Administration from the like institution. Working in Hospital Administration for the majority of her career, Watkins has also been an author of fiction literature since the young age of nine. Eventually she used writing as an outlet during her freshmen year of high school as a single parent: "In the third grade I entered a short story contest with a fiction tale of an apple tree that refused to grow despite the efforts of the darling main character. My writing evolved from apple trees to my seventh and eighth grade classmates paying me to read novels I wrote about kids our age living the lives our parents wouldn't dare let us". At the age of twenty-eight, Watkins' chronicles have matured into steamy, humorous, and realistic tales of African American Romance and Urban Fiction.

In September 2013, Jessica's most recent novel, Secrets of a Side Bitch, published by SBR Publications, reached #1 on multiple charts.

Jessica N. Watkins is available for talks, workshops or book signings. Email her at authorjwatkins@gmail.com.

Follow Jessica on social media:
Amazon: www.amazon.com/author/authorjwatkins
Facebook: www.facebook.com/authorjwatkins
Facebook Group: www.facebook.com/group/femistrypress
Instagram: www.instagram.com/authorjwatkins

EVERY LOVE STORY IS BEAUTIFUL, BUT OURS IS HOOD SERIES:

Every Love Story Is Beautiful, But Ours Is Hood:
https://goo.gl/KNyCg7

Every Love Story Is Beautiful, But Ours Is Hood 2:
https://goo.gl/wJ1yvN

Every Love Story Is Beautiful, But Ours Is Hood 3:
https://goo.gl/wJ1yvN

LOVE, SEX, LIES (COMPLETE SERIES):

Love, Sex, Lies: https://goo.gl/FdKXXL

Love Hangover (Love, Sex, Lies 2): https://goo.gl/fwoB6A

Grand Hustle (Love, Sex, Lies 3): https://goo.gl/CQ58VL

Love Drug (Love, Sex, Lies 4): https://goo.gl/ZTmqy3

Bang (Love, Sex, Lies 5): https://goo.gl/WxNSCD
Love Me Some Him (Love, Sex, Lies 6): https://goo.gl/J7GYDU
Good Girls Ain't No Fun (Love, Sex, Lies FINALE):
https://goo.gl/BCuhFu

COLLABORATION WITH NAKO:

No Fairy Tales: https://goo.gl/57RkyV

In order to receive a text message when future books by Jessica N. Watkins are released, send the keyword "Jessica" to 25827! Please be sure to leave your review of this novel!

Jessica would love to hear your thoughts!